S0-AHH-553

DEATH IN STYLE

I was balled up on a hard, ridged surface that smelled like leather and warm rubber and motor oil. Everything was dark and I was locked in the trunk of a car with little room to maneuver.

I squeezed my eyes shut and then opened them. Claustrophobia was an unthinkable indulgence. Certainly not an option. My head was killing me. I shook it to try to bring some clarity but all it brought was more pain. Slowly the fog cleared and I knew that if I didn't escape, I was dead. . . .

Cadillac built two hundred of these limited-edition Eldorado convertibles in 1976, and as I ran my fingers over the seams and seals and steel, I understood why most of them are still on the road more than twenty years later. They've got no give. They took all the cushioning and put it in the ride, leaving the trunk hard and functional and heartless as a whore—and as escape-proof as a Vuitton steamer trunk.

By the same author

TRAMP
CURTSEY
BAD MANNERS

NOTHING BUT GOSSIP

A LILLY BENNETT MYSTERY

MARNE DAVIS KELLOGG

BANTAM BOOKS
New York   Toronto   London   Sydney   Auckland

This edition contains the complete text
of the original hardcover edition.
Not one word has been omitted.

NOTHING BUT GOSSIP

A Bantam Book

PUBLISHING HISTORY
Doubleday hardcover edition / January 1999
Bantam mass market edition / October 1999

All rights reserved.
Copyright © 1999 by Marne Davis Kellogg
Cover art copyright © 1999 by Rick Lovell

No part of this book may be reproduced or transmitted in any
form or by any means, electronic or mechanical, including
photocopying, recording, or by any information storage and
retrieval system, without permission in writing from the publisher.
For information address: Bantam Books.

If you purchased this book without a cover you should be aware
that this book is stolen property. It was reported as "unsold and
destroyed" to the publisher and neither the author nor the publisher
has received any payment for this "stripped book."

ISBN 0-553-58046-9

Published simultaneously in the United States and Canada

Bantam Books are published by Bantam Books, a division of Random
House, Inc. Its trademark, consisting of the words "Bantam Books"
and the portrayal of a rooster, is Registered in U.S. Patent and
Trademark Office and in other countries. Marca Registrada, Bantam
Books, 1540 Broadway, New York, New York 10036.

PRINTED IN THE UNITED STATES OF AMERICA

OPM   10 9 8 7 6 5 4 3 2

For the other men in my life—
Nelson, Nick, and Harry

NOTHING BUT GOSSIP

PROLOGUE

SATURDAY MORNING · SEPTEMBER 12

Number one: I never thought I'd actually ever get married. And number two: I never thought if I actually did, that I'd spend the morning of my wedding day standing at a pair of side-by-side graves, the bodies being exhumed to be tested to see what, if any, kind of poison had been used to murder them. I had to attend the exhumation; there wasn't anybody else left who cared about the deceased, Mr. and Mrs. Bradford Rutherford. The rest of the Rutherford family—their two daughters, Mercedes and Alma, and one son-in-law, Wade Gilhooly—were either dead, dying, or in jail.

I watched quietly while the backhoe's grave-width shovel cut quickly through the soft September ground, digging like a child's toy until it got close to the slab of cement that sealed the vault of Mr. Rutherford's grave.

"I still don't see why you're here," Jack Lewis, Roundup's chief of detectives, crabbed. The early sun glinted off his Ray-Bans and bathed his narrow, eagle-like face in golden light. "You look like hell. Aren't you getting married today? I can't believe this guy's seen you in the morning and still wants to go through with it. Talk about reality."

I laughed. "Shut up, Jack."

"Don't you think you'd better get some ice or something on your face? Go home. This case is over."

"I'm here because whether it's over or not, Wade Gilhooly is still my client. I owe him this."

A team of men jumped down and began shoveling the dirt from the top of the vault and then around its sides, making way for the heavy chain that would be used to haul it out. The noise was loud, grating, like snow shovels on a sidewalk.

"Do you think she murdered them?" Jack asked.

The backhoe's powerful engine screamed as the cumbersome load rose unwillingly from its deep home, its eternal sleep violated and betrayed, and then was settled surprisingly gently on the ground, where the men went to work with sledgehammers. It was brutal, heavy, muscle work, and the men were sweating in spite of the morning chill. Finally, like an Easter piñata, the vault cracked, revealing a massive bronze casket.

No one spoke as the coroner stepped forward to witness the funeral director unscrew the small glass identification tube and remove the tiny sheet. "Bradford Rutherford the Third," he announced to the stony group as though he were presenting the deceased to St. Peter at the pearly gates.

The coroner gave a nod of confirmation and the mortician replaced the tube, uncranked the casket's lid, which gave off a breathless hiss when the seal was broken, and then with his blank-faced assistant, removed Mr. Rutherford's remains into a body bag and laid it gently in the back of his black coach. Mr. Rutherford, the founder and chairman of Rutherford Oil, one of the most successful, delightful, and powerful men in the world, was now just a bag of bones in the back of a Cadillac station wagon. Talk about reality.

Then the backhoe went to work on Mrs. Rutherford.

Did I think she murdered them? Well, I would be lying if I said I didn't feel like killing *my* mother sometimes—my fiancé described her once as being about as much fun as a cinnamon bear who lived in a cave with two rattlesnakes as her best friends—but if it turned out this woman had actually murdered her own parents, it would be one of the most remarkable cases of my career.

Wyoming stretched uninterrupted from the mesa-top where the Wind River Cemetery lay surrounded by a fence that kept out coyotes and tumbleweeds, but not the wind. Even on this crystal-clear September morning—Richard's and my wedding day—you could feel the slice of winter coming, almost smell the contracting of the permafrost tundra and bogs, hardening up like Arctic Jell-O.

I turned up the collar of my canvas jacket, dug my hands deep into my pockets, and looked at the panorama of our lovely city of Roundup at the foot of the Wind River Range. I could see everything, all of downtown and the river. I could even see out south, where the trees were smaller and the houses bigger. I could see all the way to the deep green of the Wind River Country Club golf course and the Gilhoolys' ridiculously massive house, dwarfing the tenth hole along which it lay like a big, gray slug.

That's where it had all begun, just last Sunday. When we went to meet the Russians.

ONE

SUNDAY EVENING · SEPTEMBER 6

I certainly hope Alma isn't planning to wear that cheap pink caftan arrangement again tonight," my mother said over the phone. "The fabric's so shiny you can practically put your lipstick on in it."

"Mmm," I agreed, trying not to talk so my mascara could dry. I stared out the window of my dressing room, across the dark, flat ribbon of the Wind River to the pastureland where a handful of Black Angus grazed quietly before a backdrop of golden aspen.

"Well, what can you expect after spending thirty years in Billings?" Mother buzzed along. I knew she was lying on the chaise in her bedroom, CNN muted, slicing open the mail as she talked. "But, my goodness, with all that Rutherford Oil money—you know it's one of the largest independent producers in the world—Alma could fly to New York or Paris every month and pick up a few things, and instead she goes around looking like someone's poor cousin in from Nebraska. I'll tell you, ever since she married that disgusting Wade Gilhooly, she's sunk to his level."

She paused for a breath and a sip of Darjeeling. "Her poor parents. I guess it's just as well they're dead, Alma made them so miserable. I'm so delighted, Lilly, darling, that you decided to wait and have such an outstanding career. You were so smart. That Richard Jerome is the most divine man I've ever met. Since your father, of course. I hope you don't gain any more weight before the wedding."

Well, there were about sixty things I could have responded to in that discourse, starting with . . . well, I'm not really sure which one to start with. It's a draw between the weight deal and how delighted she is that I decided to delay getting married.

Number one: I'm practically staring fifty in the eye and she has been in a state of full-blown hysteria at my unwed condition since I was twenty-two, the outer limit for a young woman to remain single. In her opinion.

Number two: She has yammered and yapped against my outstanding career since the day, almost thirty years ago, when—during my third Junior League Introductory Provisional meeting, where I was the only unmarried, unbabied member of the entire class—I rose to my feet, looking every inch the young matron in my black-patent pumps and pale-yellow, nubby-wool, Nan Duskin suit with a boxy jacket and straight skirt, and ceremoniously peeled off my white cotton gloves, laid them on my chair, announced, "I'm sorry, girls, but this just isn't me," and walked out, caught a plane for California, and enrolled in the police academy in Santa Bianca, two hours and millions of light-years away from my hometown of Roundup, Wyoming.

Since that day—in spite of the fact that I was the first female chief of detectives in the country, or that I'm now a successful security consultant (twenty-first-century-speak for private investigator) and a U.S. Marshal—until Richard Jerome and I announced our engagement in late June, I had never accomplished one worthwhile thing. In her opinion.

And furthermore, on that particular subject. There have been plenty of guys I could have married, but since I discovered the Pill when I was about eighteen and adopted the same philosophy as well-adjusted, happy bachelors, I never felt the need to get married. Until I met someone I really didn't want to live without.

As to the weight deal. I started smoking when I was thirteen and quit when I was forty. That's twenty-seven years of hopped-up metabolic bliss. And then, two months after I quit smoking, I started taking estrogen. Well, forget it. The metabolic bliss turned into a meltdown from which it looks like I'm never going to recover. The truth is: I still look fine. Good enough to lasso Richard Jerome, and he's not exactly what anyone with a brain would call ready for the glue factory.

Whatever. Things are on a sweet course now, and it's a sign of my increasing maturity that, unwilling to wreck my makeup, I did not rise to Mother's bait, but waited patiently and quietly while she carried on over the phone. Mother didn't scare me anymore. I could see right through her. She was just the opposite of those steel magnolias who are all sweet on the outside and tough as nails inside. Nope. Mother was a jelly-filled cannonball.

"What are you wearing tonight, darling?" She took a ladylike drag of her cigarette. She was somehow able to limit herself to ten a day. I had struggled to keep it down to forty.

"The black gabardine Saint Laurent Richard bought for me in Paris last week," I said, clipping on a diamond earring.

"I don't think I've seen that. I'll bet it's lovely."

"Yes, it is. What are you wearing?"

"Oh, I don't know. I'll dig up something. Your father has come up with a dozen excuses why he doesn't want to go to this shindig tonight, even though he's on the board. I know it's because of the proxy fight. I guess it's turning vicious."

"What proxy fight?"

"Rutherford Oil. That's what this party is all about, Lilly. It's Rutherford Oil stockholders. Their annual meeting is on Wednesday. That's why you were invited, because you're a stockholder. I thought you knew that."

"No, I just thought we were invited to meet the Gilhoolys' houseguests."

"Well, I wouldn't exactly call them *houseguests*. They're *Russians*."

And we all know Russians could never be houseguests.

"The proxy fight has something to do with Russia. Well," Mother said, bringing our conversation to an abrupt conclusion, as though she were the only one with anything to do and she'd just spent more than enough time talking to a complete imbecile, "I've got to scoot if we're going to get there. Don't be late."

Alma and Wade Gilhooly's dinner was one of the few parties we'd attended lately that was not in Richard's and my honor, and that was before the out-of-town guests, including all of Richard's family, arrived on Wednesday, when all the stops would really get pulled. I hadn't been the center of so much attention since I got caught in bed with the chief justice of the California Supreme Court. It was terrific.

Our wedding was in six days.

TWO

I grew up with Alma Rutherford. Her parents, Mr. and Mrs. Bradford Rutherford, lived in the large Georgian house next door to our city house in Roundup, where we all gazed like kings and queens across the windblown grassy field known as Mountain View Park, where a few cottonwoods held on to the dirt for dear life, at the graceful elegance of the Wind River Range in the distance.

The mountains floated just beyond Roundup's wacked-out skyline to which every cross-eyed, wall-eyed, jug-eared, happy-go-lucky, slatheringly insane architect who couldn't find work anywhere else in the world was evidently welcome to contribute, and evidently encouraged to discover how many different types of architecture—Greek, Gothic, Colonial, or Georgian Revival; High Victorian Gothic, Queen Anne, Italian Villa, Second Empire, Regency, Tudor, or Federal; Salt Box, Dutch, or Spanish Colonial; Mission, Prairie, Stick, or Shingle; or maybe just International—he or she could fit into one building. They all succeeded brilliantly. Roundup cannot be mistaken for any other city on earth.

Alma had an older half-sister, Mercedes, whose mother had died in childbirth. But Mercedes had distanced herself so completely from us smaller girls that it was almost as if Alma were an only child. I envied her singular status, especially when I figured out that my parents had big plans for my brothers—running the family banks, newspapers, railroads, oil fields, and ranches—and none for me, beyond marriage and motherhood.

In spite of our growing up next door to each other, playing jacks, and trading secrets as little girls, our personalities were so dissimilar we'd never grown close.

Alma's room, always neat and tidy, felt to me like a heavy-handed birthday cake with clotted buttercream icing, overtrimmed with ribbons and bows, ruffles and flowers. Stuffed animals and dolls were heaped on her bed, dolls in costumes from around the world stood on the bookshelves, and the whole affair always smelled faintly of unclean field-hockey shin guards.

My room, on the other hand, was a compendium of books—from *Misty of Chincoteague, Thunderhead,* and *My Friend Flicka* to full collections of Agatha Christie and Charles Dickens, my great-grandmother's collection of Royal Worcester teapots, and every type of beauty, health-care, and fragrance product ever mentioned in *Seventeen* magazine.

I'll never forget it: Alma's rug was apple green and everything else was pink, the full spectrum from shell to shocking. You would have thought she was from Texas.

As a girl, Alma was as buxom as her room, a big-boned, full-toothed Mr. Ed blonde whose milkmaid looks came from her mother, a postwar Danish import as sturdy as a giant wheel of Gouda. Alma's money came from her father, who was an oilman but not a gambler, which was probably why Mrs. Rutherford agreed to marry him, because from what I know about Danes—which I admit is limited to aquavit—they don't seem like high-risk-takers, something we Westerners have raised to an art form.

Alma and my older brother, Elias Caulfield Bennett IV, dated as seriously as one can at eighteen, but when Alma was twenty, she eloped with Harker M. "Wade" Gilhooly, the assistant golf pro at the Wind River Country Club. And boy, did it ever hit the fan.

I'd been off in Laramie at the time, whooping it up at the university, so I'd never met him, but Mother said he was just what he sounded like: a red-haired, red-skinned, red-tempered, hard-drinking, hard-hitting, loudmouthed, foulmouthed, fortune-hunting woman-izer, who had neatly extricated himself from service in Vietnam by marrying one of America's richest girls.

Once her parents recovered from the shock of the union and realized that there would be no annulment, no buyout, no payoff, that the newlyweds were sticking together, Mr. Rutherford bought his new son-in-law a Chevrolet dealership in Billings and shipped the happy couple out of state as quickly as possible, threatening to wrap Wade's golf clubs around his neck if he ever showed his face in Roundup again.

I explained all this to Richard as we left the ranch, the Circle B, in my younger brother Christian's big new Sikorsky S-76 helicopter. The two huge turbines whined as the copter lumbered up from the meadow in front of the house like a bulldog rising from a nap. But once airborne, we hovered delicately in the cool, cloud-less September sky, executed a precision quarter-turn, paused for a split second as though to gather our skirts together, and shot off toward town like a Saturn rocket. A speck of indigo flashing across the setting sun.

"I sure did luck out on that deal," my brother Elias said, reaching over to take one of the Glenfiddichs on the rocks I'd poured for him and Richard. Elias is two years older than I am and still looking for the right girl, whom we all suspect he may have found in my secretary. "I hear Alma looks sort of like a big old wrinkled hog now. But you're not completely right about Wade. He's a nice guy, and he did serve in 'Nam."

"What? You're kidding." I poured myself a Jameson's as the Wyoming hill country raced beneath us. We clinked our yellow plastic mugs.

We used to stock dozens of bright red mugs emblazoned with the Circle B brand all over the ranch, wherever people might conceivably be drinking outdoors, which was basically everywhere, as well as in the helicopter, the jets, the barns, the trucks, and the wagons. But the customized cups became collectors' items for people we'd never heard of (and some we had) and disappeared quicker than we could order them. Finally, when my mother came upon a boozed-up, toothless, unwashed derelict who made his home in a series of Maytag appliance boxes beneath a viaduct by the Wind River in downtown Roundup and who had a dozen Bennett family Circle B Ranch mugs hanging by a thong from his suspenders like a gigantic, noisy, gaudy, red plastic charm bracelet, she called Christian, who she evidently felt wasn't busy enough running the newspaper and the railroad, and told him to handle it. None of us ever asked Mother what she was doing down there under the viaduct having a conversation with the fellow in the first place—some Junior League do-gooder deal probably, handing out toothbrushes and dental floss as though that would solve all his problems—we just took her word for it.

"Yeah, he went in about the same time I did; of course, he was in the Air Force." Elias, now a general in the Marine Corps Reserve, paused, giving us time to reflect upon what torpid louts the Marines found the boys in blue, although they seldom came out and said so. "And I ran into him a couple of times in Saigon. He was some general's aide. Last I heard, he was ending up his tour as the golf pro at Clark in the Philippines until he got caught in some motel in Angeles City in bed with the commandant's wife. Immediate honorable discharge. No scandal, just mercy boocoo and ore vore." Elias gave me a conspiratorial look over the tops of his dark glasses. "Sound familiar?"

I knew he was referring to the judge.

"Sounds pretty smart to me," Richard said. He stretched his long blue pinstripes across the aisle and crossed them at the ankles. The well-worn leather of his black dress cowboy boots glowed with such patina, Holbein the Younger could have painted them onto his feet. They creaked comfortably. How come my boots never look like that? I wondered vaguely. Mine always look dried out and cracked and caked with dusty, straw-sprung manure, sort of like I'd just dragged my saddle all the way across Oklahoma. He brushed an invisible speck from the knee of his trousers.

A Manhattan-born Morgan Guaranty banker who'd turned just as gray and gaunt and frantic and feral as all the rest of those poor suckers who have to live in that town, Richard had finally cashed it all in and moved West to run the Roundup Opera, one of the world's top companies. He's also a champion team roper, champion lover, and serious get-down cowboy party guy. And rich.

Every time I look down at my ring finger, I can't believe it. That diamond is so big, if I had two, I could shoot craps. It sat there on my hand like a beacon in a lighthouse. I'd waited so long to get the right ring from the right guy, I hadn't taken it off since he'd put it there three months before.

All my life I've accepted only the best. And when it comes to love, the real thing—and I'm speaking character, integrity, passion, and chemistry here, not diamonds—I'd been willing to wait forever, which it was beginning to look as if I was going to have to do, until Richard showed up last year and things simply fell into place.

"We're about there," I told them as I looked out the window and watched the green links of the Wind River Country Club unroll beneath us like a high-speed golf documentary. We came to a dipping pause above the whopper of a concoction the Gilhoolys had constructed on the edge of the tenth fairway.

America's Mountain West—Montana, Wyoming, Colorado, and Utah—has no look of its own beyond log cabins and tepees. And unlike downtown Roundup, a structural free-for-all, architects have recently developed and assigned us a residential style, which we locals refer to as Santa Fe Gumdrop Yodel. It is taught in architectural schools as a joke, as one more hilarious example of what gullible, tasteless Neanderthals we are here in the provinces. Gumdrop Yodel characteristics include high, heavy, thick-lipped archways for all windows and doors, except for those in the shapes of circles and octagons and triangles; universal grayness in a maximum of three shades of stucco (the gray is evidently to remind us of cloudy days, which we seldom have); and rough wooden beams shooting out here and there around the roof line like straw stuck in a board during a tornado, to provide the Southwestern touch. All topped off with gray, glazed-tile roofs. It's a silly, graceless style, but the people who move here from the East don't know any better and think it's great because they can see the sky for the first time in their lives.

Alma and Wade had taken Gumdrop as far as it could conceivably go in their twelve-thousand-square-foot, one-story sprawl that squatted in the sun like a dirty plaster of paris model. And, as the chopper began its shuddering descent, Alma stood with a hand shading her eyes at the edge of the flat, emerald lake of a lawn, between the putting green and the lap pool. The windy wash plastered her shiny pink caftan to her big, sturdy body. Wade was nowhere in sight. Probably in the powder room banging one of the guests.

THREE

A number of dressy couples chatted in small groups by the pool among gigantic pots of red geraniums, and Alma, who already seemed a little bombed, took Richard and me around to make certain we met some, but not all of them. I assumed the ones she wasn't introducing us to were on the other side of the Rutherford Oil proxy issue. The stockholders included a gaggle of oil people, RV dealers, Wall Street types, golf junkies, former U.S. senator Duke Fletcher, media time salesmen, and the Russians. Six of them.

"I'd like you to meet Sergei and . . ." it sounded as if she said Sergei five more times. She kissed each one familiarly on the cheek as she presented them. They reminded me of Steve Martin in *The Jerk*. Gucci thugs. Hairy-pawed yetis, sasquatch siblings from the Far North with slanted brows and bad teeth, who rocked and rolled as they spoke and eyed the women as if they were sausages in the local GUM, or whatever they call their markets.

"You visit Siberia?" Sergei One inquired as his hand

headed for my bottom. "Furs are very beautiful there. You like lynx? You like vodka?"

What did he think? That we lived in gangster television shows? That "American Justice" on A&E was real life, that all American women were round-heeled mob girls you could buy at cocktail parties?

"Sergei, my dear." I removed his hand. "Let me explain something to you. Life in America is not one big Bill Kurtis gangster documentary. Do not handle the women, particularly this one, or you will find your family jewels hanging out the back instead of the front."

He smiled sheepishly, showing off his teeth, each one rimmed in gold as precisely as an expensive dinner plate. "Sorry, we just arrive America today. Want to be friendly." His voice was thick and guttural, as though he needed to clear his head and throat and spit, and the Rs rolled off his tongue as if from a stutter machine. "You man's secretary maybe, or wife?"

"No, I'm a federal police officer." That got him to back up a little farther. "Are you really from Siberia?" I asked.

"Da." He nodded and indicated the rest of his contingent. "We let Rutherford Oil come in and do some business. Big project. Bigger than North Slope. We build pipeline to Manily, very beautiful. I am chief petroleum engineer for Magadan, my province. You come visit."

"Well," I said—Richard had taken my arm and was pulling me away—"good luck. Enjoy your visit. Mind your manners. The police are watching."

"Da." He laughed. "That I understand."

"Aren't they a scream?" Alma asked as she steered us across the room. "I never thought Siberia could be so much fun. And the vodka is to die for. Have you met Johnny and Shanna Bourbon?"

Johnny Bourbon is Roundup's one and only world-famous televangelist. His ministry, Johnny Bourbon's Christian Cowboys, had miraculously managed to survive his thirty-six months in the federal clink for selling each timeshare condo in his Christian retreat/theme park—Christ's Corral—a remarkable twelve times.

I could tell that most of the guests found the Bourbons as exotic as Martians. They circled the get-down, ex-con, high-roller, high-country preacher and his show-business wife as if they were the fat man and bearded lady at the circus, but never actually got close enough to talk.

It's like the time I met the comedienne, Joan Rivers, and we were laughing about the horse races at the state fair in Montana—the Midland Empire State Fair—and the fact that the track at the fairgrounds was so short, the horses had to go around it eight times to make a mile and a quarter. And she said, "I was booked there very early in my career, and I think I was the first Jew ever to visit Montana. People kept sending their children up to touch me for luck."

That's what the Bourbons brought, maybe a little touch of the forbidden.

I'd never met Johnny Bourbon, but now I could see that he had it. His eyes were as fiery blue and intense as cattle prods, and I felt their power instantly when we shook hands and he turned those eyes on, burning them into mine. But mine are Bennett eyes, the color of Bisbee turquoise, and immune to unsought charms. I also saw in him the wariness that no former prisoner ever can hide around law-enforcement officers. That flicker of animal fear and longing and begging that comes from the horror of incarceration, the personal knowledge that a stranger can exercise absolute, impersonal control over your life. Even the deepest faith cannot erase that memory.

"I've heard your name for years and years from Alma," Johnny said, holding my hand in a powerful grip.

"Really?" I asked, trying to imagine why Alma would ever have any reason to mention me to anyone.

"I know you're her oldest friend."

"Really?"

"God bless you." He was medium-tall, in good, trim shape, had a black moustache and short beard, and was decked out in a snow-white Western-cut suit, white shirt, white string bow tie, and white cowboy hat with a silver coinband. His boots were shiny gray eel-skin. "I'm awful pleased to meet you. And you," he turned to Richard. "You both look like you know what you're doing, getting hitched. It's a great state of being, marriage. Shanna and I"—he slung his arm around his wife's wasp waist and drew her close in a brusque sort of yank—"have been married for twenty-five years. Haven't we, darlin'?"

"Sure enough have, sugar darlin'." Shanna's enthusiasm sounded to me as if it had a "you idiot" hanging at the end of it. Her rodeo-queen hair—as black as midnight—exploded like a Clairol commercial from beneath a white beaver Stetson, and her sleeveless baby-blue doeskin dress draped her curvy body like soft butter. Long strips of fringe fell from beaded emblems across her back, and bracelets of downy eagle feathers circled her wrists. She had on false eyelashes, television makeup with the flawless sheen and smoothness of fondant icing, and her teeth were so shiny they looked as if they'd been capped with mirrors. I remembered that she played the guitar and sang her own Christian compositions on the daily television show she and Johnny broadcast all over the world from their own studio. Shanna and her husband looked a little more like brother and sister than I thought was quite right or healthy.

"Shanna's going to sing for us a little later," explained Alma, who hadn't taken her hand off Johnny Bourbon's forearm. An edge had crept into her voice.

"Great. I'll look forward to it."

"Come on," Alma suddenly ordered me. "There's something I want to show you."

"God bless you," Johnny said again as Alma seized my arm in a painful clench and pulled me away.

"That miserable motherfucking son of a bitch," she muttered.

Wow. I turned to see if Richard had heard, but he'd vanished in the direction of the bar and my brothers.

On Alma's neck, ears, and arms, masses of gold jewelry flashed in the setting sun like signs at a truck stop as she marched me double-time through a narrow, twenty-foot-high archway into a vast solarium. There were eight or ten seating areas of natural bamboo armchairs with yellow and green palm-leaf-patterned cushions and glass coffee tables, each with an arrangement of wide, floral scented candles of different heights and what looked like black teak African fertility artifacts. But the artifacts weren't what made the room memorable. It was the fact that actual zebra-, tiger-, and leopard-skin rugs covered the gray terrazzo beneath the tables and chairs, and hundreds of stuffed heads of rare, beautiful African game stared out blindly from the walls. It made me sick at my stomach.

We stopped at a black-lacquered sideboard where a number of pictures were displayed in black-lacquered frames.

"We used to go to Africa every year on safari," a

calmer Alma explained. She tapped her fingernail on a photograph of herself leaning against the neck of a dead elephant; a long Weatherby elephant rifle rose from between her legs in case anyone missed just what a macho-girl she really was. "Got a Grand Slam in cats."

She raised a cigarette to her glossy pink lips, making her heavy gold bracelets clank into a solid stack on her strong, tanned forearm, and inhaled deeply. Her face was thickly made up and evenly taut, what looked to be the result of a recent face-lift that had turned the jowly pouches on either side of her mouth into smooth, slightly swollen balls about the size of chestnuts. And although her lips were plumped by collagen, tiny lines around them deepened into cracks as she dragged on her cigarette. She had wide, square hands and feet, stubby fingers and toes, and all her nails gleamed with the same bright pink as her lipstick and caftan. "But now they won't let you shoot anything, so we just go to Scotland and Nebraska and Texas bird-hunting. Last year I bagged two hundred quail in one afternoon."

"What do you do with that many birds?" I asked.

Alma shrugged. "They give them to the Mexicans or something. I don't know. We give away lots of stuff."

I bit my tongue and followed her through more vaulted, cold, dead rooms. I'd been in friendlier morgues. Alma's high-heeled sandals slapped against her callused feet like hands methodically slapping a face. One slap. Two slap. One slap. Two slap. One slap. Two slap. The sound was so cheap, it made me want to scream.

Alma's mother's lovely Danish country antiques—not the knife-edged Danish Modern junk everyone fell in love with in the late fifties, but graceful, pale pine pieces with clean, simple lines—were everywhere. But they'd been trampled, killed with the gray by Alma, or her decorator, and seemed to struggle for air. Even the animals in the large painting that had hung in her parents' living room, of Denmark's wild ponies racing along the banks of a swollen river beneath an endless threatening sky—a work so easy to confuse with our own wild mustangs dashing through the Wind River— looked as if they'd turned into one more herd trying to escape the Gilhooly slaughterhouse.

God. The whole place was gruesome and depressing, overwhelmingly dreary. And in spite of all its height and open space, it made me want to hunch over, as though I were walking through a dark tunnel.

"This is Wade's room." Alma punctuated the words matter-of-factly with exhaled smoke, as though she were saying, "And this is where we keep the dog."

We walked along a gray-leather sectional sofa that snaked through a grown-up boy's ultimate playroom, where one wall danced with images on twelve television monitors. Another wall held framed photographs of models wearing little more than lip gloss and posing with high-speed Harley-Davidson and BMW motorcycles between their legs. What I would consider to be a serious gun collection, ranging from antique dueling pistols to plastic Glock handguns, was mounted above the bar. Below, a glass-fronted refrigerator displayed countless brands of beer, canned margaritas, and piña coladas.

"Where *is* Wade?" I asked.

Alma, who'd been flicking ashes onto the floor the whole time, now ground out her cigarette in an ashtray set in the inlaid edge of what looked like a brand-new pool table. A few live sparks jumped onto the smooth green felt and burned tiny holes, but she didn't seem to notice or, more probably, didn't care. Alma was just a complete pig.

She looked me in the eyes for the first time, and the toughness and cynicism I saw there said it all. "He was so upset. He got an emergency call from one of the dealerships and had to run up to Billings. He's going to try to get back, at least in time for dessert."

We both knew she was lying. He wasn't upset, and he wouldn't be back.

"Too bad," I said.

"Oh, what the heck, I can't lie to you, Lilly. You're my oldest friend and you know me better than anyone." She removed a gold case from her pocket, lit a fresh cigarette, and, once she got a coughing fit behind her, continued. "The truth is that ever since I found Jesus, I've been able to forgive Wade for the life he leads. I know he strays, but he can't help himself. I have trouble staying on the straight and narrow myself from time to time. Besides, I love him too much to let him go, and as the Lord says, 'People who live in glass houses shouldn't throw stones.' "

I half-smiled at her, not trusting myself to speak for a moment or two. Where was all this best-and-oldest-friend stuff coming from? Johnny had said it, and now Alma. We hadn't seen each other for twenty-five years and didn't know each other at all, not even a little bit; only those fading memories of early acquaintance and our parents' close friendship connected us. And how can anyone who falls in love with Jesus rationalize—with pride, I might add—killing two hundred birds in one afternoon just for fun? Once you've been a cop, it's tough to rationalize killing anything for fun. A soul can take only so much carnage.

"That's great," I finally said.

"But here's what I wanted to show you." We cruised down a long, glass-walled gallery, changing wings of the house the way people change lanes on the highway, past atrium gardens and fountains, past another gun collection, and into the master bedroom wing, where Wade and Alma's bed sat in the center of the room on a raised platform like a big, round, white satin roller-derby rink. The walls were upholstered with gray flannel. If there were any windows, it was hard to tell where.

"Goodness," I said, recalling the handful of times I've slept in round beds—usually in expensive suites in Las Vegas—and spent the whole night swimming in a circle, looking for my moorings. Plus, if they have satin sheets, it's like sliding on black ice, and once you've fallen out of a round bed, it's hard to know exactly where to get back in. Besides, usually the person you've woken up with in a round bed is not one you'd especially care to crawl back in with if it's light outside. Round beds give me the heebie-jeebies.

"Dandy, isn't it?"

On we sailed into her dressing room, where she clapped the lights on with a matador's flourish, and there was a grown-up version of the room of her childhood—apple-green carpeting and pink walls with huge pink-tinted mirrors and fringed lampshades, and a bookcase of dolls, most of them dressed like Scarlett O'Hara. Off to one side, a platform bathtub sat in a glass cubicle in a walled garden that must have been designed from a description in a romance novel. Stuffed exotic birds perched overhead in the fake trees, their glass eyes angry.

"Can you stand it?" she exclaimed.

FOUR

Alma grunted herself down at her dressing table like a truck driver climbing onto a stool in a diner and powdered her face with a marabou puff between sips of her martini. Then she removed the top from a tube of lipstick with a muffled pop and applied it as though she were drawing thick circles on a wall with a crayon, slathered some peachy lip gloss over all, and that done, studied her face carefully. Finally, her eyes caught mine in the mirror.

"My life is a complete joke," she said flatly.

"What do you mean?"

"This whole thing is a sham. This house. Everything. I only moved back to Roundup to be closer to Johnny, and ever since we got here, he's avoided me." She got up and walked over to a mirrored cabinet that opened to reveal a well-stocked bar and small refrigerator, inside of which sat a crystal martini decanter.

"Want one?" she offered, waving the pitcher my way.

The sound of New Orleans jazz played quietly from invisible speakers.

"No, thanks. I will take some of the Jameson's, though," I said, splashing whiskey into my glass and glancing at my watch, wondering how much longer Richard and I had to stay and knowing it would have to be a lot longer than an hour.

"Irish. Ick." Alma grimaced. "Wade's Irish, but he doesn't have the class to drink Jameson's. He drinks ale and stout and all that affected crap." She flicked open a gold Cartier lighter with the Kenya Safari Club logo outlined in diamonds on its side, fired up another cigarette, resumed her perch on the leopard-skin dressing-table bench, and picked up the subject of Johnny.

"I've underwritten his whole stupid ministry for years, paid his stupid payroll while he was in prison, otherwise the whole stupid, fucking operation would have gone down the toilet. He and Shanna don't care about each other any more than Wade and I do. As a matter of fact, I think Wade and she even had a thing going for a few years, although I can't imagine why she'd bother, he's such a quick-fire little pipsqueak, and now he's been moping around with a case of flu for the last month. I don't know why I'm telling you all this. We hardly know each other, but I know you can keep secrets and I needed to talk to someone. I hope you don't mind."

"No," I said, and I didn't. I didn't have anything else to do, since it wasn't time to go home yet, which is what I really wanted to do. I settled into a deep-cushioned, carnation-pink velvet chair.

"I went over to see him today and he had a new secretary who didn't know who I was, or at least she pretended not to know, and she made me wait." Alma flinched as though she'd suffered a body blow, and then she began to bawl. "Stupid little wop bitch. Lord, it was so humiliating. She doesn't even speak English, for chrissakes. And then when I finally got in to see him he was very grand, very full of himself. I reminded him of his promise to leave Shanna and said if he didn't, I was going to cut off all my funding."

"What did he do?" I asked.

"He said it wouldn't make much difference," she choked out between sobs. "His donations were way back up and growing. He said he could make it up in six months or less. I can't even believe they came here tonight. Talk about mean." Alma blew her nose loudly. "Stupid, goddamn bastard." She looked at me. Tears had smeared her mascara into a black mask. "You can't imagine how stupid I feel. I left behind such a good life and so many friends in Billings."

"Mother told me you'd been miserable up there," I said. "And couldn't wait to get back to Roundup. Did Wade want to move down here?"

Alma laughed. "I know your mother cannot conceive of anyone being happy in Montana, but I was. Did Wade want to move down here?" She shrugged, pulled another tissue from her drawer, and began to blot her cheeks. "Who cares? He does what I tell him, he's such a wienie. But I'd truly like to kill the little bastard for skipping out on this party. He only did it because we're on separate sides and he'll do anything he can to humiliate me. He knows how important this Russian deal is. I've worked like hell to try to put it together, and he and Mercedes, and unfortunately your father"—finally revealing the reason she'd wanted me to accompany her on this tour down memory lane—"are trying to break my back. But they won't. I'm going to pull it off and to hell with them. Once I get Johnny wrapped up, I'll have the votes and Rutherford Oil will step up to play with the big boys—no more of this home-grown crap."

Seemingly fully recovered, Alma addressed herself in the mirror. She looked up and caught my eye. "You might just want to tell your father there's still time to join the winning side. What are you going to do with your shares?"

I shrugged. "I don't know. I don't have enough to make a difference."

"Well, whatever, Lilly. I hope we can be friends."

"Of course," I told her, standing up, smoothing invisible wrinkles from my new skirt, and thinking I wouldn't be friends with this woman if she were the last person on earth. "I hope your Russian deal, whatever it is, works out, and I'm sorry about your problems with Johnny Bourbon. But if it makes you feel any better, I've humiliated myself in front of hundreds of men and lived to tell about it, and then gone right out and done it again."

We both laughed.

"Why don't you go on back to the party," Alma dismissed me. "I'm just going to freshen up a little and I'll be right along. Can you find your way?"

"No problem," I said. I couldn't wait to get out of there and would have climbed through the nearest smoke-filmed window if I'd had to.

The temperature outside had plunged into the thirties and the party had moved to the solarium. A fire roared in the large fireplace, and Les Fielding's Combo played a cowboy lament quietly in the corner. An assemblage of fans, all men, surrounded Shanna Bourbon, but Johnny was nowhere in sight.

Mercedes, Alma's half-sister, who had become chairman and CEO of Rutherford Oil when their father died two years ago, was at the bar, talking to Richard and my parents, and I headed in their direction. She was as petite and elegant as Alma was gross and ungainly. Her shoulder-length blond hair was sleek and her face refined. She held a highball glass of what looked like Perrier and lime in her small, long-fingered hand.

"Lilly," she greeted me warmly. "I hope we have a chance to catch up once I get this meeting behind me. It's so lovely to see you. Please excuse me, there's Kennedy and I need to grab him for a second."

"What a thoroughly charming woman," my mother said as Mercedes disappeared into the crowd. "It's a pity you never knew her mother. A true English rose with a lovely accent and lovely skin and lovely, lovely manners. Such a tragedy she died so young."

"What did she die of?"

Mother thought for a minute or so. "I don't recall," she said wistfully.

"I can't believe Mercedes and Alma are sisters," I said. "They might as well be from different planets. How come you were late?" I kissed her soft cheek. She was wearing one of her old black Chanel dinner suits and a long string of twelve-millimeter pearls.

"Your father refuses to accept the fact that there are now stoplights between here and home, and he never leaves enough time."

"There shouldn't even be anything out here," my father grumbled. He was compact and wiry and wore only faded Levi's from Johnson's Western Store, or suits from his Savile Row tailor. Tonight it was a dark nailhead. He was also a thoroughly unreconstructed Western isolationist, a quality I'm proud to have inherited. "I'll never forgive Tom Wallbank for selling this land."

"He sold it fifty years ago," Elias pointed out. The

vest of his gray, three-piece pinstripe stretched around his stomach like a Lycra bodysuit. The buttons appeared cocked to go off like bee-bees. He took a chili relleno from a passing waitress and popped it into his mouth.

"Doesn't make any difference," my father retorted. "Should still be rangeland. Nothing but a bunch of damn nouveau riche oil people out here anyway."

"Well," I ventured, "we're sort of oil people."

My father and brothers all frowned at me. "We drill on our own land," my father said. "That's the difference."

When I was growing up, the Wind River Country Club and Country Estates had been built on a piece of the old Wallbank Ranch, which was then way south of Roundup. Now, of course, it's practically downtown. My mother wouldn't let me date boys whose parents were members of the Wind River club. We were strictly a Roundup Country Club family. The Old Club. Did it matter that when my great-grandfather had given the land and underwritten the creation and construction of the Roundup Country Club back before the turn of the century the Indians had probably been as riled up about it as my father was about the Wind River Club? Of course not. That was different.

"Where are our host and hostess?" Mother asked. "I would have thought they might have greeted us." She was using her vegetable-peeler voice.

"Alma will be right back," I said, "and Wade was called out of town."

"I see. Well, I would say that's no great loss to any of us."

"You lay off Wade, Katharine," my father said. "He's a nice guy."

"Did you happen to notice who's here?" Mother

asked, completely ignoring him and rolling her eyes in Shanna Bourbon's direction.

"Yes." I smiled. "Have you been over to speak to them?"

"No. I was on my way, but then he disappeared. I intend to meet him, but your father doesn't want me to. I've never met someone who's 'done time' before."

"He's nothing but a crook and a charlatan," my father grumbled. "And he's sitting on the fence on this damn Siberian vote, still waiting for the best offer. Man's got no moral compass. And did you get a load of the Russians? They all look like escaped convicts." Between all the parties for Richard and me and now the Rutherford affair, he'd had his fill. All we could do was keep bringing the whiskey.

"Alma told me you still have time to join the winning team," I told him.

"As usual, she doesn't have any idea what she's talking about."

I vaguely heard what sounded like the faint pop of a firecracker, maybe two pops. Or maybe one was an echo. But I knew it wasn't firecrackers. It was gunshots.

FIVE

I shoved my drink into Richard's hand and pulled my little Glock .26 from my purse as I ran through the reception rooms and down the corridors, pausing at each corner to look and listen, but only silence came from Alma's direction while the sounds of the party grew fainter behind me. When I reached her bedroom, I stopped again outside the door, tight against the wall, my ears straining for the slightest tip-off: a furtive footfall, a silent breath. Nothing presented itself except a scarcely audible, mournful New Orleans trumpet wail from the dressing-room sound system and the stale smell of old cigarette smoke.

"Alma?" I called.

No response.

"Alma? Are you all right?"

I crouched and spun into the bedroom, which appeared empty, and sidestepped my way over to the dressing room, where Alma slumped across the dressing table, a large, clean bullet wound in her right temple and an expression of complete openmouthed, wide-eyed surprise on her face. Her hand clutched an old horn-gripped Colt .45 single-action Army revolver. The round appeared to have traveled at a forty-five-degree angle and exited through the upper-left quadrant of her skull, slamming a big, ragged chunk of it into the mirror. Bone fragments, brain matter, and blood drenched the pink silk tasseled lampshade. Blood poured from the exit wound and soaked into the delicate pink lace doily that covered the mirrored tabletop. Several crystal perfume bottles and atomizers had spilled or smashed, their contents turning the gelatinous muck into a slick as repulsive and macabre as the *Exxon Valdez* oil spill.

I stepped slowly across to her, careful to walk where there were no other footprints in the thick carpeting, and laid my fingers firmly on her neck. Her heart was still beating. She was alive.

As I shoved my weapon back into my purse and traded it for my cell phone, I looked at the door and saw a dozen shocked, bloodless faces staring back at me. Johnny Bourbon's expression, that arctic stare, landed between my eyes over all the others, but I didn't have time to give it a lot of thought.

"If there's a doctor around, get him in here fast," I yelled as I punched out 911, which answered instantly. "This is Marshal Bennett, give me District Three Dispatch. Now."

"Yes, ma'am." At least they knew who I was. That was major progress over a year ago.

"District Three, Sergeant Holly speaking."

"Sergeant, this is Marshal Bennett. There's been a shooting at Eighteen Sunset Drive in Wind River Estates. Looks like a suicide attempt, but she's still breathing."

"We're rolling, Marshal. What's the nature of the injury?"

"Gunshot wound to the head."

"Can you stanch the flow?"

There were four physicians at the party: internist, gynecologist, urologist, and plastic surgeon—talk about the aging of America, it used to be just the sports-medicine guy—all of whom had been frantically summoned.

The gynecologist, Leo Gregory, got there first and grabbed one of Alma's raspberry-pink bath sheets as he loped across the room. He pressed the towel to the wound. Then he pulled Alma carefully into a sitting position so her head lolled back into the crook of his arm and lifted her gently onto the floor, where he knelt with her upper body reclined across his lap, cradling her like a baby, a tender pietà, keeping the bloody towel pressed tight. As he lifted her, the revolver slid off the table and tumbled to the floor beside her, landing silently in the thick taffeta folds of the dressing-table skirt.

"We have a doctor on the scene," I said into the phone as the Preservation Hall Jazz Band swung into "Oh, When the Saints Go Marchin' In" over the sound system.

"Ambulance is sixty seconds from your location."

There was nothing to do but wait.

"Do me a favor," I said. "Patch me through to Jack Lewis."

"Yes, ma'am."

"Chief Lewis," a voice barked seconds later, just as clipped and barky as Roundup's chief of detectives was himself.

"Jack," I said. "It's Lilly. I'm out at Eighteen Sunset Drive in Wind River Estates, the Gilhooly residence. Mrs. Gilhooly appears to have attempted suicide."

"So?" His voice carried the resentful attitude he always had when it slipped his mind temporarily that I was constantly saving his ass and, I might add, making sure he got all the credit. "What're you calling me for?"

"Don't be an asshole, Jack," I said under my breath. "I'm calling you because I don't think it's suicide. I think it's attempted murder. I heard two shots and, co-incidentally, one of the big floor-to-ceiling mirrors in her dressing room is shattered, starting from what looks like a little tiny hole up in the corner. It wasn't broken when I was in here ten minutes ago. And most people don't shoot a practice round before they put the gun to their head. Just thought you'd like to know." I slapped the phone closed.

I didn't add that also, when people blow their brains out, their gun hand doesn't land conveniently on the table or desktop or wherever, still gripping the weapon. The recoil generally throws the arm out and the weapon with it. Whoever did this to Alma had been watching too much television.

Moments later, we heard the sirens screaming in the distance. The pasty-faced guests watching through the bedroom door breathed a collective sigh of relief, like children rescued from a scary movie. I knew I had lim-ited time to examine the rug before the booted para-medics rumbled across it with their heavy equipment, so I stepped backward, careful to retrace my footsteps, until I could see other footprints pressed into the thick carpeting. The almost iridescent green color made it tricky to pick them out. But, in addition to the tiny holes left by Alma's sandals and my pumps and the impressions of Dr. Gregory's loafers, I could see the distinctive prints of stirrup-heeled, pointed-toed cow-boy boots: a two-inch-wide half-circle for the heel and about three quarters of the front sole. I knelt down and, with my finger, drew a line in the pile down one side of the three visible prints, then boxed them in.

"Try to stay away from these prints," I said to the paramedics in a loud voice as they rushed past me.

Alma was still breathing when they wheeled her off.

The patrolmen and officers began to take charge of the scene, and after a couple of minutes I heard Jack Lewis's dress-parade stride strutting down the gray terrazzo in his shiny lizard Tony Lamas and his voice snapping orders to his little lieutenant, Evan, who always skittled alongside him like a sand crab on a leash.

Okay. Okay. Maybe I am as surly about Jack as he is about me, but he's got all the toys of his office, toys and power I used to have before I got caught in bed with the judge. Now I've got the prestige of a marshal's badge and am—and I'm not just making this up; most of the top law-enforcement officials in the country will back me up on this—a better, smarter, more thorough, creative, competent, higher-rate-of-more-successfully-prosecuted-crimes detective than he is. But facts are facts: I am no longer the chief of detectives of a major metropolitan area (my department in Santa Bianca was twice the size of Jack's in Roundup, I might add). And he is. And it makes me crazy. And he knows it. He knows I'm better and he knows he's got the cards. So we've forged a sometimes gracious, sometimes rancorous truce, packed with mutual suspicion and resentment, like eight-year-olds whose mothers have forced them to apologize to each other but who still hate each other's guts and can't wait to trip each other on the way down the hall.

"Hey, Bennett," he greeted me. "You losing weight? You look pretty good."

"Even if I lost a hundred pounds, Jack, I'd still be more woman than you could handle." This was an exaggeration. If I lost a hundred pounds I would be dead, or at least very, very, very sick.

"Any idea whose prints these are?" He peered down at the carpet square.

"Sorry. I don't know many of the guests. Most of the men have on boots."

"You aren't going to help me much, are you?"

"Don't be silly, Jack. I just don't know."

"And you have no ideas, either. Right?"

I grinned at him. "I'll get out of your way," I said. "I know you've got a lot to do. Call me if I can help."

As I walked back to join Richard, I concentrated on the expression I'd seen on Johnny Bourbon's face, because it was so unlike the fear and horror on any of the others, and it came down to two words: Glory and Salvation.

SIX

The sun hadn't crested the hills into the main valley of the ranch when Richard and I left on our early-morning ride, he on his big palomino stallion, Hotspur, and me on my small quarterhorse mare, Ariel. The gentle wispy clouds above us were golden peach pink, the sky was a deep azure blue, and the morning star refused to leave, lingering by the wings until the last possible second before making her exit. In another week, it would be too dark to ride at five-thirty.

We clipped along at a brisk walk, our breath visible in the chilly hill-country air.

"Name this," Richard said, letting fly with some stunning aria or other. It was beautiful, but I had no clue what it was. My appreciation of opera is absolute. My ability to identify anything but the overture to *The Barber of Seville*—which incidentally had always been my father's favorite opera, if you could say he had a favorite, since he pretty much loathed them all equally, but he liked it because in the end the Bartolo didn't have to pay a dowry for Rosina to marry Count Almaviva—is absolutely nonexistent. Richard was always trying a "Name That Tune" situation with me in the futile hope that I would pick up something along the way. My standard for judging classical music is whether or not I would like to have it played at my funeral. So far, in addition to "Happy Trails to You," which even I know is not considered classical music by most people, about ten pieces have made the cut for what I sincerely hope is not my final selection.

I looked up at the trees and fiddled with my reins a second. It did sound familiar. "It's right on the tip of my tongue. Don't tell me. Don't tell me. It's from *La Traviata*, right?"

"Wrong. It's from *Le nozze di Figaro, The Marriage of Figaro*. Mozart."

"I know what *Le nozze di Figaro* is." I was getting a little annoyed with this tutoring. It had been going on for months and was clearly a complete waste of time.

"Okay," Richard said, clearly enjoying himself. "Name this." Off he went again. He had the most perfect, big, rich tenor voice. He could even sing at a trot.

"That," I said with conviction, "is Rodolfo's big number in *Bohème*."

"Wrong," Richard said. "It's from *Tosca*. And it's not a 'number,' it's an 'aria.' I can't believe you don't recognize it, Lilly. You watched me conduct it five times in Viareggio this summer."

"Really?" I said. "Well, aren't I a dope? Okay, Mr. Puccini, you name this." I held up my middle finger in Richard's general direction and gave Ariel the green light. We shot off down the road at high speed, leaving Richard laughing and singing in the dust.

Of course, he caught us; there was no way Ariel and I could outrun Richard on Hotspur. Unfortunately, in a test of physical endurance, the combination of muscle, testosterone, and determination almost always prevails over litheness, beauty, and quick wits. Besides, I like being overpowered occasionally by a well-muscled, long-legged, determined cowboy, especially when it's Richard. Also, it helped keep my mind off the fact that Alma Rutherford Gilhooly had been shot ten hours ago and Jack Lewis hadn't yet called to ask me for help. I wondered if they'd come up with anything on the boot prints. I'd measured them, and they appeared to be about size eleven or twelve, pretty standard.

We got back to the house at six, red-cheeked, robust, ornery. Even Baby, my wire-haired fox terrier, who had waited for us at the barn, leapt from one piece of living-room furniture to the next, big smile on her face, before curling up in front of the small fire in the breakfast room and going back to sleep. Her life was very good.

"When I die," Richard said, "I want to come back as your dog."

"Me, too."

I called the hospital. Alma was still holding on, but only in the barest possible sense. The prognosis was not optimistic.

"A gentleman called," Celestina, my cook, said in perfect English. Celestina uses her Mexican accent only around strangers. She refreshes the accent every year when she and her husband take their whole family to Acapulco for Easter vacation. She is the third generation of Vargases to live on the Circle B. "Wanted directions to the house, but I told him how to get to your office and said you'd meet him there at eight o'clock. *Bueno?*"

"*Bueno,*" I said, pouring Richard and me both cups of death-strong cowboy coffee while Celestina flipped the hot cakes. "*Gracias.* Who was it?"

"Wouldn't tell me."

That wasn't especially unusual in my business. People called with secret information and sometimes even wore silly disguises to deliver it in person.

After breakfast, I gave Richard a lift down to the chopper, where Christian waited in the comfortable cabin, poring over his standard three feet of paperwork and getting fed up with Richard's and my long, lingering kiss good-bye.

"For God's sake, Lilly." Christian's bushy black eyebrows frowned at me over his sparkling blue eyes. "He's just going to the office, not on a shuttle mission." He was only pretending to be perturbed, though. Everyone in the family was happy that Richard and I were about to make it official.

They were airborne practically before the door was closed. I watched, the sun at my back, until they were no bigger than a mosquito before heading back to the house to get cleaned up.

I had to go to town later to return some recovered jewels to a client, so, instead of jeans, I slipped into loose black trousers, a cashmere sweater set, and suede pumps, laid on a few pearls—every year seems to require another strand—threw Baby into the Jeep, and took off for my international headquarters in Bennett's Fort, a small tourist-trap town that sits at the edge of the ranch—a gaudy carbuncle on the Circle B's generous two-hundred-thousand-acre hips—the way Angeles City had leeched itself onto the edge of Clark Air Force Base in the Philippines.

Bennett's Fort is the kind of place that was authentic at one time, sort of like Central City or Blackhawk or Cripple Creek, Colorado. These towns used to house what little urban history we have here in the West.

They'd been boomtowns in the big silver- and gold-mining eras in the mid- to late nineteenth century and were jam-packed with a unique combination of ornate, gingerbread Victorian architecture and severe, rough-plank Wild West structures. Today, because those once-historic towns are now gambling centers, the landmark buildings have either vanished altogether or been converted into glitzy, high-tech casinos catering to people whose sense of history is limited to who won the last Super Bowl.

The history itself has been annihilated.

Even the Central City Opera House, one of the prettiest historic opera houses in the world, where grand opera is still presented every summer, is no longer worth the trip. Who wants to get dressed up, drive for an hour from Denver through a hot canyon behind a diesel-belching tour bus, and spend the evening being gawked at by some fat slob in too-tight polyester shorts and a Day-Glo Spider-Man T-shirt with a cigarette glued to her bottom lip and a tub of quarters in her grungy paw? Not me.

Bennett's Fort had once been an honest-to-God wooden fort, built by my great-great-grandfather for the cavalry to withstand Indian attacks. Then, as skirmishes gave way to cattle drives, a "town" grew up outside the front gate, and such elements of polite civilization as the GOLDEN NUGGET SALOON—SASPARILLY ONLY FIVE DOLLARS A SHOT and HOTEL—MISS KITTY AND TEDDY ROOSEVELT SLEPT HERE and JAIL—SEE WYATT EARP'S DESK AND SIX-SHOOTERS lined its dirt street.

Today, Bennett's Fort—which is owned by my cousin Bucky Bennett: Mayor for Life—is one of Wyoming's most successful tourist traps. He has added well-known Victorian/Old Western historic commercial venues such as: Ye Olde Rock Shoppe, Ye Olde Rock

Candy and Salt Water Taffy Shoppe, Ye Olde Tintype Studio, where a boy can dress up as Jesse James or Wyatt Earp and a girl as a dance-hall floozy in a black-satin corset, torn fishnet stockings and garters and stick a pheasant feather in her hair and they can get their pitcher took for twenty-five dollars. Each. And my new favorite: Ye Olde Video Arcadie.

"Doesn't it ever bother you, Buck," I said, as I joined him in his regular booth in the saloon for a quick cup of Ecstasy's coffee and a warm bear claw before heading upstairs to my office, "that all this Ye Olde stuff is more Richard the First than Victoria?"

"Nah." Buck tossed down his first shot of Jack Daniel's, daintily blotted his gray-flecked moustache with a clean, ironed handkerchief from the back pocket of his jeans, and took a big bite of pancakes and sausage and syrup. "These people could care less. It wouldn't make any difference if Alan King or Larry King or even King Arthur himself came up and whacked them over the head with a jousting lance. All they want to know is, 'Where's the bathroom?' That's why I put two million into all these fancy johns. People have been driving, kids screaming, hot as hell—'Where's the bathroom?' "

It was true, too. Bennett's Fort's dirt street, gee-gawed storefront façades and shoppes were old-fashioned-looking and historically correct (depending on whose history you chose to follow), but downstairs, underlying the entire town, were restrooms so clean and sparkling and modern that *Architectural Digest* had done a feature on them. Buck had been hoping for a cover story.

Of course, as with everything in Bennett's Fort, nothing was free. You had to show the restroom attendant a receipt for a minimum five-dollar purchase in a Bennett's Fort emporium before she'd let you in. Sometimes, in the summer, it got so crowded, people would be lined up in the street waiting to get into the rest-rooms, holding their five-dollar cups of sasparilly as if they were specimen cups for some huge insurance-plan physical. Children under twelve got in free.

"Let's get some more java going over here, sugar," Buck called over to Ecstasy, his fifty-year-old burned-out hippie sister-in-law, who shuffled across in her Earth Shoe sandals, dirty gray hair clamped into a stringy ponytail at the nape of her turkey neck.

"Hey, Lil." She smiled at me, her teeth as brown and big as fence posts, her vacant face a hundred years old. She'd surrendered her brain to LSD at a Steppenwolf concert back there in Boulder in 'sixty-eight, and it had taken her someplace very, very weird and scary and aged her overnight. Her husband, Buck's brother Bill, was so gone he now spent most of the year in the barn untangling the Christmas lights until it was time to put them up again.

"Hey, Ec." I smiled back as she shuffled home to her stool behind the bar and "Good Morning America."

Suddenly a crash and some scraping sounds thundered from my offices upstairs. Dust fell from the ceiling in long, thin, curtains, like scrims in a theater.

"What's that girl up to now?" Buck squinted at the ceiling. He was referring to my secretary, Linda Long, whose pants he was always trying to think of a way to get into, but my brother Elias had beaten him to it.

"Who knows?" I shrugged. "She's always moving things around. So what's up for you today?" I was try-ing to decide if I should join him in a shot of sour mash. It smelled delicious.

"Got that Redford crew rolling in any minute." He looked at his watch, a stainless-steel Seiko he'd worn since Vietnam. "They start shooting tomorrow."

In the off-season, which was basically the nine months between Labor Day and Memorial Day, with the exception of a few weeks at Christmas, Buck rented out the town to movie producers for an insane amount of money. Today Robert Redford's company would arrive to shoot a socially conscious, politically correct, old-time Western about cowboys who treated women as equals and believed that no meant no. And Indian braves who killed four-thousand-pound buffalo with slingshots and bows and arrows and would never, ever, consider driving a thousand head of them at a time off cliffs to kill them. And believed that no meant no. It would be another one of those history-rewrite flicks, sort of like Oliver Stone's stuff.

"How 'bout you?" He took another bite of sausage. "How's the wedding coming along?"

"Great. It still seems unreal."

"Oh, it'll be real enough all right. He slips that ring on your finger and you're fucking trapped for life. Then it'll cost you a fucking fortune to unload him. That'll be enough reality for you."

Buck obviously had had a bad marital experience.

"So I hear Alma Rutherford's party got busted up last night when she blew her brains out."

"Well, it wasn't much of a party to begin with," I said. "Have you seen Alma lately?"

Buck shook his grizzled head and lit a cigarette. "Nah. Not since her coming-out party. I was one of her escorts. She was a real load. It's her sister Mercedes who can crank my engine. Talk about a babe. She could get me down the aisle with no problem."

Neither of us had to say what the chances of that were.

"Alma didn't try to commit suicide," I told him. "Someone shot her."

"No shit. Paper said it was attempted suicide, but what do they know? So what if the family owns it?"

He threw down another shot and was about to continue when the swinging doors blasted open and Linda burst into the room as if she'd been shot from a cannon, her face as wild and red as her hair. "You'd better get up there before I kill this guy," she said breathlessly.

"What guy?"

"Wade Gilhooly."

SEVEN

Wade Gilhooly was much better-looking than I'd been led to expect by Mother's highly pejorative description. Of course, it was hard to get the full effect of his charms, chained as he was to the chimney of the potbellied stove. It looked pretty uncomfortable to me, hugging the chimney and straddling the stove at the same time.

He was so berserk with anger, his face had turned such a deep shade of crimson, I wouldn't have been a bit surprised if his eyes had flown from his head and geysers of steam shot from his ears and his tongue snapped in and out of his mouth like a window shade, except that Linda had gagged him with the Hermès scarf Richard had brought her from Paris.

"Hey, Wade," I said. "Heard a lot about you. I guess you're lucky Linda hasn't gotten the fire going yet," I joked, except that he wasn't laughing. "Exactly what's happening here?"

"Would you believe," Linda said, her fists fired into her hips like bolts in a bridge, "I offered this . . .

this . . . this *troglodyte* a cup of coffee, and when I
went to hand it to him, he tried to feel me up? *Hey!*"
she yelled at Wade, who had made an effort to speak.
"You get any spit on my new scarf and I'll rip your
fuckin' nuts off."

Here's the deal with Linda. We're about the same
age, but she's a divorced ranch wife from over near
Riverton, which means she's so tough she could make a
Marine drill sergeant weep in eight minutes flat. She
was born and raised on a working ranch and then spent
twenty-five years helping her husband run a big
spread—until the day she found him in the hayloft with
the neighbor's daughter. Linda definitely does not take
crap from anybody.

"Yup," she told me one time, "I went back down the
ladder, tossed my cigarette into a pile of hay, closed and
locked the barn door, grabbed my best stuff, and took
off for town."

"Did they burn to death?" I asked.

"Hell, no. No such luck. They just put it out with the
hose and went out the back."

And she has all this wavy reddish-gray hair that she
wears pulled up in a Gibson Girl sort of bun and thick
glasses and a brain bigger than a Pentagon computer,
and she is literally the kind of woman who, when a man
pulls off her glasses to see how she looks, looks like a
goddess.

"You stupid jerk," she said, and kicked Wade in the
ankle with the rounded tip of her no-nonsense, stacked-
leather-heel Amalfi pump, left over from sorority rush
when she attended Wyoming State in the sixties.

"Some people never learn." I untied Wade's two-
hundred-dollar gag and tossed it on a chair, then
grabbed the padlock keys from Linda's desk and freed
his hands. "Now, let's start over. Why don't you come

into my office and have a seat. Would you like another cup of coffee?"

It was hard to tell if Wade was blushing, but he shook himself out like a furious little leprechaun and had the grace to offer an embarrassed apology to Linda before picking up a silver-handled cane off the floor and following me slowly through the door into my sun-drenched office, where the wind sometimes blows straight through the glass.

"Please have a seat," I told him. "I'll be right with you." I closed the office door and turned to Linda, aghast. "I cannot believe you chained an *invalid,* who is *half* your size, to the stove. Are you insane? He could sue us into oblivion."

This was the first time I'd ever criticized Linda for anything, but I was really shocked.

"His legs may be gimped up, but there's nothing wrong with his hands, believe me," she said defensively. "It was like having eggbeaters come at me."

"I don't care. Next time, outrun him. Frontier justice is not a go around here, Linda. We do not chain up outlaws in the barn until the sheriff comes. You have a real problem, call Dwight."

"You're right," she admitted. "I got a little carried away."

"Don't do it again. He could cream us for harass-ment."

"I'm sorry. It never occurred to me."

I stared at my closed office door for a moment, pull-ing myself together, then went to join Wade, who had taken a seat and was twirling the cane like a baton, a placid, sunny look on his face.

"I'm a little surprised you aren't at the hospital with Alma," I said, sitting down behind my flat-topped oak desk. About a dozen pink message slips lay stacked next to the phone. "You could at least pretend you care a little, make a show of it. She did, after all, make you a rich man."

"I've been at the hospital all night." Wade crossed his legs. He had on a good-looking camel sport coat, a navy polo shirt, gabardine trousers, and soft Italian leather loafers. Now that he'd calmed down, although he looked pale and exhausted, with dark circles spreading beneath his eyes—I recalled Alma saying he'd had the flu for a month—he was extremely attractive. Freckles dotted his face, and bushy, sandy-red eyebrows topped his light-blue eyes. His nose looked like a boxer's, as though it had been broken a couple of times. Sexy. From what I'd learned about him, it sounded like he was both a lover and a fighter. His hands were clean and nails well manicured. Wade was, in fact, handsome, elegant, and comfortably prosperous. What looked like an old burn scar rose jaggedly on his neck above his collar, and beneath the dark circles, the yellowing remains of a black eye smudged his cheekbone.

"Let me get one thing straight." His color rose again like a crimson tide. "I'm sick of people saying I did this on Alma's back. She didn't make me rich. Her father provided the seed money. *I* made me rich. Gilhooly GMC Truck and Chevrolet is the largest dealer in the Rocky Mountain States, and Alma's never even been through the door. *And* I paid her father back every penny. With interest."

Linda brought in coffee, and Wade apologized to her again.

"I think I might have learned a lesson," he said sheepishly.

"I think we both did. I'm sorry I chained you to the stove." She smiled at him before closing the door, and I could tell he was thinking of grabbing her all over again. And I knew she was thinking if he did, she'd throw him on the floor, hog-tie him, and beat him to death with his cane.

"What can I do for you?" I said. The top message on the stack was from a major client in Italy. The marchese was missing some more paintings, a Tiepolo this time. From his Venetian palazzo. I loved it when that happened.

"I know Alma isn't expected to make it." He blew on his coffee before taking a sip, and I noticed his hand shook slightly as he raised the cup to his lips. I wondered if he were suffering from more than flu. "And the fact is, she and I had one hell of a marriage and I'm going to be the number-one suspect and I want you on my team."

"But I thought you were in Billings last night."

"I was. But I want to be careful, so I'm hiring you, just so there're no screw-ups."

Wade leaned forward, resting his arms on the desk. His deep-set eyes stared out at me with an almost lupine ferocity, and I felt a gauntlet in there somewhere, but I couldn't tell if it was a challenge or an invitation. It only felt dangerously dark and sensuous. "Alma and I went our separate ways years ago, and I won't even begin to pretend I'm surprised this happened. She was a major pain in the butt, excuse my French, and there're going to be a lot of people who say I was involved. But I wasn't. And I figure with you working for me, you can keep me posted about what's going on. Keep me out of it. Help find out who really did it."

Short of having Jack Lewis call and beg me to head his investigative team, this was the sort of invitation and case I lived for. It had all the elements of homicide that interest me: people with more money than they could possibly need so they were killing for power. For control. And when you get right down to it, murder is the ultimate exercise of power. I also knew it had been someone in Alma's immediate circle, because in 95 percent of murders—that don't involve armed robbery— the killer and victim know each other. Well.

Unfortunately, though, no matter how much I wanted to accept his offer, I knew it would be unprofessional. There was no way I could give this case the attention it deserved. I'd waited my whole life to think about my wedding gown and all the beautiful new things I was going to wear on my Burgundian honeymoon, and the fact that I was finally choosing, and being chosen, for life. I didn't want to shortchange myself—personally or professionally—in the stretch.

I swallowed. Hard. "I'm really sorry. I wish I could help, but I can't accept any new clients right now. There are a couple of people I can recommend for you, though." I scribbled the names of two other investigators on a slip of notepaper and slid it across the desk to him like a doctor dispensing a prescription.

"Whatever your standard fee is, I'll double it. You're the best in the field, and you know Alma and all the people involved. If you don't want to do it for me, do it for Alma."

Alma? I thought. From what I'd seen of Alma the night before, I wouldn't help her any more than I'd help Adolf Hitler or Idi Amin or Saddam Hussein or any other genocidal maniac, but I did like the sound of a double fee.

Here's how I feel about money: A lot of people think that if you're born with a lot of money, you shouldn't work. That you should just play golf or bridge or go deep-sea fishing or skiing or yachting or shopping all day. Have you ever had a conversation with someone who skis or yachts or plays golf or shops all day every day? They have nothing to say that is of any interest to me. I'm interested in people who do things that make a difference, and they're interested in me only if *I* do something that makes a difference, too. Also, I've always made certain that I could pay my own way no matter what my family bank account might say, because you just never know. Lots of people with much more money than the Bennett family have lost everything and had virtually no fall-back position. We Bennetts are workers. We take nothing for granted.

So, when Wade Gilhooly offered a double fee, it got my attention.

"Let me ask you a couple of questions," I said, pushing the start button on the tape recorder on my desk. "And for the record, this is all going on tape."

"Sort of like the Richard Nixon of investigators," Wade joked.

"Nothing like that," I said.

"Shoot." Wade spread his palms, indicating he'd answer anything I could throw his way.

"Who do you think did it?"

"I have a few ideas. I tossed their names back and forth all night, and all of them make some sense. By that I mean, there could be plenty of motives, but I can't see any of these people actually shooting her, trying to murder her. They aren't that kind of people. Besides, deep down, she could be a nice gal."

A nice gal who liked big-game hunting for trophies? I don't think so.

"To me, Mr. Gilhooly," I said, "someone who can look any animal, wild or tame, human or four-legged, in the eyes and then kill it, unless it's in self-defense, is a cold-blooded killer. I know too many of those types, and none of them can even remotely be described as nice gals. Let's start at the top. Who's your first possibility?"

"Johnny Bourbon," Wade answered quickly. "I'd hate to think he'd do it—we've all been friends for so long—but I must admit that his was one of the first names that occurred to me last night. I think he and Alma had some big blow-up, but . . ." He stopped to look for the right words.

"But you think Alma should have been the one to do the shooting?"

"That's what it sounded like to me. Sounded like he unloaded her, and that's not the way it usually works with Alma."

I nodded. I wrote Johnny Bourbon's name at the top of a blank yellow legal pad. "And, how does it usually work?"

"Oh, you know. She's usually the one who gets bored first, or they do something that makes her mad and she walks." His voice was flat and expository, betraying virtually no emotion.

"Who else?" I asked, thinking I'd hate to have a marriage like the Gilhoolys'. They treated it as though it were nothing but a game.

"Did you meet Kennedy McGee at the party?"

"Kennedy McGee? No. But there were a number of guests I didn't meet. Things fell apart pretty quickly after we got there."

"I don't know if he was there or not, but he's the Great White Hunter who led our safaris for years and he usually attends the Rutherford Oil annual meeting. He's not a major stockholder, but it's a congenial group and he makes it a business stop. Alma broke his heart a few years back when she pulled her money out of a big resort he'd been trying to finance, and she felt he'd been stalking her ever since."

"From Africa?"

"Well, the bottom's pretty much fallen out of the big-game-hunting business, so he was over here a lot trying to put together groups of rich Americans for the resort. I hear it's one of those places that's so expensive and exclusive they practically bring the animals to your room. But do I think he was actually stalking Alma? No. Kennedy's an okay guy, but Alma liked to live in her own world of intrigue. Most of it was made up."

"Who else?"

"Ever heard of Duke Fletcher?"

"You mean the senator from Montana?"

Wade nodded. "Former senator. They were our next-door neighbors in Billings, when they were in town anyhow. His wife died last year. Alma promised to help get him reelected, but then he did something to piss her off, some kind of environmental deal—Alma was opposed to all environmental legislation—and she yanked her pledge."

"I saw him and Alma talking at the party. She seemed friendly enough."

"Alma never closed the door. She always kept hope alive. Kept her money out there like a carrot."

"And a stick, sounds like to me," I said, recalling her saying she'd told Johnny Bourbon she would withdraw her support from his ministry if he didn't leave his wife. I also noticed that Wade kept referring to her in the past tense, as though her imminent death were a foregone conclusion.

"That's about as good a description as you could get," Wade agreed. "And then, of course, you have to keep in mind that Duke's a politician and he's running for President and money's always welcome. And then there's the proxy fight with her sister. This thing's really getting ugly."

"Tell me about it."

"Mercedes is chairman and CEO of the company, and Alma is chairman of the Executive Committee of the board. Alma and the COO, some hotshot geologist, want to develop a field in Siberia, and Mercedes is opposed. The board's split right down the middle, and some people say it won't be decided until the votes are counted at the annual shareholders' meeting. The venture would require an initial investment of about six billion—about seventy-five percent of which they'd have to borrow—and that's just to get some of the groundwork done, just to get to preliminary exploration, doesn't include up and running, with no guarantees from the Russian government. To borrow that much money could be a make-or-break deal for Rutherford Oil. I personally think it's too big a crap shoot for a company that size."

"Where are the lines drawn?"

Wade drummed his fingers on the desktop and squinted out the window. "I'm not really sure. Alma and Mercedes each own thirty-five percent of the company, and they've each been courting the other major stockholders so actively I don't think anyone knows what'll happen until the actual vote on Wednesday."

"This Wednesday?"

"That's when the annual meeting is. Day after tomorrow."

"Who inherits the bulk of her estate?"

"Well," Wade sputtered after a moment. His face splotched up again. "I do."

I wrote his name on my list after Mercedes.

"But, I mean . . ." He became as flustered as a teenager caught in the bathroom with a dirty magazine, and I imagine Wade Gilhooly has had that experience more times than most. "I don't even need it. I've made myself a millionaire ten times over. She had her money and I had mine."

"I understand," I said. "But I need to ask you where you were when she was shot?"

"Flying back from Billings." His mouth had gone suddenly dry and cottony. "I was on Frontier Flight Eight-Six-Six. You can check it. I didn't get in until nine-fifteen. We were late. I was in seat Eight-C." Wade verged on panic and was leaning so far forward in his chair I thought he would slide off onto the floor. Beads of sweat circled his receding hairline.

"Calm down, Wade," I said, laughing. "I believe you."

"Then you'll help?"

"I'll help."

EIGHT

G et Frontier Airlines on the phone," I said to Linda as
soon as the sound of Wade's slow footsteps had disappeared down the rickety wooden staircase that clung
to the back of the building like a wet cat hanging from
a broken branch. Buck said it wasn't authentic if it
didn't sag and sway and not to worry because he had
plenty of insurance. Of course it wouldn't be him doing
the falling fifteen feet.

"Yes, Marshal Bennett," the reservations supervisor
told me moments later, "Mr. Gilhooly was on Flight
Eight-Six-Six last night. He commutes with us regu-
larly."

"Was the flight delayed?" I was standing at Linda's
desk using her phone, and out the back window I
watched Wade pull out of the parking lot in a white
Cadillac Eldorado convertible—top down—with red-
leather seats and a pair of longhorns on the hood. A
blonde in dark glasses sat right next to him, her hand in
his pants.

"Let me see." The agent punched in a few numbers.

"Yes, it was delayed by twenty minutes. There were cattle on the runway in Billings."

"Thanks a lot," I said.

"Thank you for calling Frontier Airlines."

The girl's head disappeared into Wade's lap as they turned the corner.

I turned to Linda and started laughing. "Good God. Can you believe this bunch?" Wade's car was swerving carelessly down the hardtop at a high rate of speed. "This guy's wife is lying in intensive care with half her head missing and he's getting a blow job on his way to the hospital."

"Are you going to take the case?"

"Double fee," I said, and Linda grinned. "Get a retainer agreement and invoice over to him today. Make it clear his deposit has to be in my account this afternoon or the deal's off."

"You got it, chief." Linda turned to her computer and had the invoice printed before I was even back through the door into my office. She followed right on my heels. "Mrs. Van Buren is expecting you at ten-thirty. And your mother called and said please not to forget the Kellys' party tonight. It's at six-thirty. The rest of this," she said, fanning a handful of correspondence like play money, "can wait."

Mother seemed much calmer about this wedding than she had about my goddaughter Lulu's in June. She had immersed herself so deeply in the planning and execution of Lulu's marriage to the Baron, and dedicated herself so totally to the torture of everyone around her, that she never took the time to enjoy herself. I guess she felt she'd planned my nuptials for so many years, she could carry them off in her sleep. Unfortunately, deep down, of course, we all knew that this sanguine attitude masked a sleeping volcano, that the clock was ticking, and that, like a letter bomb, she was scheduled to go off any second. What she was doing was vamping for time, building up back-pressure.

I took the triple-magnification mirror out of my desk drawer, checked my makeup, and was just spinning the dial on the big, antique black-lacquered safe I'd claimed from one of my father's banks when Elias arrived with coffee and doughnut holes for Linda.

"Don't forget," he said. The tumblers fell into place and I slammed the handle down with the sound and authority of a good old-fashioned lockup, then removed a small black-velvet bag, its braided satin drawstring pulled tight. "The Kellys' party is at six-thirty."

"I know, Mother already called." I spilled Mrs. Van Buren's twelve, perfectly matched, quarter-sized, Ceylon sapphires onto my desk and counted to make sure they were all there.

"She says starting today I have to go everywhere you go. Sort of an official escort. How are you this morning, my darling?" He gave Linda a hug and a kiss that was actually more like a little peck from a shy bear.

"Elias," I said, drizzling the stones back into their soft pouch. They made deliciously solid clicks, like a slow game of marbles heard from a distance. "Just because I missed most of Lulu's parties doesn't mean I'm going to miss any of Richard's and mine. And you won't be an escort, you'll be a baby-sitter. I swear to God I'll be there."

Elias shook his head. "Sorry. You have virtually no credibility in this department. Besides, we'll have fun. I'll be your driver."

"Okay," I said. "Let's go."

"You mean right now? I just got here. What about the coffee and doughnuts and everything?"

"I'll tell you what. For today, I'll just call in every hour. How's that?"

"Yeah." Elias popped two tender, glazed, deep-fried morsels into his mouth. "I suppose that'll be okay for today. We'll start tomorrow."

I headed for town, winding through Little Squaw Canyon at a higher rate of speed than Wade, because I passed him about five minutes later. The convertible was pulled over on the side of the road. His head was pushed into the red-leather headrest. His mouth was open and his eyes were closed. I supposed that if my windows had been down I could have heard him yelling. Only the back of the blonde's head was visible, submerged as she was in the depths of Wade's Cerrutti gabardines.

"That guy is worse than a dog," I said aloud.

My lookout, Baby, stood with her front paws on the Jeep's dashboard and didn't give him more than a blink. She was searching for bigger game than Wade Gilhooly.

Mrs. Van Buren was ecstatic to recover her sapphires, which had been lifted from her neck in a suite at the Grand Hotel during an evening rendezvous, a little piece of action torn off furtively at the Arthritis Foundation annual benefit. To complicate the matter further, it was the foundation honoree, the Man of the Year, she had met in the suite, and since time was limited, he'd had to return to the ballroom before the house detective arrived, which kept his skirts nicely clean. In the meantime, Mrs. Van Buren sent a message to her husband that she had suffered a sick spell and was waiting for him at the front door, where he found her, the million-dollar sapphire necklace ostensibly safely snuggled beneath her velvet scarf and fur coat.

I had known Nell Van Buren all my life; she was only a few years older than I and was notorious for messing around on her husband. There are many things I'm old-fashioned about and fidelity is one of them. God knows, I've had more than my share of married lovers, but did I trust them? Are you kidding? Not a chance. They were cheaters. I suppose that's why I've always taken marriage so seriously: I figure a promise is a promise and playing around on your partner is simply not a go. Otherwise, who can you trust? That's the way it works on the police force anyhow, and that's good enough for me.

Her large check was safe in my pocket, my skill, silence, and discretion paid for in full, as I turned out of her tree-lined driveway across the street from the Roundup Country Club. I decided to call Richard and see what he was up to. See if he still loved me.

"He's over in the theater," his secretary told me. "They've got a *Così* rehearsal until noon. Do you want me to transfer you?"

I loved going to opera rehearsals. So much happened, so much motion and talking and music. Lighting people stood right in front of the tenor while he sang and made sure the spots hit him just right while the wardrobe mistress tugged on the back of his uniform jacket to make sure it didn't bunch up during that particular aria where he'd have to wave his arms around, and in the background the director moved the rest of the cast here and there and then descended into the front of the house to examine his work like a painter, and then motioned to the movement trainer that the ladies should be doing little dips and twirls with their fans, "Like this," not big swooping ones, "Like this," and all the cast members who weren't singing would laugh at his exaggerated antics, and then he called out to the stage manager, who was having a conversation in a normal voice with his assistant about the lighting cues, that Yes, that was just right, and all the while the orchestra was booming along at full pitch. The incredible thing to me was that everyone always seemed to be on the same page, because at some point during all this turmoil, the conductor would give his baton a little ding on his music stand and all would come to a complete and silent halt and he would say quietly, "Okay, fine. Let's try that again from the . . ." and I never could figure out what he said at that point but everyone else could and always went right to the perfect spot. Sometimes it even seemed they started right in the middle of a note. And they kept on like this for hours every day, for weeks, when finally the music, the voices, the costumes, the lights, and the action all melded together into an opulent spectacle. To me it is miraculous.

"No, that's okay. Just tell him I'll drop in later and see if he can grab a quick lunch."

I decided to pay a visit to the crime scene.

NINE

A squad car blocked the brick gateway that marked the entrance to the Gilhooly residence across the road from the tenth green. Two patrolmen—one younger, one older—leaned against the black-and-white in the warm late-morning sunshine sipping coffee and talking, no doubt about the Colorado Rockies and their bid for the pennant. One more win and everyone was sure they'd go all the way to the Series. I flashed my badge.

"Good morning, Marshal," the older patrolman said. "Did Chief Lewis clear you in?"

"Sure did," I lied.

"Fair enough." He signaled for his partner to back their car far enough for me to pass.

"Thanks," I said and headed down the gravel drive. Wade's Eldorado was visible in one of the bays of the four-car garage, while a white forensics van and another squad car were parked at the front door. Directly behind them sat a bright red Jaguar XJR-S convertible, its passenger seat stacked with expensive canvas luggage. A uniformed patrolman was eyeing the car enviously.

"Good morning," I said. "Nice wheels."

"Morning, Marshal." He smiled. "Too rich for my blood."

The Gilhoolys' gray-pine front door was open and just inside, a gigantic, wildly ornate, white-wrought-iron Victorian birdcage sat in the entry hall like a snowbound jail cell, a stuffed bald eagle perched on the bird swing. The more I saw of this place, the worse it got. The house was quiet. Wade was nowhere in sight.

"Ridiculous thing, isn't it?" A cultured English accent startled me from behind, and I turned to see a tall, tan, handsome man, whose ruggedness reminded me of Richard's, but whose sea-green eyes had a Me Tarzan–You Jane attitude that made me feel like a heifer at a cattle sale. An old scar curved down his cheek, from the corner of his eye to just below the corner of his mouth, which was chiseled and square, and he was rakishly dressed in khaki safari gear, meticulously tailored to show off his flat stomach and tapered waist. Knee-high, tight leather boots strained over his muscled calves. I felt as if I were looking at Indiana Jones. He was too glamorous to be true.

Two heavy-looking, oversized canvas ski-carriers, same style as those in the Jag, were slung over his shoulders, and he put them down with a solid clunk and stepped forward.

"Kennedy McGee." He extended a knotted, rough hand. The Great White Hunter.

"Lilly Bennett."

"Pleased to meet you. It's you who was at the party last night with all the police and whatnot."

"Yes," I answered, curious about what was in the

carriers. "I'm sorry we didn't get a chance to meet. Are you leaving?"

Kennedy nodded. His face hid a million secrets. "I'm just on my way up to hospital to see Alma before I make my way to Jackson. I have a client there. They have a large ranch outside of town."

"Everybody in Jackson has a large ranch outside of town," I said.

"Yes." He smiled uncertainly. "Quite."

Here's the deal with ranches around here: If you're an actual Westerner, as I am, you consider anything up to a hundred acres a yard and anything between a hundred and five hundred acres a farm or feedlot or something like that. It's possible to have a small ranch with a thousand acres, but you'd better have some pretty fine real estate and some pretty fine cattle or sheep on it to call it a ranch, and even then, you call it one with an aw-shucks attitude: "It's really too little to call it a ranch," you apologize. "We just call it that. It's really more of a small property." From there you move on up into real ranch territory until you get to spreads like the Circle B, which at two hundred thousand acres is bigger than some national forests. There are only a handful of places like ours left in the country, so I don't expect everyone's ranch to be the size of ours—anything over a couple of thousand acres is certainly respectable ranch property—but when I come across outsiders (usually New Yorkers) who say they have a ten-acre ranch in Jackson, I can't help laughing right in their faces because they sound like idiots and they're just parroting what their stupid developers and *People* magazine have told them.

"May I ask what's in the ski bags, Mr. McGee?"

"Skis, of course," he said lightheartedly. I heard the

bravado in his voice. "Alma has been storing them for me."

"May I see them?"

"They're just skis."

"And what else?"

"Nothing that would be of any interest to you. Just some personal trophies."

"I'm sorry," I said, pulling the navy-leather wallet from my purse. The United States Marshal badge glittered like brass knuckles. "I should have started with this. Unzip them, please."

"Oh, I forgot," McGee delivered his most beguiling smile. "Alma told me you were a sheriff or something. I've always loved women in uniform. Don't you need some sort of paperwork, some sort of warrant to search my luggage?"

I gave him *my* most beguiling smile. "You think this is a game. That I'll handcuff you and lock you up and maybe even spank you or talk dirty to you until you do what I tell you. Just like all your girls out there in the Serengeti, or whatever you call it."

McGee laughed, a big, hearty bellow. His teeth were white and straight. "Oh, you are truly delightful, Miss Bennett. I'm so sorry your fiancé met you first."

"But alas, Mr. McGee," I concluded, "I'm not playing. I am a real marshal, and I want to see what's in your bags. It'll be easy enough for me to get a warrant—might slow you down a little—but if that's what you prefer." My heart was thudding, racing. I was afraid I knew what the bags hid, and I dreaded being right. My fingers rested lightly on the weapon in my pocket as the smile left McGee's face. He wiped sweat from his hands on his pants legs before kneeling to unzip the first carrier.

I wanted to throw up. I wanted to shoot him. I wanted to cry.

The elephant tusks screamed like the skeletons of Auschwitz. Ghastly, gruesome, deathly, savage.

"Oh, Mr. McGee," I said, losing my breath. "How can you sleep at night?" I went to the open door to signal for the patrolman to join us, then I read the animal his rights. "Kennedy McGee, I'm placing you under arrest for possession of contraband. You have the right to remain silent. You have the right to an attorney. Anything you say can, and will, be used against you in a court of law. Do you understand what I've just said?"

"These aren't actually mine," he said easily. "They're Alma's."

"Do you understand what I've just said?" I approached him and snapped a handcuff around one wrist.

"Yes, of course I do. But I'd like to explain."

"I understand that for someone in your business lying becomes a way of life." I led him over to the birdcage and snapped the other handcuff around one of the bars. "But don't say another word to me unless you want to incriminate yourself further."

"Do you want me to take him downtown, Marshal?" the patrolman asked.

I looked Kennedy McGee in the eye. I wanted to say, "No, I want you to take him out behind the house and shoot him," but said instead, "No thanks. He's in federal custody. This is a federal matter. I'll take it from here."

"They're Alma's," McGee insisted.

I called my deputy, Dwight Alexander, the handsome, stupid, sexy U.S. Marshal Service poster boy, and told him to get his pants on and get on over to the Gilhoolys' to transport a prisoner back to the little jail in Bennett's Fort, and if the prisoner put up any resistance or was disrespectful, to feel free to shoot him (I looked Kennedy McGee in the eye as I said this). Then I called Jack Lewis.

"Chief Lewis," he yapped.

"Jack, it's Lilly. I'm at the Gilhooly residence, where I've just arrested a fellow for smuggling elephant tusks, and I wondered if there were anything you'd like me to check out while I'm here."

"Excuse me?" he said. "Do we have a bad connection? I think I just heard you say you were at the Gilhooly residence."

"Yup." I grinned. I could picture him perfectly. At the sound of my voice he'd jumped to his feet and was now standing arrow-straight at his desk, white-knuckled hand gripping the phone. "I am. And, as I'm sure you know, Alma Gilhooly's not going to survive, so you'll have a murder investigation on your hands and it doesn't look like anyone's out here working on it very hard." I loved sticking it to Jack.

As I explained the circumstances, the postman drove up and handed me the mail. "Here you go, Mrs. Gilhooly," he whispered. "Nice to meet you finally."

"You, too," I mouthed back while Jack ranted and raved and laid down the terms and conditions of our cooperative arrangement of Alma's homicide investigation. I flipped through the large stack of letters and bills. Nothing too earth-shaking, except two items: an agenda for the Annual Stockholders' Meeting of the Rutherford Oil Company addressed to Alma as chairman of the Executive Committee of the board, and a typed letter addressed to Alma R. Gilhooly from the Freedom Wyoming Coalition, our own homegrown militia wackos. They'd be funny if they weren't so dangerous.

Dwight arrived shortly, and after placing large evidence stickers on the canvas bags, we loaded them into his white government Suburban with the blacked-out windows. Then he shoved Kennedy McGee into the backseat.

"I swear to God, these are not mine," McGee was clearly frightened. He'd lost his color. A little tremor appeared in his hands, and a little sweat appeared around his brow and stained the back of his starched shirt.

"It's really too bad," I said through the open car door. "You look like a man, but you act like a girl. Next you'll probably start crying. Where were you when Alma Gilhooly was shot?"

"I don't know. With Mrs. Bromley, I suppose."

Velma Bromley was one of Roundup's richest widows: a perfect mark for a Great White Hunter.

"At the party?"

"No."

"You were not at this party last night?" I repeated.

"No. I'm staying at Mrs. Bromley's. We were probably having dinner or something."

"You were not at Alma's party and you did not have a conversation with Mercedes Rutherford?"

"Never."

"We'll see." I knew he was lying.

I slammed the car door. "That's it, Dwight. Take him to the Fort."

"I don't know anyone here," Kennedy wailed. "At least give me the name of a lawyer."

"Call Paul Decker," I shouted as the Suburban pulled away. "Dwight'll give you his number. He'll have you out in a day or two. You shithead."

I was just about to go back inside, find Wade, and tell him good-bye, when a pearl-gray Cadillac Seville barreled down the driveway and slid to a noisy stop in the gravel by the garage. The car door flew open and a man in a yellow-plaid sport coat and green slacks jumped out and raced through a side door. I decided to follow him.

He was about halfway down the hall when Wade's voice called from the study, "I'm in here, Jim."

I stopped outside and leaned against the wall.

"I just heard about Alma," Jim said. "I can't believe it. This is terrible."

"I know," Wade answered. His voice sounded tired, slightly incredulous. "I can't believe it either."

This was followed by one of those long, uncomfortable, self-conscious pauses so typical of men trapped in emotional circumstances. "How are *you* feeling, boss?" Jim asked. "You don't look too good."

"Like hell. Doctor said if I don't get any better in the next few days I'm going to have to go in for some tests."

"Is there anything I can do?" Jim asked.

"I'm counting on you to run the operation for the next few days. I know it's just a matter of hours for Alma, and I need to get her funeral and stuff worked out. I hired that cookie, Lilly Bennett, to look into whoever shot Alma. She's supposed to be pretty good."

Cookie. Huh.

"Help yourself to a drink. I have to go find my briefcase. I think I left it in my car." Ice clinked into a glass. "Vodka's in the freezer."

Jim poured what sounded like a lot.

"You're booked on the three o'clock."

"You want me to go *back* to Billings?"

"Yeah," Wade said testily. "I want you to go, and I'll tell you when I want you to come home. Clear?"

"Yes, sir."

I slid around the corner and concealed myself behind an armoire as Wade headed down the hall in the direction of the garage. Once he was gone, I let myself out the front door.

Richard was sitting about halfway up in Bennett Auditorium listening to the stage manager, lighting designer, and director straighten out the garden scene between Fiordiligi and her sister Dorabella, two of *Così fan tutte*'s three divas. Unlike the new breed of glamour divas, these two were a couple of tanks, but they were the only set of identical twin sopranos in the world, which, according to Richard, was what the guest conductor and director wanted. I slipped in beside him.

"Hey," he said, and took my hand. "What a nice surprise. Come on, let's go grab a sandwich. This is going to drag on for hours."

Over a club sandwich and some Jamesons on the rocks at the Cattlemen's Club, I explained all that had gone on so far.

"Look at this." I pulled the Rutherford Oil agenda from my purse. "Alma's chairman of the Executive Committee. I had no idea of the scope of this proxy fight—it's unbelievable. Wade filled me in this morning. Initial investment of six billion dollars."

"Let me guess," Richard said. "Mercedes is in favor. Alma's against."

"No. Other way around. Plus, she's yanked cash patronage from Johnny Bourbon for his ministry unless he divorces Shanna and marries her; from Kennedy McGee for his African resort unless I don't know what; and from Senator Fletcher because he voted in favor of some environmental bill, which should be no surprise to anybody since environmental protection is his whole platform in the first place. They're all furious at her. And to top the whole thing off, she's making big gifts to a Wyoming militia group."

Richard laughed and shook his head. "She's a one-woman tsunami. The Leona Helmsley of the Rockies."

"Exactly."

Richard sipped his Glenfiddich and looked me in the eye. "Speaking of hotels," he said. "What have you got on for this afternoon?"

"I was sort of thinking about a small suite at the Grand."

He smiled. "Me, too."

TEN

Well, the suite had been a fine idea, but as Richard signed the luncheon check, the hundred-year-old waiter handed him a note from his silver platter that said the *Così* twins had thundered back to their hotel like a brace of hysterical elephants and would not return until the wardrobe mistress was replaced.

"I don't know how you put up with all these prima donnas," I said. "I'd just tell them to get a damn grip."

"If I can withstand the Moscow State Orchestra getting loaded on vodka and beer during the *Tosca* intermissions at Viareggio," he said taking my hand—his neck and hands were still covered with red bumps from all the mosquito bites he'd endured in the pit as the star guest conductor at the Puccini Festival—"a couple of fat, spoiled twins from Düsseldorf are nothing."

At least we had time for a lingering kiss in the elevator.

"I'll see you tonight," he said.

•   •   •

No matter how hard you pray, nor how powerful your connection to God, it is simply not possible to keep a tent standing in Wyoming for more than two minutes. Especially a big tent. So Johnny Bourbon had built a glass-walled, prestressed-concrete tent—The Cowboy Cathedral—to house his ministry safely indoors but also to give it that old-time-religion, tent-crusade ambience. The offices were in a modern building out back. Miles of completely full parking lots surrounded the complex.

I parked in a tow-away zone by the front door.

A young man in a powder-blue jumpsuit, white cowboy boots, a white cowboy hat, and mirrored dark glasses rolled to a silent stop in a golf cart next to my Jeep. "Sorry, ma'am, you can't park there. But it'll be my pleasure to lead you to the closest spot and give you a lift back."

I flipped down my marshal's visor. "Official business." I smiled back.

"Sure thing." He pulled onto the sidewalk and dismounted, came over and held my door while I climbed out. "What can we do for you?" His face was unblemished, his expression untroubled, and his blue eyes could have had rhinestones sparkling from them.

"I need to see Reverend Bourbon," I told him.

"He's on the air right now. 'The Cowboy Crusade' is on from two to four every afternoon." As he spoke, he opened the glass doors for me to pass into the cathedral lobby, and then he ambled down a thickly carpeted corridor, its walls filled with blown-up photographs of Bourbon-induced miracles. "He does the two-to-three slot and it's pretty close to three now, so he'll be wrapping up pretty quick. I'll take you in and then let his secretary know you're here. Is he expecting you?"

I shook my head, wondering in the back of my mind

if I should enter what many people considered a den of wild-eyed, Bible-thumping, snake-handling, eye-rolling, bathtub-baptizing, tongue-speaking, foaming-at-the-mouth, wigged-out religious fanatics. I'd never been in such a place, and I felt nervous. Afraid they might grab me, hold me down, and not let me go until I repented, which could keep us all busy for several days. The fact is, to tell the truth, deep down, I was afraid I might like it.

Of course, it was nothing like what I expected. Things seldom are. Although he called it a cathedral, more than anything it was a large, state-of-the-art broadcast studio—comfortable, well padded, muffled, with large video screens on the walls so the audience could see what was going on onstage. At the moment, white-suited Johnny Bourbon was sitting in an arm-chair wrapping up a conversation, in a normal voice, with a young, nicely dressed woman whose little daugh-ter sat on her lap.

The three of them stood, and he placed his hands on their foreheads. "God bless you," he said, and they left the stage to enthusiastic and sympathetic applause. Many people were crying.

Then he turned to the camera and said a brief prayer, basically for the whole universe. Once the broadcast had cut away to a taped fund-raising commercial, he walked down a few steps to the audience level and said, "I'm done for today, but if any of you would like to come down here and just pray quietly with me for some special problem or need, I'll just stand here for a couple of minutes and pray with you." He held open his arms.

Slowly a handful of people came and huddled quietly around him. I looked at them, and at all the faces in the room, and I got the feeling that this was the last stop for many of these people. They'd tried everything else—

sex, drugs, alcohol—and finally had found solace in the Lord.

It was powerful and moving and extremely simple. There was nothing weird or embarrassing or funny about it. These were people in need whose faith had brought them here. I'd never felt the power of such a communal commitment, nor seen the sort of childlike trust and faith they had in Johnny Bourbon, and I questioned every word Alma had said about him.

Above them, the broadcast monitor silently showed a video of more miracles, mostly in Africa from what it looked like, while an 800 number flashed constantly across the bottom of the screen. I realized the fundraising effort was probably not directed to the hometown audience. They came every day. They'd already given their all.

After a final embrace, Johnny let go of his parishioners and left the room with a wave, calling out "God bless you."

Another blue suit appeared by my side and touched my arm. "Marshal Bennett?" he asked. "Come with me please."

I followed him across the studio and through an unmarked door into a busy backstage area where I saw Shanna getting ready to make her entrance, out another door, and down a noisy linoleum-tiled hallway to a bank of elevators where two armed guards stood on duty at a desk. One of them handed me a visitor's badge while my escort put a key into a lock next to the button for the fifth and top floor. The doors slid shut and we rose silently to the executive offices, which, I guess, looked a little like heaven—all white and gold. A large, curved white reception desk with a huge crystal vase of calla lilies sat in front of a thick glass wall embossed with the Johnny Bourbon's Christian Cowboys logo: a lone cowboy on a pony looking up at a cross on a hill.

The second I stepped into Johnny Bourbon's office, those ultramarine eyes locked onto me, and I must admit that after seeing him in action, even briefly, it was hard for me to evade their power. Through the windows, the Wind River Range extended behind him and he was illuminated in such a way that I wondered if there might be some boosted lighting effects involved, because the golden glow stayed on his shoulders when he approached and took my hand.

"Welcome to the Cowboy Cathedral. That'll be all for now, Judith Ann," he told the thick-waisted, low-slung, locomotive of a secretary who'd been taking dictation. She had the air of long-term propriety over Reverend Johnny, and she flipped her notebook shut and gave me a disapproving What-Jezebel-have-we-been-visited-with-now? glare as she left the room.

Maybe there was some sort of hidden signaling system, I don't know, but a split second later yet another door opened and a beautiful young woman with long dark hair, large black eyes, and red, heart-shaped lips appeared. A short black shift did little to conceal her figure.

"Not yet, darlin'," Johnny told her. "I'll buzz you."

"Okay, Reverend Johnny," she answered meekly. She had an accent that sounded Italian to me.

Then we were alone and the room was quiet but for the hum of Johnny Bourbon's personal energy. He walked over to a bar, pulled the stopper from a crystal decanter, and filled a tumbler with about three fingers of liquor, which he drank off neatly. Then he drew in a deep breath, shrugged it off, and turned to face me.

"This is a pleasant, but not unexpected visit," he said, refilling his glass. "Would you like a drink?"

"No, thanks," I responded, feeling slightly breathless under the heavy gaze. "I'm here to ask you a few questions. I'll try not to take too much of your time."

"Please, have a seat." He indicated one of the chairs in front of his desk, and once I'd sat down, he came and sat on the edge of the desk directly in front of me, one foot on the floor. The other white boot swung as slowly as a pendulum. His crotch was on the same level as my eyes, a short reach away. He was not wearing underpants. He cradled the drink in both hands.

I got up and changed seats. I wanted to tell him this kind of stuff was simply not a go anymore, and he had too much going for him to act like that, but it wouldn't have made any difference. I was confused by him. By his power to love, the incredible sincerity and compassion he'd exuded from the stage, and now this crude display. I also must admit I found the overtness slightly erotic, and if I weren't in love with Richard, and marrying him in five days, I would have seriously considered calling Johnny Bourbon's bluff, which I suspect was not a bluff at all but a serious invitation to what I also suspect would probably have been a wildly and mutually satisfying roll.

Instead, I laughed. "You've got the wrong girl, Mr. Johnny. I'm beyond temptation." I took my glasses and notebook from my purse.

He smiled at me. "I understand," he said, but he stayed where he was, and he was ready.

"What's your real name?" I asked.

"You mean my given name? Bud Hutchinson. I got Johnny Bourbon when I was a cowboy and the trail bosses realized I was better at singing around campfires, especially after a couple of belts out of the bottle, than wrangling. Then I started preaching a little, because when you're out there for weeks at a time, you need to invite the Lord in and hear what he has to say."

"Where were you when Alma was shot?"

"In the bathroom."

"Which one?"

Johnny shrugged. "One of them. There're so many of them, I lose track. I could lead you to it, though. Lots of mirrors."

"Alma told me you'd had a fight yesterday afternoon and she threatened to stop her gifts if you didn't leave Shanna."

"That's true. God knows, I couldn't have survived without Alma's backing while I was in prison, but we never had an understanding that I'd leave Shanna for her. I'd never leave my wife, and she'd never leave me."

"How much money do you raise every year?"

"About two hundred million. All from the show, 'Johnny Bourbon's Cowboy Crusade.' I got out of the real estate business the same day I walked out of prison." He smiled. His teeth were white against the black beard. "I'm a quick learner. Which is also why I wouldn't shoot Alma or anyone else. I've done my time, and I'm not going back there again."

"Were you in the bathroom alone?"

"What makes you ask that?"

"I can't imagine. Intuition, maybe. Were you?"

"No," Johnny said sheepishly. "I wasn't alone. I had a lady with me."

I waited. Staring him in the eye, tapping my pen slowly on the pad to the same tempo as his swinging boot.

He broke our gaze and looked at his hands. "I was with her sister. Mercedes."

I bit back a laugh and the urge to say, "In your

dreams," and instead asked how much Rutherford Oil stock he owned.

"A few thousand shares."

"Where do you stand on the Russian project?"

"I haven't totally made up my mind, but I'll tell you, Mercedes certainly can be persuasive. There's nothing like the passion and fervor of a determined woman."

As I left his office, he picked up his phone. "Come on in, Marcella," he said to the little Italian. The door locked automatically behind me.

ELEVEN

MONDAY EVENING

Y ou can't wear the copper organza," Mother said. "You wore it to one of Lulu's parties. Besides, you can't wear organza after Labor Day."

I was lying in the bathtub, inhaling deep breaths of calming, stress-reducing, eucalyptus-scented steam, trying to remember whether Mercedes had said she was going to talk to Kennedy McGee or Johnny Bourbon, while Mother frowned upon me over the speaker phone, carrying on about how I was the guest of honor and should look my best. All in all, between the eucalyptus and Mother, I was spending a completely contradictory, self-defeating, waste of time.

Marsha Maloney, coanchor of the KRUN evening news, having been struck dumb by my mute button, rattled along soundlessly from the small television on my dressing table. Unfortunately, since I could read lips, I could not entirely escape her long-faced, droop-eyed, sob-sister story about how some woman had gone on to long-term disability and was collecting Worker's Compensation, permanently traumatized by some fellow in a ski mask who came into her office, exposed himself, and masturbated onto her desk. Thankfully, a full team of psychiatrists was called in to make sure everyone else in the company was able to continue working, and they all had one of those big, sappy, sharing sessions when they all sit in a circle and tell the worst thing that ever happened to them, and then they hold hands and cry and take the rest of the day off. Sweet Jesus. Excuse my French, but what in the world are people thinking? Why didn't she just tell him to put it back in his pants or she'd call his mother? I think I'd say, "Gee, that sure was quick."

"It's one of my favorite dresses," I explained to Mother. "It's my wedding, and I'm wearing it."

She let the moment pass. "You'll look perfectly lovely."

"Thank you. We'll see you there."

"Now, Lilly, don't forget, Richard's parents arrive at noon tomorrow."

"Did you really think I was going to forget that?" I ran more hot water in to plump the bubbles back up. The sight of my naked body scared me to death. At least if the bubbles were there I could pretend it looked pretty good, that gravity hadn't grabbed it and wasn't beating it to death like Raggedy Ann. That it wasn't starting to look like that old hag's in *The Shining*.

Mother was off again about how simply delightful my new in-laws were and how lucky I was to get them. She sounded a little defensive, and it occurred to me that maybe she was a bit nervous about having Mr. and Mrs. Richard Welland Jerome, Sr., of Manhattan, of Jerome Guaranty Bank & Trust, one of America's oldest and most venerable banking houses, marry into her family, and then I realized what a cockeyed thought that was, since she'd spent most of her life trying to get me hooked up with Prince Charles until Camilla came on the scene and she had to admit that he was obviously blindly in love. I mean, if having the Windsors spend a week at your ranch doesn't make you nervous, why would some Upper East Side aristocrat?

Back in the studio, Marsha Maloney shook her head sadly as the insulted victim sobbed uncontrollably into a reporter's microphone from a remote hookup in her front yard. From the looks of her, in her tight shorts and a tank top that was too small to reach her waistband and cover up several rolls of blubber, with strings of dirty hair tucked behind her ears like hanks of spaghetti, the guy in the ski mask was undoubtedly the best opportunity she'd ever had. It was probably her father or brother or something, trying to cheer her up.

The story changed to a crash on the interstate, and what I saw made me sit up instantly. "I've got to go," I said to Mother, hanging up on her mid-self-help idea. It had been a one-car crash. The car, a pearl-gray Cadillac Seville, had lost control and spun out, slamming nose first, into a heavy cement divider. The driver was Jim Dixon, a senior executive of Gilhooly GMC Truck and Chevrolet. It appeared that alcohol was involved.

I toweled off quickly, stepped into an old pair of jeans, boots, a flannel shirt, and a pullover sweater, and ran down the stairs.

"Going to Elias's," I called to Celestina, who was sitting on a stool in the kitchen, sipping a cup of tea and talking to her daughter on the phone. Baby and I jumped into my Jeep and raced so fast the half mile down to ranch headquarters that when I left the truck outside the main cattle barn where Elias kept his office, dust from my spinning tires was still rising at my front door.

I tore up the steep stairs, past the life-size bronze of

Wind River Ranger, Elias's Grand Champion bull, who had a gray Stetson hanging from one horn and a dark-gray pinstripe Brooks Brothers suit vest hanging from the other. I found Elias standing in front of a mirror, tying his tie and smoking a cigar. The darkened cattle ring lay below us, past the wall of glass behind his messy desk.

"Hey, little sister." He examined his work, approved the knot, took the cigar from his teeth and laid it in a clean ashtray, and poured us each a shot, splashing a few drops of liquor on what looked like an oil lease. "What are you doing down here? Why aren't you dressed? We're leaving in"—he looked at his watch as we both listened to the helicopter settle and land in the meadow—"fifteen minutes. Soon as Christian and Mr. Wonderful get their clothes changed. What the hell happened to your face?"

Mud mask. I'd completely forgotten.

"Listen, Elias," I said, "I need you to go downtown."

"Right now?"

"Yes."

"What about the party?"

"This is more important. I'd go myself, but it'd just get everyone all riled up."

TWELVE

There was no shortage of suspects, but most of them were accomplished gunmen. Wade, Kennedy, the militiamen—their pride in their marksman skills would not permit them to miss on the first shot. Johnny Bourbon seemed, on the surface anyway, to lack the blood instinct, but I wasn't so sure about Mercedes, especially after Johnny pointed out she'd do anything to secure the proxies. And I knew Duke Fletcher. His Senate career had been more distinguished than some, less than others, and using primarily his strong environmental record as his platform, he planned to run for President. Duke wasn't stupid enough to gun down a major contributor because she'd welched on a deal. No. There were still too many possibilities—not one had been eliminated.

It was only seven-fifteen, but I knew my father would be on his way to the bank. I called him in his car. "Please explain this Rutherford Oil proxy fight."

"Sure, but I'll call you from the office. I don't want to spend six-fifty a minute explaining it from the car.

It'd cost me a fortune. These cell-phone rates are ridiculous."

"Daddy," I said, "I'll send you a check."

"I'm just pulling into the lot. I'll call you right back."

Five minutes later, my phone rang.

"Okay," he said. "What do you want to know?"

"Pretty much everything."

"Hmm." A long pause ensued. "Do you remember when we bid on the Prudhoe Bay project in the early seventies?"

"Vaguely."

"I'll try to put it in a nutshell: The Prudhoe Bay oil fields are north of the Arctic Circle in Alaska, and they're among the richest fields in the world. But getting to them, exploring them, developing them, building the pipeline to get the oil out of them to the closest ice-free port—in this case, eight hundred miles south to Valdez—was the most costly and challenging logistical and technological undertaking in the history of man. This was a place with virtually no infrastructure for humans, let alone for the production of oil and gas. Plus, Prudhoe Bay is accessible by water only three weeks a year—late July and early August—so, all those megasized oceangoing freighters and barges have to haul in as fast as they can and then get the hell out, or they'll be there till spring, literally. And spring won't come for another eleven months."

"You're kidding."

"It was superhuman. Still is. You should see all those huge vessels pushing a little farther north every day until the ice breaks and clears and then they run like the devil into port and offload a year's worth of supplies—spare parts, food, toilet paper, you name it—and then reload with a year's worth of trash because there's nowhere to throw anything away up there. It's just a big snowbank most of the year and a swamp the rest of the time. You ought to see it."

"That's okay," I said. "There's enough winter in Wyoming for me. I don't even like to go as far north as Montana. How much did it cost?"

"Well, we're talking over twenty-five years ago, you know, and in 1970 dollars, it cost five billion to put in place. Just to give you an idea of the production capability, at that time the field was projected to produce nine-point-two billion barrels of oil a year. Today, because of technical and environmental improvements, production is at twelve billion barrels a year. It's one hell of an operation."

"And Rutherford Oil wants to do the same thing in Russia?"

"Not that easy." I heard him puffing as he lit a cigar. "First of all, Rutherford is not what's considered to be a major oil company—it's a major independent. Big difference. It took ARCO and all its resources to develop the North Slope. Look at a major like Exxon: Its annual revenue is a hundred and thirty-four billion and its net income is seven and a half billion. Exxon could afford this gamble. Rutherford's annual revenue, on the other hand, is twenty-three billion and their net income is nine-hundred and fifty million. You with me?"

"So far."

"If they were to undertake this deal, the initial push—about six billion—would take most of their cash. Plus they'd have to borrow about five and a half billion of it, which is one hell of a lot of money, and they'd have to put up most of their hard assets, their proven producing fields and wells and refineries, as collateral. They'd have no net. No cushion. If they lost it, they'd be out of business, and no matter how great this field looks on paper, there's never any guarantee that the oil is where you think it's going to be, or if it's there, that there's as much as you expect."

"Would your bank lend them the money?"

"We'd probably be the lead bank in the deal, but I'd make sure we had the smallest participation, probably about ten percent. Rutherford's got a steady production history and one of the strongest balance sheets in the industry, but I see this as way too big a gamble."

"Well, that's pretty much what the oil business is, isn't it?" I observed. "One big gamble?"

"You know, I've never been averse to taking risks, Lilly, but I happen to see this venture as foolhardy. Of course—and this is what Alma's contingent contends— if it works, Rutherford will become a major-major."

I was making notes like mad. "What do they get for their six billion?"

"Very little. Six billion pretty much gets the lights on. This field is way the hell up north near the Kolyma River Delta at the Arctic Ocean, and would require a thousand-mile pipeline down to some rinky-dink town named Manily. Plus . . ."

"You mean it gets worse?"

"They'd be doing business with the Russians."

"So?"

"Russia used to be the number-one oil producer in the world, but then, because of their own greed and stupidity and mismanagement and paranoia, they started putting all their money into weapons. Their oil industry is still using 1930s equipment. And there's always the question as to exactly who it is you're doing business with and who has the right to sign the contracts. Is it Moscow? The provincial government? The Oil Ministry? No one's too sure, which means the amount of cash required for the ongoing payoffs is more than a lot of big companies generate in a year. It's

one hell of a big deal, with everybody and his brother—
in two different governments, theirs and ours—involved. Hold on a minute. I've got to take this call."

He put me on hold. The project was mind-boggling.
Can you imagine hauling virtually everything through
the Arctic Ocean into far northern Russia? How much
money were we talking about overall? Even the 1970
prices could inspire murder.

"Lilly?" Daddy's secretary, Faye, interrupted my
thoughts. "Your father's going to be a while and wants
to know if he can call you back?"

"No problem. I'll track him down later today."

I sat at my dressing table and stared at the sky reflected in the mirror. There were elements, and possible
motives, to this case that reached way beyond anything
I'd ever been involved in before.

Siberia? Six billion dollars? The Kolyma River
Delta? What the hell was that?

I put on a brown-tweed business suit and brown-
suede pumps, perfect greet-your-future-in-laws garb,
and headed into the office.

My head ached a little from the fifty glasses of champagne I'd drunk at the Kellys' the night before, and my
eyes looked sort of like someone had pasted puffy little
omelets onto them from the half-wheel of Brie I'd inhaled. But other than that, I was ready to roll. I felt
good.

THIRTEEN

Hollywood-style dressing-room trailers and equipment trucks jammed the Bennett's Fort parking lots, and some self-important little sawed-off security guard practically tackled my car as I turned into the dirt lot behind my office and found it wall to wall with limousines. Big letters on the front of his Windbreaker announced, SECURITY—*Range of My Heart*.

"You can't park here," he squeaked into my window like Barney Fife. He had on a hunting cap that was two sizes too big, with fleece-lined earflaps that stuck out like bedroom slippers on either side of his head, and cheap wraparound, mirrored sunglasses I'm sure he thought were intimidating, and might have been, if the frames hadn't been iridescent turquoise.

I pulled out my U.S. Marshal's badge. "This is my office."

"I never heard of you, and Mr. Redford has rented the whole town, and you can't park in here." He was a jabbery, chirpy monkey, and he was making me mad.

"This is my office," I said again, as calmly as I could.

"No, ma'am. I'm sorry. You can't park here." With that he crossed his arms over his narrow chest and frowned. "You'll have to park over in the big lot with everyone else and go through security over there."

I took a deep breath and considered him for a moment, then opened the console between the seats in my Jeep, removed the Glock .44 that was as big as a small cannon, and pointed it at his stomach. "Get out of my way."

I guess I didn't feel as good as I thought I did.

He dove under the nearest stretch limo, and I blocked three of them when I parked. I slammed my car door as hard as I could and stomped up the stairs.

"This is so exciting," Linda said. She was in my office watching all the goings-on from the window. There must have been a thousand miles of cords and cables down there and a hundred people bumping into each other. "I saw Robert Redford a few minutes ago. He was drinking a cup of coffee. And look, they gave me this." She held up a dusty-rose *Range of My Heart* T-shirt. "Isn't it neat?" Her eyes sparkled.

"Very. Anything big happening in our little corner of the world?"

"No." She flipped through the messages. "Just the normal stuff. Your mother called twice. Your father called and said he'll be in his office and doesn't have any meetings scheduled until noon, so if you have any more questions, call him back whenever you want. Elias said not to leave until he got here. Wade Gilhooly called just to check in . . ."

We heard footsteps on the stairs. When the door opened, the form of an Old West lawman—cowboy hat tilted way down, holstered six-shooters riding low on slim hips, wide shoulders, long legs—paused for effect, silhouetted in the backlight. Then he stepped inside, kicked the door closed, and ambled toward us, thumbs hooked in a wide gunbelt.

"Morning, Dwight," I said. "Looks like you've hired on as an extra."

"Yup." He smiled, a matchstick stuck in the corner of his mouth. "How do you like it?" He held out his hands and twirled slowly on his heels. The string tie and leather vest rose in the air. "I'm playing a deputy marshal."

"You are a deputy marshal."

"You're right about that, Marshal Lilly." He looked me in the eye and rolled the match between his lips. "I'm *your* deputy marshal. Your wish is my command." He drummed his fingers on his belt buckle and rocked slowly onto his toes. Dwight was a wild thing if ever I'd seen one.

Linda swallowed loudly, and I wondered what I would do if he decided to expose and handle himself across my desktop like the man on the evening news. I think I might lock the door and tell Linda to hold my calls. I sure as hell wouldn't call a psychiatrist.

"Dwight," I said, my mouth a little dry. "How is our prisoner this morning?"

"Who? Kennedy?"

"You mean Mr. McGee?"

"Yeah. I mean, yes. I mean, yes, ma'am. Mr. McGee is fine. Paul Decker came out to see him yesterday afternoon and said he'd have him out on bail first thing this morning. I think Paul might be over there now."

Linda offered a fax from her stack of papers. "The release order came in five minutes ago."

"Let's go have a visit." I put on my dark glasses as Linda answered the phone.

"One moment, please, Miss Rutherford," she said

into the receiver and raised a hand signaling me to stop. "Miss Bennett will be right with you."

"Something's arrived," Mercedes told me without preamble when I picked up my extension. "I'd like you to come by the office."

I glanced at my watch. "I'll be there at ten."

Stunt men crowded the tiny jail, filling up the air with testosterone, quizzing one of their real-life heroes, Kennedy McGee, who sat comfortably in his cell answering their questions about hair-raising escapes and near-misses with dangerous, wild animals—mostly big cats. I didn't want to bust their balloon by telling them that the most dangerous wildcats he came in contact with were rich and two-legged.

"Excuse me, fellas." I shouldered my way through the crowd. "Sorry to break up your tea party. Official business."

"You guys better clear out. Now," Dwight said importantly. "When Marshal Lilly says business, she means it."

"Morning, Mr. McGee," I said once we were alone, except for Paul Decker and Dwight, who unlocked the cell. "I've got the papers here for your release, but I'd like to ask you a couple of questions, if your attorney doesn't mind."

"We don't mind." Paul settled himself comfortably at the old scratched oak conference table upon which, according to legend, Wyatt Earp had a bullet dug out of him by Doc Holliday after the Gunfight at the OK Corral. If you looked carefully, you could make out Marshal Earp's bloodstains in the wood.

These large lakes of discoloration were renewed every spring by Cousin Buck with a mixture of double-

strong espresso and red wine. He had a whole reper-
toire of bloodstains around town, which he restored
when the weather was bad. When it was good, he
regrooved the wagon-wheel tracks right outside the fort
on the Oregon Trail, a chore he undertook after every
springtime thunderstorm. He sang himself hoarse to the
Rolling Stones as he swayed back and forth for miles in
either direction in an old Conestoga wagon hauled by
his silvery-taffy Percherons and belted down tumblers
of Stolichnaya from half-gallon bottles he kept packed
in ice in a Styrofoam cooler at his feet.

Paul Decker, Wyoming's most famous, most successful, and most expensive defense attorney, placed his
black cowboy hat with its hand-hammered silver-
medallion hatband on the edge of the table and brushed
the brim lovingly with his fingers. His longish gray hair
fell toward his face, making him look like Wyatt Earp
himself. He regarded me affectionately with blue-gray
eyes. Paul and I did a lot of work together, generally on
the same side.

"Ask away," he said affably. "We've got nothing to
hide."

I took my regular chair at the head of the table and
examined McGee's sneer for a second before beginning.
He was so ridiculously arrogant and contemptuous, I
forced myself to swallow every word I wanted to say
and jammed respectful calm into my brain like a dentist
cramming cotton packing into an open filling on a giant
molar. "I want to ask you again with your attorney
present, Mr. McGee: Where were you when Alma
Gilhooly was shot?"

"Whoa!" Paul held up his hand. "What does that
have to do with the price of rawhide? My client's here
in regard to elephant tusks that belonged to Ms.
Gilhooly, but if you're wanting to question him about

her murder, well, that's a whole different bucket of oats."

Paul believed that his cowboy colloquialisms endeared him to clients, judges, and juries, and he was always testing new ones outside the courtroom. Some worked better than others.

"Oh, I'm sorry, Mr. Decker," I said. "I thought you understood. The elephant tusks are a done deal: He had them. I caught him. I arrested him. And he'll go to trial and explain how he came to be in possession of international contraband. And then he'll either pay a lot of money or do a lot of time. What I'm interested in is who attempted to murder Alma Rutherford Gilhooly night before last."

"And you suspect Mr. McGee?"

"At the moment, the field is wide open. Yesterday, Mr. McGee denied being at the party, but I believe he was, and I'd like to give him an opportunity to search his memory again and possibly correct his story. Maybe he saw something that could be helpful."

McGee glanced at Paul and clenched his teeth, which made his bony jaw tighten and ripple. He clenched and unclenched his fist as well. But, to me, the Great White Hunter's handsomeness must have existed only in the context of his work. With him sitting in my little jail, lacking admirers, his chiseled features appeared sharp and cruel. Slightly counterfeit and scummy. Paul gave him the green light to answer.

"I was in the sun-room with everyone else," he said. "I heard the shot the same time everyone else did."

"Why didn't you tell me the truth in the first place?"

"Because there is some serious bad blood between Alma and me and a number of legitimate reasons why I should want to kill her. But I didn't."

"Do you remember who you were talking to?"

"Some woman. I don't remember her name."

"Mercedes Rutherford?"

"Alma's sister?" Kennedy shook his head. "I didn't even know she was there."

"When I saw Mercedes at the party, sir, she excused herself to go tell you something. Are you saying you never saw her?"

"I said I didn't know she was there." Kennedy clearly did not like being questioned by a woman and kept looking to his attorney for some assistance, for Paul to call a halt. But I wasn't doing anything irregular—Paul and I both knew the rules—other than being female, and in charge, which I imagined was a whole new experience for him.

"Mr. McGee, did you rendezvous with Mercedes Rutherford and Johnny Bourbon in a powder room for a quick assignation?"

"What?" Kennedy jumped to his feet, making Dwight tighten up a little and squint a little harder at his prisoner from where he'd stationed himself importantly at the door. Great, I thought, all we needed was for Dwight to start shooting. He'd kill all of us.

"What do you take me for? Some bloody homosexual? Of course I wasn't in the bathroom with her and that slippery quack. Jesus, Lord, makes my skin crawl just to imagine such a thing." Kennedy walked around the small room hugging himself. "Lord. You're a terrible woman."

It had been a shot in the dark, but not an unreasonable one, in my opinion. "Tell me about your relationship with Alma."

"Not much to tell, not much relationship left after she screwed me. Financially." He grabbed the chair back with both hands and leaned over it toward me. "Let me tell you, Miss Bennett, Alma is a completely psychotic bitch. Totally mad. Everything's dandy as long as you play by her rules, but she is always moving the goal line and not letting anyone know. I'm not at all surprised someone gunned her down—could even have been the Russians. Maybe she ended up screwing them, too. But it sure as hell wasn't me. I wouldn't miss with the first shot. Whoever shot her didn't know what he was doing."

"What about her relationship with Wade?"

Kennedy shrugged and sat back down. "Not much there as far as I could tell. Whenever they came to Africa, he always found an excuse to leave after the first couple of days—always some business emergency. Never even came out into the bush. He'd just leave her there with me and take off. She'd complete the safari, usually three or four weeks. I've always found him to be a little soft."

I flipped back and forth through my notes. "What do you know about her and Johnny Bourbon?"

"Nothing, except he was her next big project after she left me holding the bag."

"Senator Fletcher?"

"Seems a nice-enough chap."

"Do you own stock in Rutherford Oil?"

"A little." He looked at me and knew that wasn't enough of an answer. "Alma gave me some shares a few years ago. I don't enjoy a major position, if that's what you mean."

I turned to Paul. "Don't let your client leave town, Mr. Decker."

FOURTEEN

Y ou just missed him," Linda said when I got back to the office.

"Who?"

"Robert Redford. He came up here to apologize for his security guard."

"You're kidding."

She shook her head. Her face was so rosy with excitement it matched her fingernails. "I can't believe you missed him. God. He is so handsome. And so *nice*. God."

"Well, where'd he go?"

Linda shrugged. "Just down the stairs. Maybe he's still out there. In the parking lot or something."

Well, shoot.

"Track down Elias and tell him to meet me at the hospital," I said over my shoulder as I thudded down the stairs as coolly as I could. I know Robert Redford is a bleeding-heart, left-wing-liberal do-gooder and needs to lighten up a little, but, jeez, he'd just been in my office looking for me, wanting to apologize. I had some great ideas for him about what to do with his Sundance Institute. He was gone, of course. So was Arnold Schwarzenegger's security guard cousin.

The drive into town was easy, so pleasant now that Labor Day was behind us and every ham-and-egger with a mother-in-law and minivan had gone back home to Nebraska or wherever it is those people come from. The sky was so high, it was almost navy blue at the top.

I pulled into one of the "Authorized Parking Only" spaces by the emergency entrance at Christ & St. Luke's Hospital and noticed I'd parked next to Jack Lewis's white Crown Victoria. I found him standing outside Alma's cubicle in intensive care, leaning against the counter that surrounded the personnel station in the center of the unit, holding a cup of cold coffee and staring into space. A uniformed officer stood by smartly, extra smartly now that his big boss was here. Through the half-open glass door, I could see Wade's hands clinging to the bed rail as though he were strangling a golf club. His eyes were scooped-out holes, nothing but divots.

"Hey, Jack," I said. "Been here long? You look a little sleep-deprived."

He grinned. "Just got here. And I am sleep-deprived because I've got a bunch of interdepartmental warfare going on. Driving me nuts. It takes all my energy and has nothing to do with catching criminals."

"Life's tough at the top."

"You look a little hung over."

I groaned. "Don't tell me. I need to look good today. I'm meeting my in-laws at noon. I need to look fabulous."

"Getting married's tough duty. Especially with all the upper-class bullshit you're trotting out. I can't pick up the paper without reading about some hinky-dinky little tea party or other for you and Prince Charming."

"He is my Prince Charming, too."

"Poor bastard," Jack said. He turned his red-rimmed eyes on me. "He have any idea how tough it is being married to a cop? Even a fancy private dick like you?"

"I'm thinking he thinks it's going to be nice to be married to me." A tiny gurgle of fear stirred in my stomach like the first bubble in a pot that has just begun to simmer and, unattended, will soon reach a full boil. An old familiar feeling that I might not make the cut, that Richard would jettison me like an empty McDonald's bag on a country highway because I got too involved with my work and didn't save enough for him. I was terrified that I hadn't really found the balance I thought I'd found. Maybe this was all fake. "I'm not exactly down in the trenches anymore, like you."

"Doesn't make any difference, Lilly. You're as addicted to the dangerous chase as I am. As you ever were. Oh, well." He shrugged and dropped the empty cup into a wastebasket. "It's none of my goddamn business. You got anything on this case?"

I looked through the glass at Alma. She lay completely flat on the stretcher-like bed under icy fluorescent lights. Tubes, cables, cords, and monitors everywhere, her head bandaged like a golf ball, face swollen beyond recognition. Only a sheet covered her torso from her chest to her knees. She looked cold and bloated and her skin was gray. How could she possibly be holding on?

I shook my head. It was the truth. I didn't have anything. I had a lot of stuff that could turn into something, but at the moment it was all conjecture. "Nothing but lots of ideas," I answered. "But I think in the next twenty-four to thirty-six hours, the small stuff will start to rattle through the funnel."

"That guy." Jack indicated Wade with his eyes. "Your client."

"Yeah? What about him?"

"Guilty as hell."

I couldn't disagree, but I didn't say anything. He was, after all, my client. He said he'd been in Montana and the airline confirmed it, and he said he'd hired me to find the truth, but I couldn't shake the feeling that all roads would lead to him. But why?

"I just can't figure out how he did it, is all," Jack admitted.

Me, either. I looked at my watch and wondered where Elias was; maybe he'd have some news.

Jack glanced in at Wade, who had moved to the sink and was holding a cold washcloth over his face, struggling to stay awake. "You checked out his alibi, right?"

"Yes. He was on a plane. Commercial. They know him and they saw him."

We both stood there and watched him, full of our own private theories and thoughts.

Down at the far end of the hall, a bell dinged, the elevator door rolled open, and Elias strolled off, hands deep in his pockets. He stopped and stared and smiled compassionately into each cubicle, and I'm sure the family members who stared back with their tired, frightened eyes thought he was a doctor, just bringing them a whisper of understanding as he went on his rounds.

"Jeez," he said under his breath when he reached us. "What's wrong with that guy?" He indicated over his shoulder with his thumb. "Have you seen all that equipment? I was watching his monitor, and his heart's hardly going at all. I think they ought to pull the curtains and give them all a little privacy."

"Most people don't stand and stare at them the way you do," I said.

"Heart-lung transplant," Jack told us with an authoritative weariness that sounded as if he came across heart-lung transplants every day and found them tiresome. "Just did it yesterday. Took 'em fourteen hours. It'll be touch and go like this for two weeks. Guy looks to me like he's going to crater any second."

"Man," Elias said. "Rough." He let the moment pass and said to me, "You should have waited. You know I'm supposed to stay b-y . . . y-o-u-r . . . s-i-d-e until the wedding," he sang and then turned to Jack. "Family's afraid she'll miss a few events."

"Good idea to keep an eye on her, she could bolt. I know the type. I'd better get back to work." Jack fitted the gray Stetson firmly on his head. "I just came up to the hospital to interview a prisoner and thought I'd stop and see if there was any change in Mrs. Gilhooly. Oh, Lilly, you were right about the boot prints, nothing special to help narrow anything down. So far this is a go-nowhere case. Let me know if there's anything you need." He shook hands with Elias. "Glad I ran into you."

We watched him step into the elevator and give the man who was already on board his tough-guy look. His macho shoulder-shake that said, You wanna fight? You wanna fight? Go ahead. I dare you. Typical Small Man Complex.

"What did you find out about Jim Dixon?" I asked Elias once the doors had closed.

"Nothing. Wild-goose chase. It was booze. His blood alcohol was point-four-oh. That's why he didn't get killed—too relaxed."

I shook my head. "I don't think it matters. I think the accident was a coincidence and got us rabbited off in the wrong direction. I think the shooting was directly related to the Rutherford Oil proxy fight. The politics surrounding this Russian deal are unbelievable, definitely the kind of stakes people kill over." I looked at my watch. "Let's go see Mercedes."

Elias looked at *his* watch. "Listen to me," he said. "It's almost ten. I swore on my life that I'd have you at Richard's office at eleven forty-five, and by God I will even if I have to smack you on the head and drag you in by the heels of your little Italian pumps."

"Fair enough. We've got plenty of time."

FIFTEEN

The Rutherford Oil Building was one of the few sky-scrapers in downtown Roundup that I liked. Al-though it was nothing more than a big glass-and-steel box, it had been designed by a local guy no one had heard of before or since, and, to me, it had always rep-resented the Westerner's nature: clean, upright, no hid-den surfaces, tricks, or agendas. It was what you saw, pure and simple. Unlike most of the other florid piles that dipped and looped and shot off in all different di-rections like a bunch of architecturally defective spark-lers built by Easterners on holiday.

The building sat back from the street, fronted by a beautiful, parklike plaza where the wind blew around the corner at about a hundred miles an hour all the time and sent the water from a series of high-flying fountains into a permanent state of fine spray. In an urban tribute to Old Faithful and our Western heritage—or some other sort of high-minded explanation cooked up by our local arts council—the fountains were timed to go off every quarter hour for ten minutes. And they did.

The water misted our faces as we crossed toward the entrance. The air smelled like the stockyards on the edge of town.

"I've always been in love with Mercedes," Elias confided in me as we rode the executive express elevator to the top floor. "I think she's the most beautiful woman I've ever seen. I used to watch her sunbathing in their backyard when I was little. Her body was absolutely perfect."

"Why don't you ask her out?" I suggested. "She's never gotten married."

All the color drained from Elias's bearded face. "Are you crazy? She'd never go out with me. No. Forget it. I'm sticking with Linda." I could tell that just the idea of being in the same room with Mercedes scared Elias as much as if he were alone with, say, Madonna. He'd just stare and sweat.

I wasn't in love with Mercedes Rutherford, but I have always thought she was extra-cool, and this visit to her office just reconfirmed that opinion. She was definitely way-cool. And maybe even heartless. Detached enough, certainly, to have shot her half-sister and not chipped a nail. Her figure was boyish, completely straight up and down, and she had on a chocolate Armani suit. I could easily picture her slipping a small handgun like my little Glock in and out of the jacket pocket. But not the actual murder weapon, a Colt .45. Too crude.

Her airy, penthouse office overflowed with tall, orderly stacks of bound reports.

"Sorry for the mess," she greeted us, not really sorry but needing to offer something by way of a welcome before she got down to business. "Need to keep these confidential till the annual meeting tomorrow. No easy way."

Mercedes was friendly without being effusive, clipped without being rushed, professional without being frigid, and precise without being precious. Power suited her. She never looked at her watch, but I knew she'd allotted a specific amount of time to this meeting and would move us all along until she got where she needed to be, and then the meeting would be over.

After taking her seat at the end of the conference table, Mercedes indicated we should sit wherever we wanted. A white-noise machine, a necessity in today's world where privacy is nothing more than an arcane concept, was built flush into the center of the table and whirred soothingly.

"I appreciate your dropping by." She slid an envelope across to me. "This arrived this morning."

I removed my glasses, a pair of tight latex gloves, and a magnifying glass from my purse and examined the envelope carefully. It was plain white, the sort available in boxes of ten at the 7-Eleven, and addressed on what looked to me to be a standard laser printer:

Mercedes Rutherford, Chairman and CEO
Rutherford Oil Company
Rutherford Oil Plaza
Roundup, Wyoming 87023

The postmark was Roundup, the time and date the afternoon before. The stamp was a self-adhesive American flag. I got out my long-nosed tweezers, slid the sheet free, and spread it on the table. Plain white paper. Nothing immediately identifiable about its weight or texture. I examined the message, which was handwritten in Cyrillic letters and meant absolutely nothing to me.

Голосуй "ЗА" ули — диета.

I slid the paper across to Elias, who put on his glasses and studied it, then laughed and shook his head.

"What does it say?" I asked.

"It says . . ." The oddly guttural words flowed from Elias's lips like a ballad from Mars. Then he grinned.

"That's very nice Elias. But what does it mean?"

"It means, 'Vote yes or you'll diet.' "

"Excuse me?" Mercedes said.

"Yeah." Elias shook his head. "Obviously this was written by someone who was in a hurry and copied down the wrong word in the dictionary."

We all laughed, even though it wasn't especially funny.

"Did this come through your regular company mail delivery?" I asked.

"Yes. My secretary said it was delivered with everything else."

"Who do you think sent it?"

"I haven't got the slightest idea." She seemed bewildered by the message. "I suppose it could be just about anyone, even some of our Russian colleagues who are desperate for this investment. They'll have a large, vocal contingent at the meeting. It's a wild group, but they aren't fumbling idiots who would send a note like this." She leaned her forehead into her fingers and closed her eyes. "This person is a complete dolt."

"Mercedes, where were you when Alma was shot?"

My question was purposely from left field, and I asked it slightly aggressively, not belligerently, but certainly straight out—a quick snap of the buggy whip.

The change in direction did not catch her off guard or force her to hesitate while she sought a suitable answer. "I was in the powder room with Johnny Bourbon trying to get his proxy." She met my look dead on and started laughing. "This struggle has become shameless. You wouldn't believe how high the stakes are."

Elias blushed.

"How high?" I asked.

"The company's survival is at stake. My grandfather started Rutherford Oil in the twenties." As she spoke, Mercedes rolled a gold Cross pen in her fingers. They were long and slender, and her small oval nails were enameled in pale salmon. "He was a roughneck on Blackmer's crew when the Teapot Dome was developed, and then when Blackmer took off for France rather than go to jail, Grandfather hammered together whatever leases he could from the government and ranchers, and started Rutherford Oil. We have crews and fields all over the world now. Our annual production is almost seventy million barrels. And that's just oil. We're diversified into all fields of energy."

"Jeez," Elias said. "That's up from fifty-five million when you took over just two years ago." Then he got a little flustered. "At least, that's what I recall."

Mercedes smiled at him affectionately. "You could turn your operation into something if you'd leave home now and then, Elias. You'll never find a billion barrels under the Circle B."

"Nah. I know. But we've got enough for now."

Here's the deal with Elias: He holds a B.A. in Russian Studies from Harvard and a degree in English Literature—Shakespeare—from Oxford, and when he got home from Vietnam and Cambodia, China and Laos, and a few other places the CIA never was, he took over running the ranch and has not ventured far since. "I've seen more of the world than I ever needed to. More than enough to last my lifetime," he says by way of explanation.

"I understand you and Alma each hold thirty-five percent of the stock?" I said.

Mercedes nodded.

"Help me out with the math."

"The company has two million shares of common stock, fully issued," Mercedes explained. "Alma and I each own seven hundred thousand. The company pays an annual dividend of five dollars per share."

"So for each of you, that's only three and a half million a year in dividends," I said. Then I clamped my mouth shut and waited for her to tell me the rest. Saying nothing is the hardest thing in the world, which is why it is also so effective, which was not news to Mercedes Rutherford. She and I stared at each other. Who would blink first? She thought I didn't know what the next question should be, and she wasn't going to help me. "What about the preferred stock?" I finally asked.

"She and I own one hundred percent of the preferred stock."

"How many shares are there?"

"Two million."

"Dividend?"

"Twenty dollars."

Forty million. Twenty million each. "Nice," I said. Elias whistled.

"Now you see why I'm so opposed to this Russian

venture. Rutherford Oil is solid as a rock, and for us to borrow five and a half billion could be disastrous. It's too big a risk."

"Tell me about the other major stockholders and where they stand."

SIXTEEN

Mercedes slid a wide sheet of computer paper toward me. It was stamped in red with CONFIDENTIAL in six different places. At the same time, she pushed a remote and the information appeared on a large screen on the wall.

"We printed out a copy of this for you. As you can see, besides Alma and me there are only a handful of major individual and institutional investors who make up the remaining total shares of common stock."

I scanned the list.

NAME	# SHARES	%
Bourbon, Johnny	50,000	2.5%
Entek Mutual Fund	50,000	2.5%
Fletcher, M. B. Trust	50,000	2.5%
Fletcher, Duke	50,000	2.5%
Gilhooly, Alma R.	700,000	35%
Gilhooly, Wade	50,000	2.5%
McGee, Kennedy	50,000	2.5%

Rutherford, Edith	25,000	1.25%
Rutherford, Mercedes	700,000	35%
SIBA Fund	175,000	8.75%
Less than 1% — 375sh	<u>100,000</u>	5%
	2,000,000	100%

What surprised me most was the size of Johnny
Bourbon's and Kennedy McGee's holdings. They'd
both implied their holdings were insignificant, when in
fact they each owned two and a half percent, fifty thousand shares of Rutherford. Dividends of two hundred
and fifty thousand a year. Not insignificant in any sense
of the word. They held the same stock positions as
Alma's husband. I also wondered how Duke Fletcher
and his late wife had come to have such a large position. A total of five percent.

Mercedes walked over and stood next to the projected image, staring up at it.

"Entek is a mutual fund," she explained. "It invests
only in environmentally responsible corporations, such
as ours. Rutherford's a new breed of corporation: We
spend almost as much on environmental technology to
keep our fields clean as we do on exploration and production. Entek's very opposed to the Russian venture."

"Why?"

"The Russians are eco-pigs. They won't invest in
cleanup, removal, disposal, protection. You should see
their fields, it would scare you to death. They're toxic
wastelands where the ecology has been obliterated. Vast
expanses of nothing but sludge. No earth, no water, no
trees, no grass. Just noxious sludge." She shook her
head. "They're in such a desperate race for hard cur-
rency, they don't believe in safety—don't have time for

it. Believe me when I say Chernobyl was nothing. The whole continent is one big environmental time bomb, and I, for one, don't want Rutherford Oil to participate in, or contribute to, a continental meltdown."

Her words sent a chill down my spine. On top of that, the noise machine disturbed me. Not the sound so much as the necessity. It felt as if we were meeting in Berlin in the sixties, in the hottest part of the Cold War, when visitors to Russia and iron-curtain countries joked that if they wanted to have a conversation, any kind of conversation—family, personal, business—and keep it private, the only possible way was to turn their radios on high, put their heads under their pillows, and whisper to one another. Now it's the same in America. Virtually every communication is vulnerable, and you can be assured someone is listening. Executives with noise machines used to be considered paranoid. Now if they *don't* have them, they're considered stupid. It gives me the willies.

I studied the chart. "How long ago did Duke Fletcher's wife die?"

"Two years. Duke's record and platform are environmentally based. His whole presidential opportunity hinges on that message, so I can't see him compromising himself for profit. But"—she smiled—"he is a politician, and we all know how that goes. Actually, I shouldn't say that about him, because I don't mean it. Makes me sound more cynical than I am. He's a nice guy. He's consulting for us until the campaign gets rolling. Do you know him?"

"A little," I answered. "I've always liked his stand-up-and-take-it-like-a-man approach."

"You mean like John Wayne? I agree. He's as tough as this table." Mercedes knocked on it to make her point.

I kept going down the list. "What's SIBA Fund?"

"Ah, SIBA." Mercedes sat back down. "This is seriously problematic. SIBA is a one-hundred-percent bottom-line-oriented, extremely high-risk mutual fund. High-level, high-risk investors. The fund's director, Penn Holland, sits on our board, and he's made it clear he'll vote in favor of the Russian venture because the payoff potential is so enormous. And when I say 'potential,' I mean it in the broadest sense of the word. This is a long shot nonpareil."

Again, I was impressed by her cool. What she had just told us about how the SIBA shares would be voted was beyond "problematic," it could be disastrous. But in spite of the fact that she was, after all, fighting for the survival of her company, she displayed no daylight. No chink in her armor.

"What about Alma's block?" I said. "Now that she's not going to be there voting it herself, is there any chance there will be any give in the vote?"

Under normal circumstances, this would be an especially key question, because how the person being questioned reacted would give some sense of involvement or culpability. But with Mercedes I expected no reaction and got none. She could have been talking about a tree, except she might be more interested in a tree than she was in her sister.

"She made a big production about signing her proxy at the last board meeting, drawing her line in the sand. We can't touch that stock. If we could, there wouldn't be any problem. Here's how I see it happening." Mercedes removed the sheet from my hand and, with the gold pen, checked off names. "My camp—which we call the Company Camp—includes me, seven hundred thousand shares. Entek, fifty. The Fletchers, a hundred. And Wade, another fifty. That's nine hundred thousand.

"The Challengers, Alma's group—those in favor of the Russian venture—include Alma, seven hundred. SIBA, one seventy-five. McGee, probably, he's such a low-life, fifty. That's nine twenty-five." She tossed the list back. "You can see why Johnny Bourbon is so important."

"You're sure Wade will vote with you?"

"Always has," Mercedes answered.

"Don't you find that even slightly curious?" I asked, because I surely did. "To vote against your spouse, so publicly?"

She looked up from the sheet. "Lilly, I don't think you know either one of them at all. I mean, when was the last time you saw Alma? Twenty-five, thirty years ago? And I don't think you'd even met Wade until Monday. Am I right?"

I nodded.

"He and Alma have the most toxic, recriminatory, retaliatory relationship I've ever seen. They fight like cats and dogs. Publicly. It's ridiculous. It's as though they're addicted to the pain."

"Physical pain?" I asked. "Or mental?"

"All pain. Alma . . ." she began, but then closed her eyes and wrinkled her nose as though she'd just taken a bite of spoiled meat. I could tell she wanted to say more but discretion, or family loyalty, or some private knowledge stopped her. "It's just sick," she finally said and swallowed.

"Alma what?"

"Nothing. It's nothing but gossip."

"Wade was at the hospital this morning," I said. "He looked like he'd been there all night."

"I doubt it. He'd probably been up all night, but not with her. Listen. Wade's not a bad guy, he's just married to the wrong person. He's the kind of man who shouldn't be married at all because he can't seem to keep his pants zipped, but he wouldn't kill his wife. He's worked too hard to get where he's gotten."

"Who do you think shot her?"

"I don't know." Mercedes shook her head. "But I know it wasn't Wade. Why would he? Why wait till now? He doesn't need the money and, as I said, I think they both love the brutality. Frankly, I think she was shot either by one of the ex-lovers she screwed or some tree-hugger she'd offended or some militia member she ticked off, or maybe she shot herself and was too drunk to realize she'd missed the first time. You know"—Mercedes looked me straight in the eye—"some people never amount to anything. They just fiddle away their lives oblivious to everyone around them. Alma is one of those people who won't be missed if she dies because she's never exactly been around to begin with."

Well, Mercedes was right about that. From what I'd seen of Alma, she existed only as a black hole, sucking life into her maw.

"Who's Edith Rutherford?" I asked, looking at another name on the list.

"Oh, heaven help us," Mercedes groaned and rolled her eyes, which for the first time showed a little sparkle. "My aunt. She was married to my father's brother. He left Roundup right after the war and moved to New York and went into the meat-locker business or something equally distinguished. He died several years ago. And I haven't got the slightest idea how she'll vote—she stopped communicating with Alma and me when I refused to put her on the board after Father died. Aunt Edith is a complete living, breathing, walking, talking nightmare. I'd rather have Mike Wallace and 'Sixty Minutes' show up than Aunt Edith because she simply will not shut up. She is the most obnoxious, antagonistic, argumentative person I've ever known in my life."

"Does she still live in New York?"

"No. She moved to San Diego a few years ago." Mercedes shrugged. "Maybe her plane will crash. I should be so lucky. She doesn't have enough shares to make any difference, but the way she acts, you'd think she was the chairman emeritus. Who's next?"

"Let's talk about Johnny again." I said it with a straight face, but the picture of this elegant Armaniesque swan mindlessly, passionately entwined with a jamboree-suited, country-western satyr like Johnny Bourbon in a mirrored guest bathroom was so *surreal,* I wanted to say, "Are you insane? I just can't even believe you did such a thing."

"All I know, is that I think I got to him last. I might take one more run at him this afternoon, though." She laughed. "I think I have the energy, and it's not as tough duty as you might imagine."

Just then the door flew open and Duke Fletcher's lanky presence filled the room like Goliath Gone Western. He spun in with all the *con brio* grace of a duded-up trail boss—his trademark flat-brimmed cowboy hat hunkered firmly on his head like a barrel cactus on a plate. He waved a sheet of paper in his hand.

"Look what came in this morning's mail, ladies, Elias," he thundered with obvious relish. "The plot thickens! This looks like a note to me. Doesn't it look like one to you?" He waved it in my face. "Is everyone still present and accounted for, Mercedes honey?" He tousled her hair in a familiar way that I would have thought would have caused him to lose his hand to a meat cleaver. "No overnight fatalities?"

"Not as far as I know." She smiled up at him. Mercedes Rutherford was in love with Duke Fletcher.

"Then the little red-ass commies are getting nervous. Good. They can't intimidate us, by God." Duke sailed the hat across the room, where it circled and landed on the brass hook of a coatrack.

It was the same message Mercedes had received.

"What do the conniving little fellow-traveler peckerheads want now?" he demanded.

"Vote yes or you'll diet," Mercedes said calmly.

That stopped him. "Whoa there. Say again?"

"We think whoever sent it meant, 'Vote yes or you'll die,' but copied down the wrong word." Her voice was acerbic, and she pursed her lips as if she'd just bitten into a lemon.

"May I see that, please?" I took the sheet in my tweezers and smoothed it out on the table next to Mercedes's copy. They appeared identical. I wondered if all the major stockholders and everyone on the board had received the same communiqué. Even though the message was mangled, the meaning was clear: Vote yes or you'll die. What did all this mean? A mass murder at the annual meeting? A terrorist bombing? A methodical elimination of each stockholder between now and ten o'clock tomorrow morning?

Adrenaline surged into my veins, tightening my stomach and sharpening my wits. I felt I was on the brink of a case that could launch me into some serious international business beyond the marchese's missing Tiepolo, which I loved, but it wasn't twenty billion barrels of oil in a frozen land where espionage was still a way of life and vodka and sable were legitimate commodities.

I reached for my cellphone to call Jack Lewis and tell him to get on the ball and notify forensics, when Elias passed a note across to me. "Eleven thirty-five," it said. He caught my eye and tapped his watch.

Oh, God. Not now. Not now, I wanted to scream. My heart started to pound. I thought it would jump out of my chest. I looked at Elias, and his eyes said, Okay, Lilly. This is it. Time's up. What will it be? And I knew I was staring at the most important decision I'd make in my life. Until now, my life had been my career, period. Did I want more or not? Could I fit the two together and make it work? Or did I have to choose between Richard Jerome and the Russians? I was just hours from promising to forsake all others, a promise I would keep if I made it. It didn't mean my career would end, only that it would no longer be my top priority. My decision right now would be a pretty good gauge of what the future held.

Elias stared hard at me and I stared back. My breath grew short. My hands began to shake and the sea roared in my ears. I opened my purse. There was my phone. All it would take was one call to Richard: Something big has come up. I can't go to the airport with you to pick up your parents and sons. I'll meet you later. That would be the end and we would both know it. I reached in and my shaking fingers touched the cold plastic.

SEVENTEEN

I don't think anyone noticed that I fumbled slightly as I yanked two large clear plastic freezer-size Ziploc bags out of my purse. I slid Mercedes's Russian letter into one, the senator's into the other, and sealed them.

"I've got another appointment," I said and tucked everything back into my bag. "We'll drop these off at the police forensics lab."

"I don't understand," Duke said, insulted. A large frown creased his face, sunburned so many times it remained in a permanent state of scorch. "I just got here. Don't you have any questions for me?"

I nodded. "A few, yes. But just one big one for now: Where were you when Alma Gilhooly was shot?"

Evidently this was not the question he'd been expecting, because he drew back and demanded I apologize, in a cowboy sort of way: "Hey, hold on there, Lilly gal. I think you'd best take that back."

"Duke, do me a favor. Just answer the question. I'm late for another appointment and I know we could sit around and jaw-jack this thing to death for another hour or two, but at the moment, I'm out of time and I'm just going to have to cut right to the bottom line. I apologize, but tell me now or I promise you that neither I nor any member of my family will give you any money to run for President."

We like straight talk out West, and in less than a heartbeat, he gave me his aw-shucks grin.

"You're right," he said. "I've got nothing to hide, but the truth is, I can't exactly remember who I was talking to, or rather listening to. All these cocktail parties run together. All I do is listen and hope the fellow will give me some money and vote for me. I just know it was someone or other, and then I saw you take off like a rabbit down the hall with your sidearm waving. I'll work on remembering, though. Maybe Mercedes will recall, she's a crackerjack in that department." He grinned over at her, evidently unaware that she had been busy securing Johnny Bourbon's proxy at that time.

"Where can I reach you?" Mercedes asked.

"My office knows where I am every second," I told her. "Right now, though, Richard and I are going to the airport to pick up his family."

A tinge of what could have been envy flared in Mercedes's eyes. "I tried to get Richard Jerome to fall in love with me when he first got to town, but I kept having to break our dates because of business. I regret it."

I knew I didn't need any reassurance that I'd made the right decision, but her expression was thoughtful and gave me a nice smug glow, deep down.

"Do you want me to assign a security detail to you and Duke?" I asked. "In case the letter-writer decides to try something before the meeting?"

"No, thanks," Mercedes answered for both of them, although I could tell Duke was just itching to have a security contingent follow him around. "I'll have our own security beefed up. We'll be well protected."

"What about security at the meeting? Can we help out there?"

"No. It's already heavy. Always. These meetings are harder to get into than the White House."

"All right," I said. "Just call if you want us to augment it. Also, if any more stockholders or directors call to report they've received one of these letters, notify my office immediately and we'll send someone to pick up the documents."

We shook hands at the door to her office.

"You're lucky," she said to me.

"I know. I'll be in touch."

"This is an incredible situation," I said to Richard as I settled myself comfortably in the tan leather seat of his big old Mercedes convertible. Elias followed in his Suburban as we cruised out to the airport. Shortly it emerged like the Emerald City in the middle of nowhere on several thousand acres my father had sold to the City of Roundup after negotiating to retain the oil, gas, and mineral rights.

I told Richard about the magnitude of the Russian venture, the botched-up letters, the list of stockholders, Mercedes Rutherford and Johnny Bourbon in the powder room, the choice I'd made when Elias had pointed out the time.

"That was an incredible moment for me," I said. "It was like 'Okay, this is it.' And do you know why I know I'm doing the right thing?" I didn't wait for him to respond. "Because in the past I would have said, 'Well, that's the way it goes, I'll just get another guy.' But today, even though it made my heart pound a little and gave me the shakes, it was excellent. Making the decision was easy. I can't wait to be married to you."

Richard pulled my hand to his lips and kissed it and then turned it over and kissed the palm. "You know," he said evenly, "I like what you do—it's part of who you are."

"Good, because this case is a doozy. We might have to go to Siberia."

"Say when."

I reached under my jacket and unclipped my pager—it had been vibrating almost continuously since I'd gotten to Mercedes's office. "Look at this," I said. "Eight calls from my mother and two from the office."

Linda told me, as I suspected she would, that so far, Wade, Johnny Bourbon, and Aunt Edith Rutherford had called to report receiving the Russian notes. I told her to call them back and instruct them to set the letters aside until someone from Jack Lewis's office came to pick them up. We'd not heard from Kennedy McGee, who, Linda informed me, had resumed residence in Mrs. Bromley's guest room. Mrs. Bromley being an avid big-game hunter and an even more avid fan of Mr. McGee. I did not consider him to be a serious suspect. He'd been in jail in Bennett's Fort the afternoon before when the letters were mailed, and he wouldn't botch up Alma's shooting the way the assailant did. Maybe I didn't suspect him because I didn't want to. I didn't like him and didn't want to have anything to do with him. I wished he'd disappear.

"Where in the bah-Jaysus are you?" Mother yelled furiously into the phone when I called her. "I've been trying to get a hold of you for hours."

"What's wrong?" I asked.

"Well . . . for God's sake, Lilly," she gasped. "I'm absolutely frantic. You know the Jeromes arrive in half an hour, and who knows where in the world you have been. What on earth is that sound?"

We were driving around the end of the runway and Richard and I both ducked, although we didn't need to, as a Frontier 737 with a couple of polar bears painted on its tail passed overhead on final approach.

Finally, when the noise had cleared, I said, "It was a plane, Mother. We're at the airport to pick them up."

"Oh, thank God." All the air escaped. "You're at the airport. I was afraid you'd forget. You almost gave me a heart attack. Where's your brother?"

"He's following us."

"All right. I'll call him up. But now listen to me, Lilly. Don't get nervous and say anything stupid to Mr. and Mrs. Jerome. And for God's sake, don't use any profanity. What are you wearing?"

"I'm sorry, Mother," I shouted into the phone, although the reception was perfect. "I can't hear you. I think our transmission's breaking up. Bye. Bye."

The terminal came into sight, and I pulled down the visor and flipped open the mirror to examine my makeup. "Even if your parents change their minds and decide they hate me, will you still go through with it?"

"Lilly. I'm not having this conversation again."

We pulled into the lot and arrived at the gate just as their plane docked. Richard's parents and his grown, twin sons were the first people out. They all looked just alike—tall, thin, determined, good old-fashioned WASP New Englanders. Well dressed, but not chic. Kind, but not overly friendly faces. Reserved, but not cold or standoffish demeanor. And bright-eyed as new drill bits. They had never missed a thing. His parents, both in their late eighties, were slightly stooped, which only made them seem more distinguished.

I'd been to visit them back East, but this was their

first visit to Roundup, which, as we all know, is nothing like Manhattan or Fisher's Island. Nothing. And their first time to meet my family, which is nothing like theirs. Nothing.

Well, of course, everything was fine. And the boys, Richard III, and Charles, young men really—they'd both graduated from Princeton in June and gone straight to work for the family bank—were as handsome and charming as their father and seemed genuinely glad to see me.

EIGHTEEN

TUESDAY EVENING

I always think we look just like Roy and Dale when we stand out here and wait for our guests to land, don't you?" I snuggled into Richard's side as the evening breeze whipped across the meadow, causing the stampede strap on my hat to tug on my chin and my buckskin skirt to sway around like I was doing the hula.

"Younger."

The sun shone directly into our eyes, making it difficult to spot the chopper until suddenly it exploded from the brightness like a chariot of the gods—all noise and aggravation. And, in fact, the analogy was not groundless—my mother was on board and dinner tonight could be described as a parley of clan leaders. Three big chiefs: my father, Richard's father, and Richard. And three big squaws: my mother, Richard's mother, and me. As long as it didn't turn into the clash of the Titans, it would be fine. I didn't know about Richard's mother, but mine could turn a garden party into Armageddon with a flick of her wrist. Just the attitude with which she ground out her cigarette could polarize a crowd like lightning, serve notice that the fun, for her, was just getting started.

And now, with the ceremonial arrival of our parents, our wedding festivities were officially beginning. As we stood there, so close there was no light between us, it was as though I were watching the whole thing from someone else's body with someone else's eyes. The lovely craft settled to terra firma, the door opened as the engines whined down, the stairway extended. The copilot emerged, settling his cap firmly on his head, and reached up his hand to assist the passengers. Down the road, Elias's dented and rusted-out Ford pickup bumped across the deep ruts and over the noisy cattleguard, dust following him halfheartedly. His Australian shepherds, Gal and Pal, sat calmly in the truck bed, and I had the idea they had been playing cards and wanted the ride to be over so they could resume their hands. On the other side of the valley, light glinted off Christian's Range Rover as he and Mimi raced not to be late, and I had an image of Mimi pumping Bal à Versailles on herself from an old-fashioned atomizer and smoothing her already seamless blond chignon while Christian, a big cigar clamped between his teeth, squinted into the sun and floored it. And then everyone was greeting everyone else, and Richard and I welcomed them to the house, almost *our* house, where Celestina waited at the patio gate in a hot-pink smocked Mexican wedding dress with a tray of triple-shot Cuervo Gold margaritas, and no current knowledge of the English language.

"Elias," I said once everyone had settled in, "I need you to do me another favor."

"You mean *now*?" he said once I'd described my idea.

"Do you mind?"

"No, actually, I don't. I don't know how you're keeping up. I'm kind of partied out. Just seeing the same people night after night. If I ever got married, it'd be nothing like this."

"Take the helicopter. You'll be back in no time."

"Can I take Linda? She's still at the office."

"Sure, as long as she gets to work on time in the morning."

This cheered him up significantly.

I scrawled out a note, folded it up, and handed it to him. "Give this to her. Top priority. Hopefully she can go to work on it on the ride."

"Where is your brother going?" Mother asked when Elias gunned the engine, sending billows of stinking exhaust across the patio as the old Ford bounced and jerked down to the helipad.

"He's just running an errand for me," I told her. "He'll be right back."

"In the middle of a dinner party?"

"It's important," I said.

"Honestly, Lilly, if I get you through this wedding, it will be the miracle of the century. I wish you hadn't taken on this new case. I'm so afraid something will happen to you."

"You aren't going all maternal on me now, are you?" I gave her a squeeze. "Don't worry, Mama. Nothing will happen to me. I'm learning to delegate."

"Try to find someone besides your brother," she said. "Last time you almost got him killed. His leg's just now getting back to normal."

"Don't you think the Jeromes are delightful?"

"Oh, so attractive I just can't stand it."

I think she wasn't as spooled up about our wedding as she usually got about everything else because she was actually enjoying herself.

Richard came and stood beside me as the helicopter departed with Elias aboard. "Are you sorry you aren't on it?"

I couldn't answer. I turned and looked up at him, into his deep, gentle blue eyes, so full of his love and humor and maturity. "Would you have come with me?"

"In a heartbeat."

"Really?"

"Really."

I didn't deserve him.

NINETEEN

The fact was, something in this whole case stank. The more I thought about the Russian letters, the more they bothered me. Not because of what they said, but because of what they didn't say, and didn't do. It was not simply the use of the wrong word, which, in truth, made them not an actual legal threat at all: "Vote yes or you'll diet." What was that? Nothing. But they were rushed. Were they an afterthought, designed to draw us in the wrong direction because the attempted murder had been flubbed?

It was possible the annual meeting had nothing to do with anything and was simply a convenient way to attempt to salvage a seriously screwed-up situation. This idea would not leave me. It had dug itself into my brain like a too-tight waistband.

The helicopter had brought Elias home at about midnight, and at five forty-five, while Richard and I were in the barn saddling up, he and Linda drove off toward town.

"What do you suppose that's all about?" Richard

asked as the big maroon Suburban vanished into the deep shadows of the trees like a magician's trick.

"I don't know." A gnaw of worry tugged at my right shoulder blade and kinked my neck. "I wish he'd stopped by first."

We settled ourselves onto our horses and moved slowly away from the barn, stretching, breathing deep breaths of the cold, rich air that every day grew more pungent and loamy with fallen leaves. Our horses seemed to be glad for the slow start. Everyone seemed a little lumpy this morning, a little partied out and pooped. Except for Elias and Linda, evidently.

As though by unspoken consent, our mounts picked up speed, trotting and then cantering, and we all—Richard, me, Hotspur, and Ariel—headed in the direction of the pavilion, Mother's magnificent creation constructed for my goddaughter Lulu's wedding to the baron last June. It would be the scene of our reception in four days.

We loped slowly down the road, up a short rise, through a gap in the rocks, down a steep, sharp hill through the trees, and then out into a wide meadow, where the river flowed, gentle and silent, a silver ribbon in the clear morning. There, on the far side, in streamers of clean, white sun, the pavilion shimmered like a golden palace. Built of shellacked, peeled pine logs with a moss-green shingle roof, the structure was open on three sides. The sunlight had turned its vast, varnished floor into a brilliant lake. We dismounted and sat down on the wide steps of its shore.

"Well," he said. "What do you think?"

I pulled a little Thermos out of my pocket and poured us each a small mug of coffee.

"I'm thinking I'm getting drawn off by someone who wants to look stupid and bumbling, but isn't. I'm think-

ing about the annual meeting today and hoping Linda
got the SIBA stockholders' list last night. And I'm thinking that Elias and Linda must be on to something and I
want to know what it is. What are you thinking?"

"You mean besides business?"

"Yeah."

"I'm thinking I'd like to make love in the middle of
this floor."

"Right now?"

"Right now."

"Me, too."

We ripped our clothes off and made love right there
in the middle of nature with all the passionate enthusiasm and fervor of dogs who'd been eyeing each other
for months, although in fact it had been only hours.

"Maybe we could get married more often," I said.

Overnight, the *Range of My Heart* production company had mushroomed into something bigger than
Hollywood itself. Everything had doubled. Twice as
many dressing-room trailers. Twice as many eighteen-
wheelers. Twice as many pickups and customized white
Hollywood Suburbans with blacked-out windows and
drug-dealer grilles. Even the security guard at my little
parking lot was twice as big as the Napoleonic nut-case
from the day before. This one tipped his cowboy hat
and called out, "Good morning, Marshal," when I
drove in. They'd even reserved a space with my name
on it.

I parked next to Wade Gilhooly's Eldorado. Wade's
blonde was visiting with Dwight, who appeared ready
to hang his family jewels over the car door. They
awaited only her invitation, which she was in the
process of delivering. Her eyes smoldered like coals

through a wide band of terra-cotta and silver eye paint that practically stretched from ear to ear like a bandit's mask. Her mouth, with its big red lips, looked like a smiling tomato surrounding carnivorous teeth and an undulating pink tongue that curled up like a panther's. Her hair was more processed than Velveeta and whiter than a pair of Cloroxed Hanes 100-percent-cotton jockey shorts. There was no question but that Wade's blonde was Dwight's idea of the dream he'd waited his whole life to meet: She was young and hip and glamorous, she was as stacked as Anna Nicole Smith, as tall as Brigitte Nielsen, as available as Belle Starr, and she was practically yipping like a coyote hot on a scent.

They were so involved with their virtual copulation—his manhood pushing his jeans out as far as they would go; her overdeveloped, suntanned pecs and biceps rippling beneath her fringed pony-hide halter top—they didn't even notice me until I was almost right on top of them.

"Good morning, Deputy," I said.

"Whoa, Marshal." He turned with a big dizzy grin. "You snuck up on me. Didn't hear you coming."

"Right," I said. "I nearly ran over you. Who's your friend?"

"I'd like you to meet Mr. Gilhooly's personal executive assistant, Tiffany."

"Tiffany?"

"Tiffany West." The girl uncoiled herself and got out of the car, making Dwight draw in a ragged breath. Her legs were as long as I was tall, and they were wrapped in super-tight, pinto-pony-hide chaps.

"What's your real name?"

"Who's askin'?" Her voice was throaty and she was talking to me, but her eyes were on Dwight, looking as if she was thinking about eating him for lunch.

"You'd better tell her," Dwight said. "You don't want to make the marshal mad."

She looked at me and actually scoffed. "That little bitty thing?"

"You better tell her. Believe me, she gets mad and all hell breaks loose. She's The Man."

"Okay, I'll tell her. I don't want no problem with 'The Man.'" With that she laughed and punched me playfully in the shoulder.

I wasn't laughing.

"Alice Houston," she offered quickly when she figured out Dwight wasn't laughing, either, and then the words started rushing out and I was afraid she'd never shut up. "But when I went to body-building school in Denver so I could get my routine worked out, you know, get it refined and get sculpted and get enough poise to enter the Miss Wyoming Body Builder USA Pageant, the scout from *Penthouse* told me I'd never get anywhere named Alice Houston. So he told me about this radical procedure how people get their names for like porno movies. You know what I'm talking about?"

"No," I said.

"Yeah, I can tell by looking at you, you've got no clue."

"Don't make her mad. Don't make her mad." Dwight's eyes darted nervously between Tiffany and me.

"Don't worry, puddin'. I'm just joking. She knows that. Here's what you do: You take the name of your first pet as your first name and the name of the first street you lived on as your last name. You with me?"

"So far."

"All right, then. My first pet was a kitty named Tiffany and my first street was West Butte. But I didn't want to be Tiffany Butte, people would say it like 'butt.'"

So I used West instead. Pretty neat, huh? What's yours?"

I didn't want to tell them it would have been Sally State Road Four-Eight-Five, so I said I couldn't remember. "Did you win the contest?" I asked. I couldn't believe she was from Wyoming; we just don't make people like that up here.

"No." She dragged a long red fingernail down Dwight's chest toward the business end of his operation, which had shown no sign of diminishing in spite of his boss's arrival. He cleared his throat. "But I didn't mind. It's such an empty world being just a body-builder and a beauty queen. So I just keep myself up for personal fitness reasons, now. You still with me, little feller?"

"Sure thing." Dwight swallowed.

"I decided it was time to grow up and get a profession, so I went to Orky's Business School and learned to type. I figured, what the heck, it'd come in handy when I wrote my memoirs. And I've got some damn interesting memoirs, too."

With this Tiffany threw back her head and whooped like she was driving cattle. "Wooo-yow, baby, I've got memoirs!" And then she tossed her leg around Dwight's waist, like her leg was a boa constrictor with a fancy boot or something, and yanked him to her. "And I'm puttin' you in 'em."

I don't mean to be sexist, or chauvinistic, or whatever you want to call it, but to me, she looked like the kind of secretary that if she made a typo and you tried to correct her, she'd just beat you up.

"So," Tiffany continued once she'd rejoined the planet, "I kind of took to it. I type one hundred words a minute and my dictation is up to two twenty-five."

Okay, so I was wrong.

"How long have you worked for Mr. Gilhooly?" I asked.

"Only about six months, since he moved his corporate headquarters to Roundup. His secretary in Billings didn't want to leave. She doesn't know what she's missing." She cupped Dwight's face in her hand. "Does she, hon?"

"Do you mind telling me where were you on Sunday night?"

"No problem. I spend every Sunday after church at the High Plains Christian Home with my mother."

"Your mother?" This girl was no more than twenty-five, and her mother couldn't have been much older than I was.

"Well, my grandmother," she told Dwight, who listened to her as spellbound as if she were reading the latest Michael Crichton thriller out loud. "My real mother took off when I was three. Never came back. And my grandmother raised me. But she's real old now, and sick, so she has to live in the home. So I go over there every Sunday and play the piano and bingo and have dinner, flip quarters off my biceps—the old guys love it when I do that—things like that. It's fun. Everybody's extra nice. I like it." Her brow furrowed in thought. "I've been thinking about being a nurse."

Dwight smiled like a complete idiot. "Isn't that wonderful?"

"So you didn't go to Billings with Mr. Gilhooly on Sunday afternoon?"

"Nope." She shook her head.

"Do you usually travel with him?"

She had to consider that for a second. "Umm, well, I'd say I usually go with him when he takes his own plane. It's a Learjet. Like sitting on a rocket." She delivered this information to Dwight's fly.

"Will you excuse us a minute, Miss West?" I said.

"No problemo. See you in a minute, Deputy Dog." The tomato smiled wider and the jaguar's pink tongue appeared, and Dwight stumbled in the dirt as he followed me.

"I think I'm in love, Marshal Lilly," he said. "I love you more, but I think I'm in love with Tiffany, big time."

"Listen to me, Deputy," I told him. "Shift your brain back to normal, whatever that means, and find out whatever you can from her about Gilhooly's operations and family life, company executives, anything that could provide us with a possible lead to who shot Alma and what all's going on here. You with me?"

"Oh, yes, ma'am. I'll get on her right now. I mean, I'll get on *it* right now."

We're such a bunch of sex maniacs at Bennett Security International, it's a miracle we get any business done.

TWENTY

Linda was squinting at her computer monitor, thick glasses down low on her nose, head tilted back. She handed me a sheaf of papers. It was a list of names and numbers. The SIBA Fund investors.

"How did you get this?" I asked, not really sure if I wanted to know.

She shrugged innocently. "Your brother and I fiddled around on his computer a little, and this accidentally came out. You'd think they'd be more careful. This information could fall into the wrong hands." She smiled and indicated the closed door of my office. "He was here when I got here."

"Where's Elias? Did you go with him last night?"

"Question number one: downtown. He said he'd meet you at the Rutherford meeting, which, incidentally, starts at ten, convention center auditorium at the Grand. And question number two: yes. He said he'd fill you in at the meeting. I'm not sure what we found out. And, finally, this was slipped under the door this morning. I opened it first in case it was a bomb or something.

I only touched the edges." She handed me an envelope with my name scrawled on it: Marshal Lilly Bennett. I slipped out the note:

> *Dear Marshal Bennett, I apologize for any disruption we're causing in your schedule and hope you can join me for a drink this evening at six o'clock in your cousin's saloon so I may apologize in person. Cordially, Bob*

"Who's Bob?"

"Redford," Linda practically screamed. "Rob-bert Red-ford. He invited you out."

Isn't that perfect? Here I am, halfway through my life, halfway up the aisle, my wedding's in three days, and Robert Redford asks me out. I looked at the ceiling.

"You're really testing me, Lord," I said out loud. "First the Rutherfords, then the Russians, and now the Redfords. But forget it. I'm sticking with Richard Jerome and that's that. End of subject."

"Aren't you at least going to meet him?" She couldn't believe I wasn't.

"No. I'm busy at six o'clock tonight. We're going to a dinner party at the Johnsons'. Please call and give him my regrets. Now I'm going to go find out what Wade wants."

Linda was crestfallen.

"Okay, listen. Why don't you meet him for me and thank him?"

"Really?"

"Really. Now, would you bring me a cup of coffee?"

Wade worked his way to his feet when I walked in. He offered his hand. The old bruise on his cheekbone had faded to nothing, and the crooked, flattened Liam Neeson veer to his nose made his face enormously charming when he smiled and greeted me. He appeared more rested than he had the day before—he'd obviously clocked some time in a tanning bed, because his skin had a slightly healthier glow. The starched collar of his shirt concealed most of the angry red scar on his neck.

Even though Wade was dressed in a dark suit, white shirt, and Gucci tie—all expensive and perfectly fitted— and his manners were fine, in my mind, he'd never be able to shake the slickness of his past. The glibness of a second-rate golf pro hustling for hundreds. The slippery shine of a used-car dealer hustling for the hidden profit. The humiliation and disgrace of the unacceptable son-in-law hustling for approval.

"Sorry to show up so early," he said without preamble. "But I understand your brother was in Billings last night."

"Really?" I said and sat down, not surprised he'd been contacted.

"Yes, a friend of mine called. Did he find out anything?"

"Is there anything you think he should have found out?"

Wade thrust his hands deep in his trouser pockets and shrugged his shoulders. "I hope not. I'd hate to think any of our friends tried to kill Alma. I don't think we have any enemies up there." He took his cane from where it leaned on the edge of the desk, walked over and looked out the window to the movie-land maelstrom below. Buck was standing on the wooden sidewalk across the street, leaning against a post, belly drooping over his Levi's, hat pulled low, mirrored glasses shining like beacons, a longneck in his hand.

"Hey," Wade said, "isn't that Robert Redford?"

I went to look. "Where?"

"Just went into the café."

He turned and we were inches away from each other. Up close he looked even better. His eyes were sky blue and flecked with gold—the same color gold as his freckles—and they betrayed an unexpected vulnerability and gentleness. His lips were sensuous and as crooked as his nose.

The moment passed without any more acknowledgment than that of two strangers standing at the same window, and I returned to my chair as Linda gave the door a brisk knock and brought in the coffee.

"I don't mean to be pushy," Wade said once Linda was gone. "But I have paid you a boatload of money, and I'm curious if you've come up with anything? Any clues at all?"

"You aren't being a bit pushy," I answered and cupped the mug with both hands, stalling a little, weighing my words, admiring my engagement ring. Boy, it was big. "You're entitled to ask. And the answer is: I'm not sure. I haven't had a chance to talk to Elias yet this morning—he's going to meet me at the Rutherford meeting—so I don't know what, if anything, he came up with in Billings. Frankly, I doubt if there's anything to be found up there. I'm more concerned about the meeting itself. I hope Mercedes's security chief knows what he's doing, because it's starting to look like whoever tried to kill Alma has a large stake in the outcome of the vote."

"I got one of those letters. What'd it say?"

I explained the bungled message and laughed at his shocked expression. "Can you believe it? Whoever sent them copied down the wrong word out of the dictionary." As I'd been talking, I'd also been scanning the SIBA Fund investor list, and my eyes jarred to a halt. "My God, will you look at this."

There, in alphabetical order, in black and white, was

the name of America's most ardent environmentalist–politician–presidential candidate.

"What?" Wade asked.

"Duke Fletcher is an investor in SIBA."

"You can't be serious." He reached across and snatched the sheet from my fingers. "SIBA is in favor of the Russian venture. It represents everything Duke's against. They're destroyers."

I nodded, too stunned to speak. What was it with our leaders that they give us such hope and then half the time turn out to be double-crossing, underhanded, conniving, immoral bastards? Of course, if we'd just raise everybody's salary back there in Washington, maybe we'd be able to attract a higher caliber of candidate. Who wants to go live in that godforsaken climate and take constant abuse from the press for a hundred grand a year? No one, except poor schmucks looking for ways to cut corners—they're the only ones who can afford it. Or else they're too young to know much that's helpful. But Duke Fletcher. It made me sick to my stomach. He already had plenty of money. As far as I, and a lot of other people, were concerned, he was the planet Earth's last, greatest hope.

"Holy moly," I said.

Linda swept in with a fax. "Elias just sent this over."

The memo, retrieved out of the ether from some long-ago meeting, showed the genesis of the SIBA name: Siberian Associates. The fund had been formed specifically to take advantage of this venture.

"I don't believe it," Wade said. "We've been neighbors for a long time and it's not possible for Duke to be that big a fraud." He glanced at his watch. "Oh, man. Look how late it is. I've got to go, I want to stop by the hospital and see how Alma's doing. I'll see you at the meeting. You can sit with me if you want, but I'm going to be working the crowd pretty steadily, trying to keep this vote on track. Look out for the Russians, they're loose cannons. They'll feel you up so fast you'll think you're a camp follower on a troop train."

I laughed. "I know, I met them on Sunday, but thanks for the warning. Wade, why are you voting against Alma?"

He grasped the top of the chair back in his hands and leaned over it toward me. "Alma only cares about herself. Always has, always will. She's a bully who doesn't think anything is bigger than she is, but most things are. Mercedes has consistently led the company on a responsible path. She could have made more money short-term, but she makes long-term decisions, decisions that work for the company, the environment, the employees, the stockholders. That's why the stock stays so strong. She's a big thinker. Long-term, everyone benefits.

"But Alma won't accept responsibility for herself"— Wade seemed almost out of breath—"much less for the actions of her own company. I've always voted against her plank. And now there she is, lying up in the hospital, still breathing in spite of the odds, and still making everyone's life hell."

I suddenly felt sorry for Wade Gilhooly. I don't know what sort of lingering illness he had, but he looked and sounded exhausted, and he spoke in such a babbling rush it was almost as though he were on speed.

"I was sorry about your vice president, Jim Dixon. What's the latest report on his condition?"

"He's in bad shape. You might not believe this, but if he dies, I'll be a lot sorrier to lose him than Alma. Jim's the glue in my whole operation, but sometimes he drinks more than he should. I was hoping to hand off the business to him in a few years. Now I'm not so sure." Wade gave an ironic snort. "Life sucks. You bust your butt to get everything you want, and then by the time you figure out that's not what you wanted, it's too late."

"Yup," I said. "That's pretty much the way it works. One more question: Why did you fly commercially to Billings instead of taking your own plane?"

"Three reasons: Their schedule worked for me, which saved me a few thousand dollars—that's reasons one and two—and three, my jet's in for maintenance. And four: I did not shoot Alma."

TWENTY-ONE

A few scraggly pickets—GIVE THE LAND BACK TO THE NATIVE AMERICANS, DEATH TO AMERICAN CAPITALISTS, DOWN WITH DOW CHEMICAL, SUPPORT GROCERY WORK-ERS—stuff like that, shuffled back and forth behind a police barricade across the street from the hotel's main entrance. We're so behind in Wyoming, I love it. Bored camera crews from the local television outlets kicked invisible pebbles off the sidewalk.

"Sort of a disappointing group of protesters you've got here," I said to Curtis, the doorman. Curtis was the Scatman Cruthers of doormen. A Roundup institution born at the door of the Grand in his brown-twill coat and gold-braided cap. They did a story about him in *National Geographic* once, and the picture they took of him was so good he kept it taped inside the key cabinet instead of a mirror.

He shook his head. "They've been using those same signs for years. I don't think they dare carry any that say anything agin' the oil business, 'cause they're all a bunch of oil-business trust-funders. But you'd think with all this Russia business going on, a few interesting people would show up. We've got all the networks set up inside, and nothing happening. Makes us look bad." He pocketed my twenty and patted Baby on the head. "Don't worry, I'll keep an eye on the dog. Hey," he said as an afterthought. "You seen those Russians yet?"

"Briefly."

"Well, hold on to yourself. They're staying here in the hotel and the word's out: They're such grabbers, they scared off all our best girls, and even the five-dollar street hookers won't come near the place."

Just then a black stretch limousine glided to the curb. Before Curtis could open the door, it flew open, cracking him in the knee, and a spry, tiny, wiry, old woman in a miniskirt and purple lace stockings leapt out and made a beeline across the street for the TV crew. She was a little bowlegged crab homing in on a dead jellyfish, and she'd flatten anyone or anything that got in her way. The camera lights blinked alive.

"My name is Edith Rochester Rutherford," she shouted into their faces in the most grating New York accent I've ever heard in my life. "And I live in the Del Coronado Hotel in San Diego, California. My suit is a Galanos." She extended a lilac-tweed arm. "Nancy Reagan wears lots of Galanos, but she wears too much red."

It didn't matter if the reporters knew who she was, she was alive, and that was better than any other story they had at the moment. I crossed the street and huddled up with the team.

"Are you related to the Rutherford family?" someone asked her.

"I *am* the Rutherford family," she declared. "These girls—Mercedes and Alma—are a couple of ingrates. They've destroyed everything my husband—James

Rutherford—ever worked for, and I'm here today to see that they get their comeuppance."

"I thought Bradford Rutherford was chairman before Mercedes," said another. "What did your husband do for Rutherford Oil?"

"He was a Wall Street stockbroker and meat-packer, but what does it matter what he did?" Aunt Edith blew him off from behind white-rimmed dark glasses so large they made her look like an ant. "The fact is these girls have headed the company down a very slippery slope."

"Do you care to elaborate, Mrs. Rutherford?"

"Yes. Come to the meeting."

"How do you plan to vote today? Are you in favor of or opposed to the Russian deal?"

"Russian deal, smussian deal. That's nothing." Aunt Edith opened her lilac Kate Spade tote and pulled out sheets of typed paper, which she waved around with an arthritic, red-tipped claw. She had on a pearl ring so big it looked as if she'd glued a golf ball to her hand. "I plan to propose an entirely new slate of officers and directors and clean house." She handed out the copies, which the members of the press studied diligently. "I already have commitments from every single one of these individuals, and once they elect me chairman, we will turn Rutherford Oil into the largest, classiest oil company in the world."

"This is impressive," Tom O'Neill said. He was the half-brain former coanchor of the KRUN-TV Evening News who'd gotten fired for staging pit-bull fights and then covering them as news. Now he was the catchall for the local community-access cable channel. "You say you have commitments from all of these people?"

"That's what I said."

"This is *big*."

What a dope. I dropped out of the crowd and scanned the list. Here's who was on it:

King Saud—King of Saudi Arabia
George Bush—Former President of the United States
Margaret Thatcher—Former Prime Minister of Great Britain
Julio Iglesias—Mexican diplomat
Barbra Brolin—Singer
Norman Schwarzkopf—Former General of Desert Storm
Werner Erhardt—Guru
Rosie O'Donnell—Media mogul
Daniel Baker, M.D.—Plastic surgeon
Jake Steinfeld—Personal trainer
Michael Jordan—Former Basketball player

Here's the thing with some of the media that makes me crazy: They have no judgment, no discretion. They are just big vacuum cleaners that suck up information and then spew it out in high-fidelity, Surround-Sound diarrhea without a single thought as to the legitimacy of the information or the credibility of their sources. Hey! they exclaim. First Amendment. It's news. While anyone with any sense knows it's not news at all. It's nothing but a load of crap.

Regardless, they all went on the air live at that very second, interrupting whatever oral sex was going on in their network soap operas, to announce the Rutherford Oil takeover by what they interpreted to be a legitimate new group that included *Michael Jordan*. This would really put Rutherford Oil on the map.

Wait till the actual business reporters, who were inside covering the actual meeting, get a load of this slate, I thought. They'll fall on the floor in hysterics.

I followed Edith Rutherford into the hotel. She barreled along like a little door-slammer cloaked in a heavy cloud of Tea Rose perfume. I trailed her across the lobby and up the escalators, during which ride she opened her purse and, without looking in a mirror, ground a tube of smashed-up bright-red lipstick onto her mouth. I followed her to the mezzanine, where she passed the check-in tables and announced to the surprised receptionists with a wave of her hand, "I don't need any of that junk," then cruised through the metal detector and disappeared.

So far as I could tell, in spite of Mercedes's claim that Security would be so tight it would be easier to get into the White House, it appeared minimal to nonexistent, and I decided whomever they'd used was either very, very good or not there at all. When I reached the entrance to the convention center/ballroom I noticed two gorillas in too-small cheap blue blazers with the Rutherford logo on their breast pockets, and too-tight gray pants. My first thought was that I hoped they didn't have any weapons.

Three airport-type metal detectors stood at the open doors into the convention-hall lobby. I showed my badge to one of the fellows.

"We're ready for anything, Marshal," he informed me as I passed through. "Don't worry."

Ha. This was Mercedes's show, not mine, but if those two goons were her idea of beefed-up security, we hadn't communicated. A little hole began burning in my stomach.

TWENTY-TWO

'd never been to the annual meeting of a major, publicly held company before. All our businesses are family-owned, so when the Bennetts gather officially once a year at the main ranch house, we sit down around the thirty-foot-long dining-room table where the ranch hands have their meals, suck up a number of cocktails, tell a lot of lies, laugh a lot, get into a few shouting matches, listen to my father report on the banks and say how much we made or lost overall (although we've never actually ended up in a deficit position), listen to Christian report on the newspapers and railroads, listen to Elias report on the ranch and the oil and the cattle, and listen to Cousin Buck tell us what a bunch of assholes he thinks we all are. Then we vote to keep everything the way it is and have some more drinks and rib eyes and pineapple upside-down cake. So even though I own stock in a few corporations and get invited to their annual meetings annually, this was my first time to attend.

And I was totally unprepared for the chaos.

The lobby was like a political convention, a mob scene of Americana, a combination of Wall Street, downtown Boulder, and Barnum and Bailey. Granola-heads, tree-huggers, and bean-counters, everything from people wearing hats in the shapes of oil derricks and oil-well pumps to a giant, very friendly looking Russian bear who was followed by a curvy young woman in a tiny, mink-trimmed Russian peasant outfit carrying a tray filled with shot glasses. The bear waved Wyoming and Siberian flags in one paw and handed out vodka from the tray with the other. Another young woman—heavyset, hirsute, simian, and arrayed in a large rhinestone crown and a mink-trimmed silver-lamé bathing suit with a banner introducing her as Miss Manily-Siberia—was kissing all the men, which none but a handful of the company's oil-field workers brought down from Alaska for the meeting looked too crazy about.

I spotted Wade having what appeared to be angry words with Kennedy McGee, who towered over him and spoke directly into his upturned face. Judging by Wade's expression, his breath smelled like onions. Wade had just handed him an envelope with something written on its front.

"We had a deal, McGee. So just give me the proxy and get the hell out of town," I heard him say through clenched teeth as I approached them.

"Not bloody likely, you mewling little mole-butt." Kennedy slid the envelope arrogantly into his jacket. A cruel, defiant grin curled his lips. "I've changed my mind, and there's not a bleeding thing you can do to stop me. The Russians' offer makes this look like bus fare, you stupid gull. As far as I'm concerned, you can go screw yourself. It's not as if you weren't used to it."

"Hey, good morning, Lilly," Johnny Bourbon yelled

from behind. He spun me around by my shoulder and took my hand. Diamonds sparkled from the gold cross that held his leather-thong bolo tight to his throat. The brim of his white beaver Stetson shaded his eyes. I wondered if he knew the whole shebang now rested on his vote. "Praise the Lord," he declared.

Shanna hung back a little in her curvy powder-blue Western suit with bleached deer-antler buttons, a frilly little white crinoline-lined peplum, which needed to stick out at least six more inches if it were going to match her bosom, and oceans of fringe hanging from her sleeves and skirt. I wondered if she had as active a libido as her husband, and if she had a young Italian as her assistant. The more I looked at her, the more I decided she probably had two young Italians.

"Excuse me." I pulled away to see what had happened between Wade and Kennedy, but Kennedy was gone, and Wade, still red-faced, was trying to have a friendly conversation with someone else. I turned back to Johnny and Shanna. "I guess I shouldn't be surprised you're here," I said. "I mean . . . well, I don't know exactly what I do mean."

"You mean why would a man of God, a man with feet of clay who begs for a living, be at an occasion that so concerns itself with earthly matters? Don't you know, 'Even the rich are hungry for love, for being cared for, for being wanted, for having someone to call their own'? Mother Teresa herself, God rest her soul, said that."

"No, I had no idea she'd ever said any such thing."

"And I'll tell you something else," Johnny pressed his case. "Over the years, Alma gave Johnny Bourbon's Christian Cowboys plenty of stock in this fine company, and I believe, although we won't know until she's gone—whenever that day is that the Lord decides to call her home—that she left our ministry a significant endowment. Now, I don't know that for sure—you and I both know what our Alma's like, that girl can change her mind quicker than the weather—but she loves the Lord, sure enough, and I pray He'll have mercy and restore her to us."

"Praise the Lord," said Shanna in her best television voice: long on delivery and short on conviction. I'm not saying she wanted Alma to die, and I'm not saying she didn't. But I also didn't think she especially cared if she lived or not, because Shanna and I both knew there always had been, and always would be, Almas orbiting Johnny. Just as there are always people anxious and willing to pay for salvation.

Wade was now surrounded by a group of men who looked as if they'd been dressed by Hopalong Cassidy's wardrobe person. All six of them were big, stocky, sturdy, muscular. Much too hefty for the wildly expensive high-slide-heeled, gila-monster-skin cowboy boots that kept them constantly rocking over backward and scrambling for balance. They had bandannas at their necks, color-coordinated with skintight shirts cowboy-trimmed with silver medallions and fringe and different-colored piping—red on white, white on red, white on black, black on white, saddle brown on Wedgwood and vice versa—tucked into matching skintight piped pants tucked into the boots, and absurd, old-fashioned ten-gallon hats.

The Russians.

They were yelling at Wade and towering over him like giant cannibals getting ready to snatch him up and stick him in the pot.

"Wade," I said. "How're your friends?"

"Hey!" They all turned and said at the same time. "It's lady?"

Then the biggest one, the chief oaf, the red-on-white, my old friend Sergei said, "Bride. She's bride."

What they tried to do was bend their knees and thrust their pelvises forward and act out a little hokey-pokey, but the boots prevented the action and simply turned them into a bunch of cheap, drunk Elvis imper-sonators.

"Gentlemen, you know Marshal Bennett."

"Oh, *da,* lady policemans. You very beautiful, noth-ing like Russian policemans." With this they all re-moved their hats and gave me a little teetering bow. Red-on-white snapped his fingers and the bear rumbled up next to him. "You want vodka?"

"Not quite yet, thanks."

"Vodka good for you." With that, they all tossed off shots.

"You want hokey-pokey with me?"

"Not at the moment, thanks."

"Maybe later?"

"I don't think that's going to be possible, thanks."

"Russian very good hokey-pokey."

"Thanks anyway. But no."

"You see. I very, very good hokey-pokey. Very big. Like bear."

"No."

"You vote yes or you sorry."

"I'll keep that in mind, thanks."

"You vote yes and you come Russia. We hokey-pokey."

I looked at Wade, who was smiling. "Can you be-lieve this guy?" I asked.

"Russian women aren't exactly what you'd call lib-erated," he answered.

"No kidding. Listen, Boris. No hokey-pokey, ever. Understand?"

Six pretty young women in matching navy suits with Rutherford logos on their breast pockets appeared out of nowhere, and each took one of the Russians' arms. "Time for the meeting to start, gentlemen," one girl said, and the six Russkis went meekly, their eyes sparkling with anticipation.

These men were funny because of their provincialism, but they were not funny. Like bears, they were determined, and because they and their countrymen were hungry for food and money, they were dangerous. They had eaten their own before, and, if they had to, they'd do it again. But they'd rather try to eat us first.

More company public-relations staffers urged stockholders to go in and be seated as quickly as possible, since the meeting was about to start. But there was a bottleneck by one of the doors because Edith Rutherford was handing out her ballots, and saying loudly over and over again, "My name is Edith Rochester Rutherford and I live in the Del Coronado Hotel in San Diego, California. My suit is a Galanos. All these people said yes."

"Does she do this every year?" I asked Wade.

"Every year like clockwork. Last year her slate included O. J. Simpson, Paula Barbieri, and Yasir Arafat. She's very ecumenical." As he watched her, he rolled and unrolled a thick annual report into a tube between his wide, flat hands, which had turned black with rubbed-off ink. "Looks like your whole family's here."

"Just my parents, I think," I answered. "Elias should be here any minute."

Before they disappeared through the door, I watched my mother, who looked just sharp as could be in navy and camel Chanel, whisper, "Paste" to my father, referring to Edith's golf-ball ring and jeweled oil-derrick pendant. Daddy studied the Xeroxed ballot, slapped out a quick laugh, folded the sheet in thirds, and slid it into his jacket pocket. "Michael Jordan," he said.

"Are you sure you don't want to sit with me?" Wade asked. The lights flashed twice, and a man's voice came over the sound system asking people to take their seats because the meeting would start on time.

"No, I'm fine, thanks."

What I wanted to know was, where the hell was Elias? I waited on the far side of the lobby, watching for him until they began to close the doors. I punched the speed dial. He answered immediately. "Yo."

"Where are you?"

"On my way. Got a lot to tell you. Big scandal. The neighbors said that Alma used to beat up Wade—always had black eyes and his jaws wired and stuff. But he never fought back because she's so much bigger. Another guy said he has all those injuries because he gets into bar fights all the time. And then another guy said Mercedes was always rushing up there pretending to meet with Wade, but it was just a cover to meet with Duke. They don't seem to have much else to do in Billings except gossip, and they sure do hate Alma."

"Where'd you hear all this, Elias?"

"Bar at the Northern. But here's the good part: After I'd drunk eight hundred thousand cups of tea with her, Duke Fletcher's housekeeper . . ." The transmission broke up.

I called him back, but he was somewhere out of range. It was 10:01. My stomach turned up the burner, the sort of aggravation that, when I was on the street, could be salved by a couple of glazed doughnuts, a cup of old coffee, and a handful of cigarettes. Now all I could do was suffer. No doughnuts. No cigarettes. And coffee by itself just made it worse. God, I wish I could smoke again. Sometimes the urge entered and tempted

me so much I wanted to scream. To make a deal with
the monkey. To throw all the research and facts out the
window, believe they were wrong. Forget it. All roads
lead to heart disease, cancer and death.

I entered the convention hall.

TWENTY-THREE

The *William Tell* Overture thundered from one corner of the darkened hall to the other. But this was no Saturday-morning movie, no Lone Ranger and Tonto racing faster than was earthly possible across the screen. Instead, a video began with a dramatic high-speed shot of a threatening and empty North Sea, spinning fast across heaving, murky whitecaps until, far in the distance, a small speck appeared and grew into a derrick, a white-metal tower, an offshore rig with the Rutherford Oil name stretching around its cement base. Men in red hard hats, yellow slickers, high rubber boots, and life jackets with lifelines that connected them like leashes to rigging bars, waved at the chopper as it circled and then landed on the rolling deck.

A narrator's voice—it sounded like Gene Hackman—boomed above the music as the video proceeded at full volume from one Rutherford oil, gas, and coal project to another—Indonesia, California, Texas, Egypt, Venezuela, West Virginia, Wyoming.

I edged my way along the paneled wall, stopped

about a third of the way forward, and leaned there, waiting for my beloved brother, whose neck I looked forward to breaking. He had something. Something big. I stood motionless in the dark, and my chest tightened as I began to feel the unmistakable rumblings of danger. It draped the hall in sticky, wet, invisible cobwebs. I couldn't see it, or hear it, but I could taste and smell it. My antennae searched the way giant receiving dishes listen blindly for sounds from space. Where would it come from? Where was Elias? It was 10:10.

The music blasted and the room grew darker as we descended into a coal mine. You could feel the damp and cold as the elevator sank deeper into the earth. It made my hair stand on end. Suddenly an after-shave-soaked bulk materialized next to me and a meaty hand grabbed my breast and squeezed. Hard. I was so shocked I didn't make a sound. I just instinctively turned and smashed my knee, hard and fast, into the man's crotch. It was one of the Russians! Mr. Red-on-White. The provincial oil minister from Watchahoochee or whatever. He sank to his knees, groaning, and, as he crawled away, the tension drained out of my chest and I started laughing to myself. I was probably overreacting, looking for trouble. I took a deep breath. I needed to relax.

Finally the video ended and the lights came up slightly, enough to see my Russian intruder slumped in his seat. Mercedes, flanked by two gray-suited men, ascended three steps to the stark dais and took her place at a draped banquet table in front of the big screen. She'd pulled her shoulder-length hair back into a severe chignon, and her charcoal suit coat absorbed the stage lights like a blotter. I tried again to picture her and Johnny Bourbon groping each other in the powder room while someone was shooting Alma, and all I could see were Tarzan and Jane. The Gorilla and the Lady. A real hanging-from-the-chandeliers deal. One big jungle yell and a lot of chest-pounding before you snap that girdle back on and return to the boardroom. This lady was all business.

The table was bare except for pitchers of ice water, three glasses, and a gavel. A large stack of thick binders sat on the floor next to one of the men, whom I took to be the secretary of the corporation. The other was the general counsel.

Mercedes stepped to the podium and banged the gavel. "The Annual Meeting of the Rutherford Oil Company is officially open. We will first have the report from the secretary of the corporation."

"Madame Chairman. Madame Chairman." Edith Rutherford stood in the aisle waving her sheaf. Her voice was nails on a blackboard. "Madame Chairman. I demand to be recognized."

"You will be recognized in the Other Business section of the agenda, Ms. Rutherford," Mercedes said evenly. "We will now have the report from the secretary of the corporation."

While the gray suit droned on about the minutes of last year's meeting and a lot of other dreary corporate stuff—punctuated every sixty seconds by Edith's demands to be recognized and Mercedes's evenly repeated answer—I made my way farther forward to look over the audience and see who was there.

The board of directors, corporate executives, and their spouses all were seated in the front rows, staring straight ahead like West Point's long gray line, ready to leap to their feet and take a bullet for the cause. I recognized a number of them: chairman and CEO of U.S. Airways; chairman and CEO of AT&T; chairman and CEO of Sumitomo, Japan's largest shipbuilder; chairman and CEO of the First National Bank of Round-up—my father (he and my mother, the senior members of the team); former U.N. ambassador Jeanne Kirkpatrick; former senator Fletcher, whom I could not accept as a turncoat; and next to him a gray, humorless man I took to be the head of the SIBA Fund, Penn Holland, Mr. Bottom-Line-at-Any-Cost.

Financial charts, spreadsheets and budgets appeared on the giant screen as the treasurer delivered his report. I glanced at my agenda; election of the officers was next. This was when Edith really went to town. She had made it halfway through her slate of nominees when the general counsel, with his thinning hair and tortoise-shell glasses and regimental tie, interrupted her.

"Mizz Rutherford," he said condescendingly, "I would have thought by now that you would have been well acquainted with the bylaws of this corporation as they pertain to the nomination of candidates for the board and officers of the corporation. But since you seem not to be familiar with them, I feel it is important to enlighten you, once again, of the rules and regulations governing this meeting."

He droned like a fly on a lazy summer afternoon, around and around and around until, finally, God bless her, Edith held her hands in the air in a T-sign, like a referee at a football game calling for time and shouted, "Okay, Frankie. What's your point?"

The point was that she had neglected to register her slate with the corporate secretary within the mandated period of time and therefore could not enter her nominees onto the ballot.

"You people are all the same," Edith groused. "You got no style. No panache." For once, I agreed with her.

Next came the Siberian venture, exploration and exploitation. Mercedes outlined the company position to the accompaniment of the Russians trying to shout her down, and then Siberian Associates' own Penn Holland, with constant interruptions for applause by the Russians, took the podium to present the opposition view. Finally the secretary took over and the voting began. It was similar to being on the floor of the House or the Senate or the Chicago Commodities Exchange, constant motion and noise, people lobbying each other right to the last second, shouting into cell phones. Giddy, tense excitement swamped the room as the roll was read, and one at a time, stockholders shouted over the din to cast their votes. The company was winning. The air boiled up and started to steam like a fragrance counter at Bloomingdale's.

Elias finally appeared.

"Speak," I said as my eyes dragged from one end of the hall to the other. Deep down, I could not shake the feeling that we were reenacting the opening scene from *The Manchurian Candidate,* that some Russian was behind the air vent over our heads with an Uzi trained on someone.

Elias had no more than gotten his mouth open, said, "Okay, here's what it looks like in Billings," than we both watched in horror as our mother stood up and trampled across half a row of people to join us.

"Oh, no," I said under my breath. "What does she want?"

"What are you two doing standing over here?" Her suit had a sort of shawl affair held in place on her shoulder by a large pearl-and-gold brooch. Her voice had an accusatory sound to it. "Elias, isn't that the same tie you wore last night?"

"We're working, Mother," I whispered.

"On what?" she whispered back. "Alma's attacker?"

I nodded.

"Oooh." Mother's eyes sparkled. "Do you think he's here?"

"Yes. I'm pretty sure." I didn't bother to point out to her that the "he" could be a "she."

She grinned conspiratorially, and her whole face lit up. "Is there anything you want me to do?" Snoop Sisters on patrol.

"Nope. I think we've got it pretty well under control."

Suddenly, out of the corner of my eye, emerging from the dark behind the video screen, I saw a movement. And then the quick, dull glint of light on blued metal.

TWENTY-FOUR

*D*uck!" I screamed, as I fell on top of my mother and a round exploded into the mahogany wall directly behind us, shattering and splintering the wood like a thin sheet of ice. But what coated my face wasn't ice. It was blood.

I raised up on my elbows and looked at my mother. Other than looking fairly squashed, she didn't seem to be wounded. And then, in all the thundering chaos, I heard a moan. It was Elias. The wound was enormous. A giant shell had smashed through beneath his collarbone, leaving a gaping, jagged hole. Blood from a severed artery geysered into the air, drenching everything within a three-foot radius. I didn't even think about it. I reached right into the wound and pinched the artery closed as Elias lost consciousness and my mother stroked his forehead and held his hand, murmuring to her firstborn, "Just hold on there, darling. You'll be fine. You'll be fine." He got whiter, and whiter, and whiter.

I dug my phone out of my pocket, hit the emergency

button, and when 911 answered I told them there was an officer down and to get the hell over here right away. Who knew how long it took? It took forever. It took seconds. Later, people said they'd never seen a call answered so fast, but I'll tell you, I've never seen one answered so slowly.

"Goddamn it, Elias," I said to him as we waited. I was sure he could hear, sure he was faking it. "If you die, I'll kill you."

When the paramedics finally arrived and relieved me of sealing his throbbing artery, he was still breathing. I stood up and backed away. My brother was the chalky gray of death. I was red with his blood. It covered my face, my hair, my clothes. It was in my mouth and my eyes and I didn't care. He was my brother, and he would not die. I would not let him. Mother was still holding his hand as they raced the stretcher up the aisle, and I scrambled for the door closest to where the gunman had appeared.

Mercedes stood in front of the podium, telling people to exit calmly and not panic.

Interestingly, the Russians talked in their small group as though nothing unusual had happened, and it occurred to me that this sort of thing was probably par for the course at Russian meetings.

I pushed through the swinging door into the wide corridor that led to the kitchens. One of the company security men, the one who looked as big and as dumb as a grand champion steer, was holding the gun.

"Put that down," I said to him, but naturally, when he saw me marching toward him like the Red Death, like the Mummy, or Frankenstein's monster covered in blood, like the bad movie that had given him nightmares his whole life, he pointed it at me. I held up my badge. "U.S. Marshal," I said. "Put down the weapon, now."

And he dropped it. I mean, dropped it on the floor, where it discharged, blasting a chunk out of the wall and filling the tight space with plaster dust and the hall beyond with screams. I couldn't even believe my eyes. I pulled my weapon.

"Get your hands in the air, you stupid son of a bitch."

Suddenly the area swarmed with uniformed officers, sidearms drawn, the security guard trapped in the headlights of their barrels. His arms shot into the air in surrender, and his whaleskin-white John Candy belly shot through his shirt buttons and over his John Brown belt.

Jack Lewis's boots made a hard, sharp, no-nonsense noise on the linoleum. He patted his hands on the air the way a speaker does to stop a crowd's applause. He and I arrived in the guard's face at the same time.

"I didn't do it. I didn't do it," the guard sputtered. "I came back here to catch him. I picked up the gun as a reflex. I didn't mean to."

"Back here to catch who?" Jack snapped.

"I don't know. I didn't see him."

"Then how do you know it was a 'him'? Cuff him," Jack ordered a patrolman, then handed me his handkerchief. But I didn't want it. I had on honest-to-God war paint. This would be personal. A blood grudge of the deepest order.

I knelt down by the weapon. It wasn't a rocket launcher, or a bazooka, but it might as well have been. It was a .460 Weatherby Magnum, an elephant gun. There was only one elephant hunter in the audience as far as I knew, and he was one hell of a shot, the best in Africa according to his fans. Not someone who would miss, which made me wonder if it were possible that

Elias was actually the target? Or—oh, Jesus—was it me? I'd dropped on Mother just before the blast, and Elias had been unlucky enough to be right behind me. But did Kennedy McGee really have the passion to kill for the sake of the Siberian environment? Why? So he could go there and hunt rare, vanishing tigers?

"I think you'll find this is Kennedy McGee's gun," I said to Jack. "He was here earlier. I saw him in the lobby arguing with Wade Gilhooly. Put out an APB for the road to Jackson and the airport."

Jack spoke into his radio as I completed the description, but we all knew McGee was long gone. The airport was our only hope. I stared at the Weatherby. Tantalizing smudges were visible on the long blue barrel, so maybe we'd get some prints. But why would Kennedy bring a gun from Africa? That made no sense. He wouldn't, and he wouldn't miss. He wouldn't miss once, and he wouldn't miss twice.

Nearby, the door of a supply closet stood open. I looked inside. Nothing much but shelves of clean table linens. The gunman might have waited there. I poked around for a couple of seconds and was about to rejoin Jack when I spotted a crumpled-up ball of white paper shoved way back between neat stacks of tablecloths. A ripped-open white envelope. There was the Gilhooly GMC logo in the upper-left-hand corner, and the name MCGEE was neatly printed in blue ink.

Why didn't he just leave a trail of bread crumbs?

"Get on up to the hospital," Jack said. "I'll keep you posted."

I slid the envelope into my pocket.

My father, dean of the School of the Stiff Upper Lip, was in the lobby telling people he was quite sure that

Elias was fine, nothing more than a flesh wound, but nevertheless he looked pale and uncertain. I put my arm through his. "Come on," I said. "Let's go."

He was silent as I bumped the Jeep up onto the curb and drove across the sidewalk to get around the fleet of squad cars and rescue vehicles.

I handed him the phone. "Call my office," I said. "Tell Linda there's been an accident and to get to Christ and St. Luke's as soon as she can."

Happy for an assignment, he explained to her what was going on as I careened up the street at about ninety miles an hour and skidded to a stop by the emergency-room door.

"You'll get towed," my father said. "You'd better let me move the car."

"It's okay, Daddy," I said. "I'm authorized."

"Oh, that's right." His smile was grateful and child-like.

A nurse was waiting for us. "Come with me, Mr. Bennett," she said. "I'll take you upstairs."

"How is Elias?"

"He's in surgery," she answered, leading us briskly down a corridor and into a waiting elevator. On the third floor, we followed our escort into a sunny lounge, where my mother stood looking out the window. Richard stood next to her, his arm around her shoulders, comforting her with his own solid brand of authority. I have never been so glad to see anyone in my life. My parents fell into each other's arms, and I fell into Richard's with such relief that if I'd been a lady I would have swooned.

"What's the word?" I asked.

Mother shrugged her shoulders and raised her eyebrows and shook her head. She had pulled herself totally back together. Fixed her hair, put on her lipstick.

If her suit weren't covered with blood, you'd think she was on her way to a luncheon. "Nothing. They're working on him. But he'll be fine." She studied me. "I think it's going to be a while. You might want to clean up a little. You have time."

Richard nodded. "Come on, I'll get you set up."

I saw what they meant when I looked in the mirror. I was so thoroughly drenched with blood, I looked like I'd been in a fatal accident. But I hadn't—and, if I had anything to say about it, neither had Elias.

A surgeon friend once told me a story about the different effects a patient and the patient's family's attitude have in surgery. He's a urologist who specializes in long and complicated radical prostate operations, a procedure that typically takes four to five hours. I mean, I think it takes about an hour just to dig past all the bowels to find the prostate in the first place. Anyhow, he said he can tell the second he enters the operating room how everyone feels about the situation. "If the patient and his family have a positive attitude—even in the face of the most dire prognosis—if they are praying for his strength and healing, and sending him messages of hope and courage, I feel it, and there is no question that it makes a difference on the length and complication of the procedure, and definitely on the healing. On the other hand, if the family has said good-bye at the door and meant it, like 'Good-bye, you're dead,' that comes through, too. I feel the dread, and sometimes there can be a lethargy that makes it a struggle for control. It seems endless. Blood loss is always greater, the risk increases. We all walk out totally exhausted, and the recovery is usually rife with complications.

"One time," he told me, "I was operating on the

Dalai Lama's number-two guy. He was wonderful, this man, and, as you can imagine, there was some serious praying going on all over the world during the surgery. The praying was so powerful, so positive, it was as though it had taken control of my hands. I finished in an hour and a half. It was one of the most incredible days of my life. If anyone ever tells you that prayer has no effect on medicine, they're wrong. And if you get the two of them working together—if the person has a ghost of a chance—you've got the hardest part behind you. You're just down to technique and healing."

I've never forgotten that story. As I stood in the hospital shower and let the warm water wash Elias's blood out of my hair and off my face and from beneath my fingernails, I thought about him every second. I sent my mind through the walls like a laser beam, into the operating room, into the surgeon's hands, and into Elias's heart and soul. "Don't be afraid," I said to him. "You're going to be fine. Keep your eye on the ball."

I also thought about the fact that it was all my fault. If I hadn't been so greedy, so enticed by Wade's double fee, so anxious to solve a juicy crime during my wedding week just so I could prove to everybody that I could still have and do it all, Elias wouldn't be lying on that table and I wouldn't be watching his blood go down the drain.

I pulled on a pair of borrowed green surgical scrubs, and applied fresh makeup with particular care. It is at times like these—times of danger and fear—which I know will require every ounce of my strength, all my intestinal fortitude, that I get and keep myself as squared away as possible. Today, more than any other in my life, called on me to suck it up. Totally. I looked in the mirror and decided I would have made a good-looking doctor. I also wished I'd become something that involved wearing such comfortable clothes.

Richard was waiting for me. A worried grin crinkled his weatherbeaten face, grooving it deeply. His eyes were unreadable.

"What?" I said, frightened.

"Nothing bad. But an amazing sight nevertheless. Johnny Bourbon and Shanna showed up, and for the last ten minutes they've practically had a revival meeting going on. Come on."

We could hear the noise all the way down the hall.

TWENTY-FIVE

I t was a hootenanny of serious proportions. The Holy
Spirit in the form of some thigh-slapping, get-down,
old-time religion had taken hold of Wade, his personal
secretary Tiffany, Duke Fletcher, Linda, and my parents.

Shanna had her baby-blue guitar strapped around
her neck and one of her white boots up on a coffee
table and was going to town with one of her own compositions—"Jesus, Take Hold of This Situation and
Heal Our Hearts"—making the fringe on her skirt and
jacket swing so wildly she looked like a car wash. Everyone was clapping and singing. I prayed Elias could
hear us through the vacuum-sealed doors to the operating suites and Jesus could hear us in heaven.

Richard and I stood outside in the hallway and
clapped and sang along until the only other thing that
could go wrong that day did.

"Oh, no," I suddenly said.

"What?"

"It's your parents."

Sure enough, my future in-laws, both lean as sticks, were striding down the corridor. *American Gothic* in London Fog. Mrs. Jerome with a large Queen Elizabeth handbag over her arm and a furled umbrella in her fist, glided toward us. They were tall ships at sail in their no-nonsense New England raincoats and -hats. As best I recalled, the day was sunny and warm, but it might as well have been raining because, for me, it just kept getting worse and worse. First my brother gets shot, then Richard's parents show up and I'm dressed in pearls, brown-suede high heels, and bright-green cotton pajamas. I swear to God, I know Richard's mother was wondering if he could get his great-grandmother's giant diamond ring back without a fuss.

"Don't worry," Richard said. "They'll be fine."

Sure they will, I thought.

The appearance of the Jeromes brought the rally to a rough, tumbling conclusion when my mother said—completely unselfconsciously I might say in her defense—"Oh, look, Dick and Alida Jerome are here."

Richard and I watched as Mother graciously introduced his parents around as if they'd dropped in to her house for tea. The fact was, they looked as if they'd dropped in from another planet, Planet Veto, actually. But they greeted everyone nicely, even Tiffany, who growled at Richard's father like a wolverine looking at lunch. Well, I thought, this is what we are, and in spite of the great time we all had last night, they are seeing we are nothing like them. This marriage is headed straight down the toilet. Except that Richard smiled and never took his arm from around my shoulders.

I followed the Jeromes with my eyes and as they stopped at each person—Wade, Tiffany, Johnny, Shanna, Duke—I tried to remember where that person had been during the shooting. I had no idea. I couldn't remember a single individual's position. I wondered where Mercedes had been and if the police had apprehended Kennedy McGee.

An orderly rolled in a covered table that looked like a body on a gurney.

"Where do you want this, Mrs. Bennett?" he asked.

"Oh, just over there by the wall is fine, thank you."

He removed the cover, and when I saw the luncheon spread—a mound of turkey, ham, and chicken-salad sandwiches, large baskets of Fritos and potato chips, a stacked-up pile of fudge, and squares of white cake with pink icing that looked as if they might have been left over from a reception on the pediatrics floor because they had little yellow icing ducks marching around the edge—I was suddenly so hungry I thought I would faint. Mother was chairman of the board of Christ & St. Luke's and, thankfully, had flexed her muscles.

"They get so bored down there in the kitchen boiling all those briskets all the time," she explained. "This gave them a little something fun to do."

I'll bet they loved it. I studied Mother carefully as she began offering sandwiches and coffee. She was so charming, so gracious, and I could see that she was scared to death. She was just brave as hell.

Halfway through our meal, a grim-faced doctor walked in and everything stopped. All the air simply evaporated. He paused in the doorway and looked from face to face, searching for a responsible party and finally settled on Wade.

"Can I see you a minute, please, Mr. Gilhooly?" he said.

"What?" Wade said quickly. He slapped his plate

down on the table so hard it sounded like a gunshot. "Is it Alma?"

"Let's talk out here in the hall."

"No, tell me."

"We did everything we could."

Oh, thank God. Thank God. Elias was still with us.

TWENTY-SIX

Wade, Johnny, and Shanna stampeded after the doctor, practically elbowing each other to be the first out the door and down to the ICU, as though they expected to find a copy of Alma's will taped to her chest.

The rest of us stayed behind. Linda—who'd stationed herself outside the surgical-area door—started her tenth full rosary.

Ever since he'd arrived, Duke had had his eye on Mr. Jerome, waiting for the right time to hit him up for a donation to his presidential campaign. But now, with most of the crowd gone and everything in position for him to make his move, Tiffany had attached herself to Duke, and while he was a tall man, maybe six-four, Tiffany, in her high heels, met him eye to eye, emoting into his face in an explicit sort of way. He gaped back as though she were a she-devil trying to trap him and wreck his whole life and career. I knew how he felt— the Jeromes had been exchanging similarly knowing glances about me for quite a while.

"I can't wait till you're President, Senator Duke. Do you really think you're going to win?"

"Don't think I don't know what you've got in mind, madam," he said to Tiffany, whose award-winning muscles strained against her skintight, miniskirted business suit with all the power of a tropical sunrise. She had hidden her blond locks beneath a short, spiky black wig, and that, combined with her exaggerated black eye makeup and dark red lips, made her look like a rock star.

"What's that, sir?" she asked.

"You're wanting to sit on my lap and get your picture taken with me like that Madonna Rice girl with Gary Hart on the monkey boat down there in Florida. Well, sugar, it ain't gonna work."

"See what I mean, everybody?" Tiffany smiled around the room. "He will be a great President. This man is power. This man is America." She tossed her arm around his shoulders and squeezed all the wind right out of him.

Richard's mother gasped. But I truly had the feeling it might have been to smother a laugh.

"I was very surprised to see your name on the SIBA list," I said to Duke once I'd finished my second piece of cake, which was semigood except that the little yellow icing ducks made it way too sweet. Unfortunately, anxiety makes me hungry. I have never in my life been too upset to eat, and the longer Elias was in surgery, the hungrier I got.

"What are you talking about?"

"We obtained a printout of all the SIBA Fund investors, and your name was included."

"Now, hold on there, Lilly girl. Is this a joke?" He glanced nervously at Mr. Jerome—who could open the door to millions and millions and who was now listening with grim intensity—and gave him a knowing smile.

I shook my head. "No. Your name is there."

"Well, that's some kind of damn mistake. The SIBA Fund stands for everything I detest, and I would not put one penny of my money toward their efforts. Even their name, Siberian Associates, is misleading, because they don't give a damn about Siberia or Siberians or the delicate Siberian environment. If my name appears, it means the little commie rats are desperate and are trying to sabotage my reputation. Little underhanded, red-ass peckerheads. They couldn't do an honest day's business if their lives depended on it."

I believed him, but I'm not so sure about Richard's father, who ripped into a celery stick like a lion devouring a bloody leg.

Pretty soon everyone was gone except for our families and Linda. We all sat quietly and read. Nobody spoke. I didn't care who'd shot Alma or Elias, I only wanted him well. As far as I was concerned, I was off the case.

Moments later, Jack paged me. I called him back. "How's Elias?" he asked.

"No word yet."

"We picked up Kennedy McGee at the airport getting on a plane for L.A., and I've got him down here in custody. He's trying to track down Paul Decker, who should be here anytime. We'll start the questioning in about an hour if you'd like to join us."

"Nah. I don't think you need my help. I'm just going to hang around here, but thanks for the offer."

After a while, Wade drifted back in. He didn't seem to know what to do with himself. He kept hanging around, as though Alma's death were an unimportant sidebar to his day. Finally, when Elias went into his third hour of surgery, I told Wade to take off. This had become a family affair, and we needed some privacy.

"Come on." I led him to the bank of elevators. "I'll walk you to your car. You need to make some arrangements for Alma's funeral."

"Done," he said.

"Done?" I looked at my watch. "She's only been dead for an hour."

"I made the arrangements yesterday. We all knew she didn't have a chance."

Outside, it was wrongly bright and sunny and warm, and life chugged along around us. He opened the door of the Caddy and sat down, but Tiffany was not there waiting for him. Probably eloped with Dwight. "Friday. Cowboy Cathedral. Two o'clock."

"I can't remember if I told you," I said. "Everything's been happening so fast. But the police arrested Kennedy McGee at the airport."

He smiled. "That's great. I hope he gets the chair. Case closed." He placed his hand softly on top of mine. "Lilly, I sure hope Elias is okay. Will you call me when he gets out of surgery?"

"Of course. Oh, I almost forgot about this. What do you make of it?" I removed the crinkled, torn envelope from my pocket and smoothed it out across the chrome and red leather of his steering wheel. "Is this your handwriting?" I pointed to the word McGEE, scrawled in blue ball-point ink.

"Yes, where did you get that?" A flush crept up Wade's neck, turning the wedge-shaped burn scar into a snow-white spade.

"I found it in a supply closet off the ballroom. I think the gunman waited in the closet. What was in the envelope?"

"That fucking McGee. He said he'd give me his proxy to vote against the Russian deal and leave town if I gave him a hundred thousand dollars in cash. So I did. And once I handed him the envelope, he told me the Russians had given him ten times that much and to go fuck myself. I'd like to kill that son of a bitch."

"Why would he try to kill me or Elias?"

Wade considered the question. "I don't know. Maybe he was trying to disrupt the meeting and wasn't exactly aiming at anybody. The votes were going in the company's favor and he knew the Russians would rip his balls off if they'd given him a million in hard dollars and he didn't deliver. Even Kennedy isn't naive enough to think the Russian character has changed along with their politics. Their approach has always been fists first. Questions if you survive." He hit the steering wheel with the palm of his hand. "I feel ridiculous giving him all that money. You know what's wrong with me? I've been living in Montana too long, gotten to trust people too much. I've turned into a country boy leaving a trail of dollar bills behind me. People see me coming a hundred miles off. Oh, here comes that dopy Wade Gilhooly. He's such a sucker, you can trick him into anything."

With that he slapped his hands on top of his head and slumped down in his seat. He looked so small and vulnerable and taken-advantage-of that I wanted to comfort him. What was it about Wade that, in spite of his Dark Ages chauvinism, sexism, and general crudity, made women want to protect him? He was Peck's Bad Boy, naughty as could be with freckles on his nose, a frog in his pocket, the gift of blarney, and the physical grace and easy elegance of Fred Astaire.

"Well"—he started the engine—"thanks again for

everything. I'm really sorry about Elias. I hope he's okay. I'm sorry I got you into this mess."

"Me, too."

"I know you and Alma weren't exactly friends, but I hope you'll come to the funeral anyway."

"I'll be there."

It wasn't true, what I said earlier about not caring who shot Alma or Elias. I cared a lot, and the more time passed, the madder I was getting. Someone was going to pay for this mess and it sure as hell wasn't going to be one of us.

I didn't believe for one second that Kennedy McGee had perpetrated any of these actions. But at least if everyone else did, the killer might relax, and maybe we'd get a few mistakes happening on our side.

Hours later, I stood at Elias's bedside in the recovery room. Christian and I had each given him a pint of blood, and they'd taken the rest—seven pints in all— out of the blood bank. He was still unconscious and, according to the doctor, would be for some time. But he would survive.

"As a matter of fact," the doctor told us, "I expect him to bounce back fairly quickly. Won't be able to use his arm for quite a while, but that shouldn't slow him down much. He's strong as an ox."

Richard followed me into the hall, where I leaned against the wall. I felt drained. Maybe it was just the blood donation, or, more likely, maybe it was that, along with the wedding, Richard's parents, their total immersion into the eccentric irascibility of life in the Bennett family, and the adrenaline crash of safety.

"I'm going to take my parents back to the hotel," Richard told me as the stone-faced battleships tugged impatiently at their halyards, moored as they were to the elevator, foul-weather gear, purse, and umbrella on full alert. "I'll meet you back at the ranch. Will you be all right?"

What could I say? No?

"I think your mother hates me."

"Believe me, if my mother didn't like you, we'd know."

I peeked around the corner to where Mrs. Jerome's umbrella was pointed at my forehead like a sixteen-inch cannon on the *Missouri*. "If you say so."

"Listen to me, Lilly." Richard put his hands on the wall on either side of me and his face close to mine. His lips were so close they started to melt me. "Your mother isn't exactly a picnic. But now that I've gotten to know your parents, I love them. Keep this in mind when you look at my parents: While my father was away in the war, my mother had a flagrant affair with Dean Martin. Met him at the Stork Club every night. Big scandal. And my father still carries black-and-white snapshots in his wallet of Tahitian natives whose breasts come to their knees. Friends from his tour in the Pacific."

I peeked at them again. "Maybe they just have jet lag."

"Maybe they're just worried about your brother. Maybe their clenched jaws have absolutely nothing to do with you. Think about it."

Deep in the pocket of my scrubs, my phone buzzed.

"How's Elias?" Jack asked.

"He's going to be fine."

"Glad to hear it. When will you be down to talk to your friend?"

"He's not my friend, and I already told you, I don't think I'll be there."

"Well, we found a Russian-English dictionary in his luggage, so we've got a good start. Why don't you come down tomorrow at ten? Paul Decker's out of town, so that's the soonest he can get here anyhow."

"Thanks, I'll think about it. Don't wait for me, though."

I had other ideas. I wished I'd been able to talk with the Russians, but by the time I called the Grand they'd checked out, and when I called the AMR Combs hangar I learned the SIBA Fund's G-4 corporate jet had taken off just half an hour after the shooting. So our big drunken grizzlies had slipped through the net and vanished into the big blue. By now they would be at forty-five thousand feet over Canada, making bear tracks for Moscow and completely out of our reach.

TWENTY-SEVEN

THURSDAY MORNING · SEPTEMBER 10

The morning line on Elias was extremely optimistic—they'd keep him one more day—and after checking in on him, I went downtown.

"Well, look who's here," Kennedy McGee snorted over his shoulder when I entered the interrogation room. "Nancy Drew."

"Nice to see you, too, Mr. McGee." I put my purse and a double espresso from Starbucks on the conference table.

Cigarette burns and ridges from handcuffs slammed on its surface by infuriated, wrongly incarcerated prisoners scarred and cracked the gray Formica. Along the center of the table, sealed in plastic bags, lay the Colt .45 that had been used to murder Alma, the Weatherby rifle that had shot Elias, and a small bright-yellow plastic Langenscheidt Russian-English, English-Russian pocket dictionary. Another zip-top held what looked like the prisoner's personal effects.

Opposite me sat Paul Decker, and he didn't look too happy to be there. Maybe he didn't know about Mc-

Gee's fifty-thousand shares in Rutherford Oil and thought that the Great White Hunter's fiduciary prospects were slim, unable to provide even a fraction of Paul's customary retainer. If it hadn't taken place already, I imagined that a serious conversation with his client about exactly where McGee intended to get the money to pay him was close on the horizon.

It would have been nice to believe that Paul's bad humor had to do with the fact that his client was accused of shooting Elias, one of Paul's best friends, and maybe he would have trouble defending him. But my years of experience with defense lawyers had taught me that even if the client had shot the attorney's mother, if the client could pay, the attorney would defend.

"Morning, Counselor," I said.

"Marshal," he answered.

McGee, decked out in jailhouse orange, was slouched in his seat, glowering up at the slice of sky visible through the high, wire-mesh windows. He had chewed his fingernails completely off. He was scared, and I didn't blame him.

The evidence seemed strong. And now that I'd had a night to sleep on it, and now that Elias was going to be all right, it was possible to assemble the pieces in my head more calmly and rationally. Pieces that could be fitted for the shooter to be Kennedy: He'd been at both scenes. At least one of the weapons was his. He had clear motive to shoot Alma, though little or none to shoot Elias or me. But maybe Wade's theory about the Russians' payoff had been correct and he had to find a way to stop the meeting before the vote was complete. The dictionary that could have been used to compose the ersatz Russian threat was in his possession.

I couldn't say one way or the other. A lot depended on the upcoming interrogation.

Directly across from Kennedy, a guard stood at parade rest, hands clasped behind his back, feet slightly spread, and watched him, a measure of reverence in his gaze. I wondered how many people observed us through the mirrored wall panel. The large round clock above it read a minute before ten.

Sixty seconds later, ten o'clock on the nose, the door clicked open and Jack appeared, dapper as ever in a knife-pressed brown cavalry twill suit, crisp white shirt, lizard boots, and a string tie with a silver bolo of longhorns. He placed his coffee carefully on the table and cleaned his glasses with a white handkerchief from his back pocket before pulling his chair over tight to McGee and sitting down. I wouldn't have been surprised if he'd dusted off the seat first.

Lieutenant Evan fussed and hovered next to him as though he were balancing on a pogo stick, ready to boing into action at the slightest rise in his boss's eyebrow. I wandered over and half-sat on the edge of the table, in tight on the other side of McGee. He was totally impinged upon. And he couldn't do anything about it. All our faces were in his, and they were implacable.

"Mr. McGee," Jack began, "this conversation is being recorded and videotaped, and I want to reiterate that anything you say can and will be used against you in a court of law. Understood?"

"Yes, sir," Kennedy answered.

"Let the record show, it is ten-oh-five A.M., Thursday, September tenth. Present are the prisoner, Kennedy McGee; the prisoner's attorney, Paul Decker; U.S. Marshal Lilly Bennett; Detective Inspector Lieutenant Geoff Evan; myself, Jack Lewis, Chief of Detectives Roundup P.D., and a sergeant-at-arms. We are questioning the prisoner about the murder of Alma Gilhooly and the attempted murder of Elias Bennett.

"Mr. McGee, why don't you begin by describing your relationship with the victim, Alma Rutherford Gilhooly."

"I've already done this a hundred times." Kennedy looked at Paul to get him off the hook, but no help was forthcoming. Paul was just like a damn cash register. He'd been happy to help with the elephant tusks, but a lengthy murder investigation and trial were more than he'd bargained for. Ethically, he couldn't back out. He was trapped, and he knew it. It was almost physically painful to watch him. I wanted to laugh.

"And I'm afraid you'll probably have to do it another hundred times before we're through," Jack told him.

Kennedy drew in a deep, peevish breath and relayed the facts of his and Alma's relationship—the African safaris, the love affair, the resort hotel she promised to underwrite, and her backing out at the last minute.

"So you decided to come to America and have it out with her?"

"Not at all. I'm here to talk to clients, do a little hunting, attend the Rutherford Oil annual meeting. Alma and I remained friendly. It wouldn't accomplish anything to 'have it out with her,' as you put it."

Jack led him through the same interrogation I'd had with him three days earlier. Nothing new.

"Tell me about the threatening letters." Jack said.

"What threatening letters?"

"The ones in Russian warning Rutherford stockholders."

"I don't know what you're talking about."

Jack dragged the dictionary across the table to him. "You've never seen this before?"

"Not until you pulled it out of my luggage."

"Where did you leave your luggage that the dictionary could have been put in it?" I asked.

"I left it in the hotel lobby while I went up to meet with Wade."

"What did you and Wade fight about?"

"When?"

"In the ballroom lobby before the meeting."

"I don't know what you're talking about. I didn't have a fight with Wade."

"I saw it with my own eyes, Mr. McGee," I said. "Mr. Gilhooly says he gave you one hundred thousand dollars."

Jack and Paul and Evan all looked at me.

"What hundred thousand dollars?" Jack asked.

Paul didn't say anything, but he relaxed considerably, cleared his throat importantly, and leaned forward a little, engaging himself somewhat in the process.

Kennedy would have killed me if he could have. "Wade gave me some cash in exchange for my vote against the Russian venture," he said grudgingly.

I eyeballed Kennedy. He knew there was more and he knew I knew it, and he realized if he didn't speak, I would ask.

"And the Russians gave me some cash to vote in favor," he concluded.

"How much?" Paul asked, but McGee didn't answer.

"So what did you do?" I asked.

"I left. Went to the airport."

"Before the vote?"

"Certainly," Kennedy said. "I could care less if Rutherford Oil drills in Siberia or not. My stock goes up either way."

This guy was as low as Pleistocene goo.

"What stock?" said Paul.

"Did the Russians threaten to kill you if the vote failed? Is that why you shot my brother?"

"I didn't shoot your brother," Kennedy snarled. "I wasn't even there. Ask the cabdriver."

"Cabdriver corroborates his story," Paul jumped in.

"That doesn't mean anything," Jack and I said at the same time.

"You didn't bag his hands," Paul said. "There was no gunshot residue."

"That doesn't mean anything, either," Jack fired back. "We didn't catch him for two hours. Anyone with a brain would have washed his hands by then."

I think Jack washes his hands at least twice an hour and wants to believe everyone else does, too.

"How did you get the rifle into the hotel, Mr. McGee?" Jack questioned.

Kennedy groaned. "I did not 'get' my rifle into the hotel. It had been stolen at some point out of my car. But the fact is, Chief Lewis, just for your information, I am a hunter. Hunters travel with their weapons—sporting rifles, shotguns. The guns have special cases. It's simple to walk into any hotel with them. Not a bit unusual. The hotel people know you're not carrying a semiautomatic rifle. Especially in Wyoming, hunters come up here all the time. Hell, it's elk season right now. The hotel's full of hunters."

Well, he was right about that.

"This happens to be your rifle, Mr. McGee," Jack said. "And it's an elephant rifle. We don't have elephant season in Wyoming."

"It's part of my sales pitch. Prospective safari clients like to see things like that. And, as I've already said:

Someone stole my Weatherby. I have the empty case to prove it."

As Jack questioned him more about the shootings, I slid the plastic bag with Kennedy's personal effects closer to me and shoved the contents around inside it. British passport. Thin leather wallet with no big wad of cash visible. Comb. ChapStick. Airline tickets. Address book and calendar. And an empty white number-ten envelope with McGee's name written on the front.

I opened the baggie and removed the envelope. "What is this?"

"What does it look like?"

"Please just answer the question, Mr. McGee," I said.

"That's the envelope the money was in."

"Which money?"

"Wade's."

"Are you sure?"

"Sure I'm sure."

"How do you know it's not the Russians' envelope?"

"Maybe it is. What difference does it make?"

"Maybe none. But try to remember which one it is."

"I think you're being a little hard on my client here," Paul chimed in, now that he could smell his fee getting close to his bank account.

"It could be the Russians'. It could be Gilhooly's. I don't know. What I do know"—Kennedy's eyes raked the table—"is that I did not kill Alma Gilhooly. She was not worth it. And I did not write any letters in Russian. And I did not take a shot at you or your brother, although I must say I'm glad someone did. But I wish it had been you. And I wish they'd not missed."

I gathered up my gear. "When's the arraignment?" I asked.

"This afternoon."

"Good luck, Mr. McGee," I said. "You're in for a long day."

I went into the observation room, where three detectives leaned against the rail in front of the mirror.

"What do you think?" I asked.

"Evidence doesn't lie."

TWENTY-EIGHT

C an't you get this thing to go any faster?" I yelled into the cockpit at the pilot over the roar of the S-76's powerful turbines.

"One hundred and seventy-five miles an hour is our top speed, Miss Bennett. We'll touch down in about fifteen minutes."

We'd stopped at the ranch long enough for me to pick up a couple of changes of clothes and then took off again immediately. We'd been airborne for twenty minutes, and I was ready to move.

I've never bitten my fingernails in my life, but now I was tempted. A lot rode on this particular boondoggle. Not only was I going to be late for the Kendalls' party for Richard and me at the country club tonight, I was still pretty sure his parents hated my guts and this would finish the whole deal, not to mention the fact that if I stood up Richard, none of my family would ever speak to me again. But also, even though it was certainly possible—even obvious, if you chose to believe the evidence—that Kennedy McGee had killed

Alma and taken a shot at me that very nearly killed my brother, it was simply not plausible. Whoever took that shot did so because the information Elias had discovered was something very important, information worth killing for that the killer did not want him to say, nor me to hear. I intended to find out what it was before Wade or Johnny or Shanna or Duke or Mercedes figured out that the case was not closed and started hunting again.

Besides, I couldn't ask Elias. He'd have tubes down his throat until tomorrow morning and wasn't talking. And one arm was incapacitated and the other was full of IV needles, so he wasn't writing. And they had him all loaded up on heavy prescription drugs, which he loved, so he wasn't thinking, either. Basically, he was useless.

The airframe shuddered slightly as we changed airspeed and floated to the ground, a heavy, harried feather, in front of the general-aviation hangar at Billings's little Logan Airport. By the time I'd popped the airstairs, the rental car, a white Ford Taurus, was parked next to the chopper and ready to go.

I hadn't been to Billings for years, but I was pretty sure it hadn't changed much. I mean, parts of Montana have become incredibly chic and precious, especially around Livingston and Bozeman and a little up toward Missoula, but the sad truth is that Billings will always be the state's haunch, its hind end, a mail-order bride deceptively pretty in a blurred photograph taken in the gently screened light of summer, (which in Billings, like Siberia, is comprised of three weeks in July and the first week of August). But, in reality, it's a living, freezing hell on earth—dusty, windblown, and cold as a brass toilet seat—for the other eleven months of the year. I think they probably have more alcoholics in Billings, per capita, than in any other town in the country.

I gunned the Ford's engine and peeled out of the airport onto Rimrock Road, which led steeply down the face of the butte and then turned right and wound along the edge of the Yellowstone Country Club golf course, until I found the Gilhoolys' street: Strawberry Tree Drive. The cul-de-sac contained five good-sized, split-level, ranch-style houses, all of which looked as though they'd been built in the sixties. According to the Remax Realty sign, the Gilhooly house, number eighteen—"Pool. Gourmet Kitchen. Lots of Extras"—was still on the market. The driveway was empty, the lawn starting to turn brown with the approach of winter. Large picture windows reflected the north country's gray, unfriendly sky.

I parked at Duke Fletcher's house, next door to the Gilhoolys' and rang the bell. I knew the senator wasn't there, but Elias had mentioned drinking tea with a housekeeper. An older woman, who looked a little like a tiny white bird, opened the door. Bright blue eyes peeked out through heavy wrinkles and rimless glasses.

"If you're with the newspapers,"—her voice was not especially inviting—"Senator Fletcher is not here."

I showed her my badge. "No, ma'am," I said. "I'd just like to ask you a few questions about the Gilhoolys."

"Like what?"

"I don't know if you've heard or not, but Mrs. Gilhooly was shot a few days ago. She died yesterday afternoon. I'm working on the murder investigation, and I was wondering if you could tell me a little about what she was like."

"Someone was here night before last. I already answered all the questions about them I'm gonna."

"Yes, that was my deputy, and now *he's* been shot, so maybe you could tell me what you told him."

"Well, I'm sorry to hear that. He was a polite young man." Her implication being that I was an impolite old woman, but she relented. "I suppose you'd better come in. We do believe in cooperating with the authorities in this house, unlike some of the other nuts who live around here." She scowled up and down the street.

"Thank you, ma'am, I appreciate it." I thought adding a "Gee" might be gilding the lily. But I did make a big show of wiping my boots on the mat before I stepped inside.

Half an hour later, I rang another neighbor's doorbell.

"She was some kinda piece of work," the man said once he'd gotten his Rottweiler, whose name sounded something like Gut, calmed down. He was neatly dressed in golf clothes and looked like every man I've ever known from Billings: bald, with a big beer belly. Maybe I've just had a bad run of eastern-Montana men, but they remind me of people in Maine, where the winters are so long, all they do is eat a bunch of potatoes and drink.

"She had one hell of a feud with the Fletchers. Well, first they had a love affair, not literally as far as I know, but the Senator, God bless him." The man squelched a belch. "Say, do you want to come in and have a beer?"

"I'd like to come in, but no beer. Thanks."

The house reeked of baked ham and buttered microwave popcorn. The dog lay down on the kitchen floor and watched me as if I were the change in menu he'd been being promised for a long time.

"Jerry Pierce." He extended his hand. "Sorry about

the mess, but my wife's visiting her parents up in Ekalaka for a few days."

Ekalaka's near Baker, which is basically nowhere.

"Yes, old Duke, he's a dear, but he's so money-crazy he loses his place sometimes. He and Martha Belle moved in here about five or six years ago. Kept the ranch in Cut Bank, but by then Martha Belle was pretty sick and I guess he felt they needed a place in town closer to the hospital. When Duke saw that he was living next door to a Rutherford, you could see those wheels turning. See him thinking, I'm gonna get some of that. And, the fact is, Alma helped him out a lot, started pouring money into his campaigns and PACs and all, until one time she asked him to vote against some new strip-mining law or other—can't remember which one it was, we've got so goddamn many of them now—and he said no. Well, you know, Alma's so far to the right she makes right-wingers look like communists. She went completely haywire."

If there are contests for belches, which I am quite sure there are, this one was an Olympic gold-medal contender. The windows rattled and the dog howled. Jerry patted his belly appreciatively.

"What exactly do you mean by haywire?" I asked once he'd stopped.

"Well, for instance, she's got that big gun collection, and if the Fletchers' maid didn't get the trash barrels moved back in their garage the second the trash truck left, Alma would go out in her driveway and start using the barrels for target practice. She was a mean old bitch. We're still convinced she poisoned our last dog. Probably has it stuffed and on display with all the rest of the things she's killed."

I think the dog died of beer fumes. "Did she and Duke Fletcher ever make up?"

"Well, I'm pretty sure she never gave him any more money, but when Martha Belle died and then he left the Senate, he joined the board of Rutherford Oil, so they must have come to some sort of understanding."

"What about her and Wade?"

"I miss old Wade. He's a hell of a nice guy. One of my best buds." He lobbed the beer can into a tall plastic barrel that had a big recycling emblem on its side. "You recycle?"

"Excuse me?"

"Do you recycle? You know. Newspapers. Cans. Milk bottles. So forth."

"Well, yes we do."

"Waste of time, except aluminum. Unless you reuse, of course." He popped open another Coors Light and proceeded to lecture me on the perils and costs of recycling.

"Did they fight?" I finally asked.

"Who? Alma and Wade? No more than most completely incompatible, unhappily married couples who hate each other's guts. He always gave Alma a real wide berth. And a lot of the time, she'd be off traveling in Africa, had something going with some big-game hunter, and then she got real tight with Johnny Bourbon, the televangelist, you know him? He was hanging around a lot to keep her company. I'd hate to imagine how much money she gave those two. Wade and I played golf three, four times a week and, you know, he just never talked about her at all."

"How is Wade's business? Pretty strong?"

"Money machine. He slipped a little last year, got caught along with a lot of us in underestimating this whole Internet deal. Ford dealership started selling cars by computer. Can you imagine? You can just walk into your kitchen or wherever you've got your computer and call up the dealer's home page and just buy a damn truck. You could be sitting on the toilet and buy a damn truck. Oh, excuse me, ma'am. I didn't mean anything by that."

"It's okay."

I asked him a few more questions, but the answers were all inconclusive. No rumors. No gossip. This guy was loyal.

On my way back to the airport, I stopped in at the Northern Hotel, Billings's only enduring landmark and, according to Wade's neighbors, his bar of choice. I'd visited the place a number of times in the far past, and it had never changed—same whorehouse decor with run-through red carpet on the floor, grease-stained red-and-gold cut-velvet wallpaper, and a medium-large, hammered-bronze, Rank Organization–style gong to announce the arrival of flaming dishes, which included most things on the menu, and which meant that the lights in the dining room were constantly flashing on and off while the gong gonged and the waiter circled the room with flaming swords of shish kebab or chafing dishes of blazing lobster Newburg. The bar still had the same dead plants in its window and the same long bar rail lined with the same combination of local drunks, cowboys come to town to do their banking, and a few out-of-towners.

I ordered a Jameson's neat, which won me an admiring once-over from the boys at the rail and the bartender, whose moustache was so long it looked as if he'd hung Spanish moss on his face.

"Do any of you fellas know Wade Gilhooly?" I asked, and then tossed off the shot.

"Sure," one answered. "Everyone knows Wade Gilhooly. Who may I ask is asking?"

"I'm Lilly Bennett. I'm doing some work for Mr. Gilhooly, investigating his wife's murder."

"You're a private investigator?" another asked.

"Yup, sure am." I gave them a second or so to let that sink in. "Do any of you know if Mr. Gilhooly ever got into any fights?"

I decided to take the direct approach, because Westerners are not easily duped by pretty faces the way Southern gentlemen are, and I knew right off that these guys would tell me nothing and that sooner or later in this conversation I was going to have to pull rank and use threats to get what I was after. Besides, I was running out of time.

"Never."

"How'd he get all those bruises on his face?"

"You'd have to ask him."

"I hear his wife gave them to him, but I'd hate to think someone as well liked and charming and successful as Wade Gilhooly used to get rumbled on by his wife—it's just unseemly, a man like that. I'd rather think he got into scuffles over the Broncos or the Minnesota Vikings. You sure he never got into fights in here?"

They all looked at each other and by mutual consent shook their heads at the same time, especially the one with the healing split lip.

"Okay, look, fellas," I said. "Let's cut the crap. You can tell me here now, or you can tell me in court. This is a murder investigation. You don't want to be accused of obstructing justice, especially where your friend's involved. Let me ask you one more time: Is Wade Gilhooly a brawler?"

•   •   •

My last stop was the Billings National Bank, where I scanned the Gilhoolys' banking records for the last five years. Alma had moved so much money through there it was unimaginable. Millions and millions of dollars. It looked as if she used her checking account for everything. Huge deposits. Huge withdrawals, most of the most recent ones to the order of the SIBA Fund. Wade's accounts, while sizable, were modest compared to Alma's. I noticed what the neighbor was talking about in the Gilhooly GMC account. The business generated a huge amount of cash flow, but overall, deposits had been down significantly over the last two years.

Did it make a difference? I didn't know, but I was pretty sure I had what I needed. At least I thought I did until my phone rang on the way back to the airport.

"Kennedy McGee's escaped."

I've never heard Jack Lewis sound so low in my life.

TWENTY-NINE

The setting sun burned through the windows as the helicopter raced south to Roundup and the Kendalls' party, the first major event on the calendar of our wedding festivities. Tom and Sparky Kendall were our best friends, and I knew she had really pulled out all the stops for tonight's black-tie dinner-dance bash.

"I just want to be sure all your out-of-town guests will be comfortable," Sparky had said earlier. "Most of them think they're going to have to survive on beef jerky and hardtack all weekend. But, by the time I'm done with them, they won't think they've even left Palm Beach, until they get to the main event, of course."

The Main Event. Thirty-six hours to go. I couldn't wait. Once we lifted off, I hatched a double espresso—no way I could afford to slow down now. Do you know they have Starbucks in Billings? I can't even believe it.

I rang up Richard on his car phone. "Hey," I yelled over the engine noise. "What's up?"

"On our way to the club." His voice was tight.

" 'Our' as in your parents?" I pulled off my boots and jeans.

"Yup. Where are you?"

I looked out the window. "Starting over the Bighorns. Is everything all right? Everybody happy?"

"Very, very happy." His voice had that tone that implied he'd gotten a few things straightened out and everybody had decided to have a very fine time indeed.

I put on my stockings and black-suede heels. "I can't wait to see you. I love you so much."

"I love you, too. Hurry up. Everything's fine."

I slipped into my new navy-satin gown and had just finished hanging Grandmother's diamonds around my neck and clipping on the matching earrings when we touched down on the putting green at the Roundup Country Club. Richard waited at the bottom of the steps to greet me in his double-breasted tuxedo, looking as if he'd just walked off a runway in Milan.

"Well?" he said after he'd kissed me and handed me a drink. "You don't look like you've been in Montana. You look beautiful. Tell me what you found out."

"I'm a lot closer. I think I've got a couple of people I can eliminate at least. Have you been here very long?"

"Only about five minutes. We stopped by to see Elias on the way over. He's in and out, but Linda's there holding his hand. We'll go by and see him on our way home."

I didn't have the nerve to ask him about his parents, and frankly, even though I was excited about the party and all the rest of the festivities, I was also a little jittery and preoccupied and stressed out about Alma and Wade and Elias, and I didn't much care about his parents at the moment. If they were upset, they'd just have to deal with it.

I tucked my arm through Richard's and we joined

the party. Sparky had indeed outdone herself, filling the club with mounds of flowers—over the mantel was a cascade of white orchids so enormous it must have defoliated an entire tropical island, and the centerpieces on the dinner tables were small gardens of gerbera daisies surrounded by picket fences. Peter Duchin was playing the piano at top speed and talking at the top of his voice to some old friend or other from the Gulf Stream Club.

We said hello to our friends and finally made it through the crowd to Richard's parents, who, while not exactly effusive, were certainly warmer than the last time I'd seen them. Once the perfunctory greetings were out of the way, Richard deserted me almost immediately for a conversation about grazing fees and water rights with his father, my father, and the governor. I was stranded with his mother.

"I'm so glad your brother is so much better," Mrs. Jerome said. She had a very long, thin face, the longest neck I've ever seen in my life, and very high eyebrows, and when she pulled them all up at the same time, I felt as if I was about to have my eyes pecked out by a jeweled whooping crane. I tried to picture her in bed with Dean Martin. It would have made me want to shriek with laughter if her eyes hadn't been cauterizing my face like Flash Gordon's death rays. "We haven't really gotten to know him well, or you either, for that matter. You're always rushing off somewhere. I was concerned you might not make it this evening. You have such an exciting career."

"Mrs. Jerome," I said. This was ridiculous. I was nervous, my hands were sopped and shaking, my mouth was dry. "I want you to know something. I absolutely adore your son, and I'm going to take such good care of him that he'll think he lives in heaven. Believe me, it's not always like this."

"I know, dear." Her tone was unsure. "Richard has never been so happy nor looked so well in his life. It's just all so different from what we're accustomed to, but Dick and I are thrilled for both of you."

"Well, you sure don't act like it," I snapped. I'm sorry, but I was really tired and didn't have time to break her down one teaspoonful of sugar at a time. This conversation was long past due. I had to establish my relationship with this woman now or I'd be forever doomed, and I wasn't going to be browbeaten and intimidated. Life was too short. This was it. "All you do is frown at me. I'm actually a very nice person who happens to be going through a sort of rough, complicated patch at the moment—which I admit is all my own fault; I know I shouldn't have taken this case, but I did—and I need friends right now, not foes. You're supposed to be here loving me, not marching around looking like you just ate a lemon."

Mrs. Jerome listened closely. People simply did not speak to her that way. This was a woman of power. But so was I. Her face betrayed nothing. I knew mine was red.

"I'm sorry," I said. I'd stepped off the end of the board, and there was no crawling back. "But that's the way it is. Right at the moment, you think you'd like a daughter-in-law you can mold and direct, someone who'll convince your son to move back to Manhattan and have lunch at Mortimer's and get involved in your charities. Well, he already tried that once, and it didn't work out too well. And I'm nothing like that. I'm way too old to be anything but what I am—a cop from a good family. But I'm telling you, I'm going to be such a terrific daughter-in-law you won't be able to get enough of me."

Everyone had drawn back, giving us plenty of room, and was ignoring us studiously. We were basically alone in this glittering crowd. Two wild sheep, dug in deep, about to smack our horns together.

"I know, deep down, Alida, if you were really the type who wanted some garden-club-joining, muffin-baking, bridge-playing, madras-skirted matronette as a daughter-in-law, you wouldn't have a son like Richard in the first place. He'd be in some country-club bar somewhere back East in Greenwich rolling dice for drinks instead of out West roping steers and running the opera."

Those eyebrows now quivered like batwings close to the chandelier, and I was afraid they were going to lift her right off the ground.

"I'd appreciate it if you'd give me a chance. Come on along for the ride. We'll have fun."

The standoff continued for what seemed forever. But there was one thing I knew from watching and listening to my mother and being her daughter: When it comes to relationships, decide what it is you want. If it's respect you're after, meet power with power. Backbone with backbone. Eye with eye. And courage with courage. If I were ever going to win Alida Jerome's respect, I had to meet her head on. And even if she wouldn't admit it, she knew it, too.

I'd said my piece. Now all I could do was wait. It turned out to be only for a moment. I could tell she was thinking about what I'd said and using all her fortitude not to follow her first instinct: gather up her skirts and demand of her husband that she be taken home imme-diately. We looked into each other's eyes. Her nostrils flared slightly. Frankly, if I'd been her, I would have smacked me in the face.

"You know, I like you much better than you think I do. I always look like I'm frowning because I'm too vain to wear my glasses." She put her hand on my cheek and studied my face. "But I've never known any-one quite like you before, never met quite such an inde-pendent spirit. Anyone quite so outspoken." Her hand was gentle and cool. "We don't exactly have people like you in New England."

"No kidding." I took a huge gulp of my drink.

"I'm beginning to see why Richard loves you so much."

"Ditto."

"And I'm absolutely mad for your mother."

We both drew in deep breaths, let the moment pass, and smiled at each other.

"Let's start over," she said.

I wanted to burst into tears.

"Well, dear," Alida continued, since tears would never do, "tell me, now that the killer has been caught, does that mean you'll be able to relax and enjoy the next few days? It is your wedding, after all."

"You mean Kennedy McGee?" My pulse began to approach normal. Talking about work helped a lot. "I'll tell you right now, he's not the killer. The police want to believe he is because all the evidence adds up, but there's a problem. He escaped this afternoon."

"Oh, goodness."

"Don't worry. He's not going to hurt anyone. He's probably on some rich widow's private jet right this minute sipping champagne and telling her whatever she wants to hear. Unfortunately, this case is far from over, and I'm afraid I'm going to have to ride this horse all the way back to the barn."

"Who do you think did it?" By now she was becoming legitimately interested.

I grinned and shook my head. "It's a big mess. First I think it's one person and then another."

My mother slipped her arm around my waist. I could tell it was her arm before I saw her, because she's the only person in the world I know who wears Miss Balmain perfume. I kissed her cheek. It was soft as velvet. A wide collar of emeralds circled her neck and lay flat against the peach shantung of her evening gown. "I think I may have what's known as a hot tip," she told me.

"Oh?"

"Go look in the Buckhorn Room." Mother winked as broadly as Charlie Chan's Number One Son. "There are some people having dinner in there that I think you will find very interesting."

The Buckhorn Room is the discreet little dining room where members never, ever discuss what they've seen because it's smoky and dark and you never can be totally sure if you've seen what you think you have, so you keep your mouth shut. You can practically get away with murder in there. The Buckhorn Room is a gleaming beacon of closemouthed clubdom.

"Isn't it against the rules to see *anything* in there?" I asked.

"I believe we need to disregard the rules from time to time. Don't you agree, Alida?"

"Completely."

"All right. Excuse me, I'll be right back."

"Don't you worry about your daughter?" I heard Mrs. Jerome ask as I left the ballroom.

"What good would it do?" my mother answered.

I crossed the lobby and headed down the carpeted hall, past glass-fronted cabinets packed with tarnished golf trophies and color portraits of club champions decked out in a variety of sportswear and holding a variety of athletic equipment: tennis rackets, drivers, putters, bows and quivers, ice skates and hockey sticks. At the end of the gallery, just before I turned to go into the Buckhorn Room, I glanced over my shoulder and caught my mother and Alida Jerome actually tiptoeing behind me. I put my finger to my lips, and they stopped and giggled. I knew Mrs. Jerome had never behaved like this in her life, with or without Dean Martin, and I had a feeling she also had never had so much fun.

The room was almost empty, and murky as ever, but as my eyes adjusted, I squinted into the darkness. Back in the far corner I made out a seriously inebriated, very happy Duke Fletcher having a very public grope of Tiffany West, who had on a blunt-cut red wig with long, straight Yvette Mimieux bangs. Oh, well. He was a widower, after all, and if he got elected, it would be the first Republican presidency on the order of—and with all the excitement and verve and hog-wild copulation diplomacy of—the Kennedy-Johnson-Clinton years. Now those guys could get down and party. Big time.

"Duke," I said with a big smile. "Just the man I was looking for."

He turned his head in my direction, but his eyes couldn't focus very well because Tiffany had sucked one of his fingers into her cherry-bomb lips like a piece of spaghetti. She opened her mouth, and his hand plopped onto the table.

"Hell," he said. "Don't you ever take a break?"

"I'm really sorry to interrupt, but I have just a couple more questions I needed to ask you. Tiffany, I think your lipstick is a little smeared. By the time you get back, I'll be done."

"You run along, sugar," he told his Amazon. "Big

Duke's got a little business to do, but I'll be here when you get back."

She actually blew him a kiss.

"I hear you were up talking to my housekeeper and the neighbors this afternoon."

"Is it true what she told me?"

"About what?"

"About that Alma used to beat up Wade."

"I don't know anything about that. I think it's probably nothing but gossip. Wade's always been a scrapper. Bar fights and so forth. I don't think he'd take it from a woman, even one as big as Alma."

"Your housekeeper said Wade used to come over to your house and she'd patch him up."

"Never when I've been around."

"She also told me Mercedes used to come up and stay with Wade when Alma was out of town, and the three of you often had dinner and sometimes talked all night."

"So what if we did?"

"Senator, did you and Wade and Mercedes conspire to murder Alma Rutherford Gilhooly?" It was an educated shot in the dark, and the reaction was disappointing.

Duke looked at me with complete incredulity. I might as well have punched him in the solar plexus, his breath was so gone. "What in the world are you talking about?" he finally said.

"I'm not sure," I admitted. "But I know I'm headed in the right direction. Sorry to interrupt."

The ladies were gone by the time I got back into the hall, but fortunately Richard was there. He had a big smile on his face.

"What have you done to my mother?"

"What?" I asked, thinking maybe she was missing. Or dead.

"She's acting like a complete fool."

"I don't know what you're talking about," I insisted, all innocence.

Well, at least I could take that problem off my list.

THIRTY

FRIDAY MORNING · SEPTEMBER 11

Sunlight crept silently through the open doors, across the bedroom floor, up the side of the bed, and into our eyes, waking us with a start. I sat up and leaned across Richard to see the clock and then fell back into my pillows.

"Can you believe we slept this late?" I said. "It's ten of six."

"We needed it. The last couple of days have been killers."

Sparky and Tom Kendall do not speak to each other in the morning until each has been at his or her office for at least an hour. They get up, walk the dogs, have breakfast, watch the "Today" show, read the papers, shower, get dressed, and they don't say a word. Even on their birthdays. They talk at night. We're the opposite. Richard and I both wake up speaking in complete sentences. Just open our eyes and start yakking away.

"I wonder how Elias is doing." I dragged the phone off my bedside table and called the hospital.

"He had a good night," the duty nurse reported,

"and has been awake since five-fifteen. Do you want to talk to him?"

"Sure."

The phone only rang a half. "Yo," Elias answered. His voice sounded strong.

"How're you doin', honey?"

"Fine, but I'll tell you something, little sister. I don't think I'm going to work for you anymore unless I start to get some hazardous-duty pay. Some kind of benefits. My leg is barely right from the accident down at the theater, and now I've just about gotten my arm shot off."

"I know. I'm sorry. But I'm so glad you're going to be all right."

Richard began kissing my neck, working his way across the top of my shoulder.

"Hell, it's not as bad as it sounded. I'll still be able to sign checks and drink. I'm just waiting for the doctor to come in and tell me to go home. Now, did Linda tell me you went to Billings, or did I dream that?"

"No, I went." I was having trouble concentrating, because Richard had hooked his finger under the strap of my nightgown and slipped it slowly down my arm.

"So you heard all about the Gilhoolys? About how she used to beat the daylights out of him? And how Mercedes used to visit whenever Alma was out of town?"

"Yes." I was having trouble getting my breath. Richard slowly lowered one side of my gown, the fine satin no more than a balmy breeze on my skin. "But I really think that's nothing but gossip. The big problem is, Wade was in Billings when Alma was shot and Mercedes was in the powder room with Johnny Bourbon. And Duke Fletcher isn't sure."

Satin slid up my legs and around my waist.

"I know there's a path to the truth, and I'm on it, but . . ."

Richard pulled the phone from my hand and said into it. "Your sister has to go now."

"I'll see you when you get home," I yelled at Elias, but by then Richard's lips had covered mine, so I don't know if Elias understood me or not and, frankly, I didn't much care.

The chief wrangler, Art, had an old kitchen chair tilted against the barn door. He sat in the sunshine reading the morning paper and sipping coffee around the home-rolled cigarette that's permanently embedded in his lower lip. "I thought you all wanted to ride before breakfast, not lunch," he said, not looking up from the paper. It was six-thirty. "You going to start sleeping this late when you're old married people? Day's half over."

I laughed. "Okay. Okay."

We followed him into the barn, where our horses were saddled, just waiting for their cinches to be tightened. He had the team of golden Percherons—Blackie and Blondie—ready to go, too. Fully rigged for another test run, they stood ready to be harnessed to the buckboard I would ride to our wedding. Tomorrow. It gleamed with fresh varnish.

"I didn't think buckboards ever looked this fancy," I said to Art. "Even in the movies."

"Don't. Just yours. Look at this." He slapped his hand on the tufted black-leather seat. "Innerspring bench. That's what Richard here said he wanted. 'Don't want my bride with any splinters in her butt.' That's what you told me. Isn't that right, Mr. Opera?"

"Yup." Richard laughed, drawing up Hotspur's

cinch. Richard and Art had a strong mutual-admiration society.

"Don't you think this is sort of overkill on the horse-power?" I patted Blondie's thick neck. "I mean, its not exactly as though they're dragging a fully loaded stage-coach over the pass. It's just for my father and me."

"What your daddy wants," Art said, and we all knew that that was that. "Should be down here any minute. Here he comes now."

True enough. The old 1975 hailstone-pitted yellow Wagoneer bucked to a stop next to my pickup, and my father, the epitome of the West, the son of the son of the son of a pioneer, wearing what looked as if it could have been his great-grandfather's original Stetson it was so mauled, stepped to the ground and slammed the old Jeep's door with an authoritative crash.

"Have a good ride?" he asked us and moseyed into the barn. "How're my girls today?"

The massive animals gobbled up handfuls of cut-up apple from Daddy's gloved hand, and then he walked slowly around each of them the way a pilot inspects his aircraft before takeoff, sliding his hand over their glow-ing withers and rumps, up and down their legs. Rub-bing their noses and foreheads. Checking their harness.

Nobody needs Percherons anymore. In the U.S. any-way. They're a throwback to a way of life that no longer exists. No one needs horses to haul sleds full of boulders or move two-ton safes up Main Street from the railroad station to the bank. Art uses our team occa-sionally to drag one of our fancy four-wheelers out of the mud, but he could use one of the big tractors just as easily. When you go to draft-horse power-team shows these days, the only people who compete look as though they're from some lost part of Appalachia. They all have on dirty T-shirts, backward baseball caps, few teeth, and probably use the horses to haul tree stumps out of the way of their new stills or outhouse sites.

He and Art hitched up the team and led them into the farmyard while Richard and I watched.

"Your mother says don't forget the rehearsal dinner tonight," my father called over his shoulder as he and the rig rolled away at a bright-eyed clip. He'd been working the team for a couple of hours every morning so there wouldn't be any surprises when the big day came to drive me down into the meadow next to the river to give me away to my man.

THIRTY-ONE

I'm glad you're here," Linda said when I got to the office. Richard and I had decided to forget our ride. She looked at her watch. "Seven forty-five. I've got to get back to town and take Elias home."

"Back to town?" I asked.

"I spent the night at the hospital again, but I thought I'd better get out here first thing to see what's going on and get you set up for the day." She squared off a stack of faxes and marched them into my office like a teacher handing back disappointing tests. "Not much here. Wade left a message. He'd like you to come by the house around noon for cocktails and a light lunch before the funeral. Fax from London."

She handed me the sheet. Scrawled across a piece of Connaught Hotel letterhead were the words "I DID NOT DO IT."

"Kennedy McGee," I said.

"Do you believe him?" Linda asked.

"Yes. He had nothing to gain and everything to lose. Whoever did this, and I'm pretty sure I know who it was, had a scheme that was extremely well planned. It was thought out over a long period of time, but went off course with the first shot and now has gotten totally out of control."

I scanned the offered, uninteresting correspondence and tossed it onto my desk, then pulled my notebook out of my purse. I flipped through the pages that were black with my notes. "All this other stuff," I said. "Russian letters, Russian payoffs, Russian dictionaries—it's a bunch of last-minute dust. I still have two big pieces missing, but I'm going by the airport on my way to Wade's, and I think I'll find one of them."

"Speaking of the airport"—Linda pushed her glasses back up on her nose—"the Frontier Airlines crew supervisor called a few minutes ago and said the crew you're looking for from the flight Wade was on the other night came in yesterday afternoon. They've told all but one of them you'd be wanting to talk. No problem."

"Great," I said. "Why all but one?"

"One of the flight attendants didn't check in at the crew office, and they're trying to track her down now." She reached up and tucked an errant lock of hair back into the curly pile. I realized she looked completely exhausted. "Oh, and Mercedes called and wants to see you. She's at home. Do you think she did it? I do."

"I think she may be involved. I'm just not totally sure who else is, whether it's Duke Fletcher or Wade or Johnny Bourbon. Or all three."

"Duke Fletcher would never do such a thing." Linda was incensed.

"I wouldn't like to think so. If you're looking for me," I said, putting on my dark glasses, "I'll be down at Buck's."

• • •

"Redford's mad at you," Buck said once I'd sat down across from him and accepted a cup of regular coffee and a banana-nut muffin from Ecstasy, who had plucked her eyebrow in honor of the movie company. She now actually had two: one two inches long, the other three. She had also put on socks. They weren't particularly clean, but they were there, and they were cleaner than her feet.

"Why?"

"Stood him up."

"Oh, you mean because my brother got shot and I'm getting married? And because I never accepted his invitation in the first place? Tell him to get over it." I laughed and sipped the strong brew. I'll say this for poor old Ec, she sure could make a fine cup of coffee. "If there's one thing I can't stand, it's having Robert Redford always moping around me. He's such a whiner."

"Speaking of your brother, I went to see him the other night after you all had left. Few hours after his surgery." Buck rolled his empty cup back and forth between his bear-paw hands. His eyes overflowed with tears that streamed down into his beard. "Scared the shit out of me. He's too tough of an old bull to be laid up like that, all helpless. We already did all that shit in 'Nam. He doesn't need to do it again." Buck ran his arm across his face. "I told him good-bye. I love that old bastard so much. I hope when you catch that son of a bitch that killed him you'll bring him by here so I can kick the shit out of him."

I reached over and put my hand on his. "He's fine, Buck. He's coming home this morning."

The look on his face was worth a million dollars. I'd given him a shiny red bike on Christmas morning. He didn't want to look as if it was true, because it was too good to be. His chin quivered and his eyes sparkled.

"You serious?"

"I am."

"Praise God." Buck buried his face in his hands and burst into tears. "Oh, Lord, I'm so happy. I didn't know what I was going to do without him. I haven't slept in two days." He pulled a large handkerchief out of his back pocket and blew his nose and wiped his wet cheeks. "You serious?" he asked again.

"He's going to be fine. Linda's on her way to get him now."

"You aren't shittin' me, are you?"

I shook my head.

"Hey, Ec," he yelled. "Bring me a double. Elias's comin' home."

Buck tossed off the shot, slammed the glass on the wooden table, and stared out the window for a minute without speaking. "Well," he finally said. "Tomorrow's the day. You can still bolt."

"I'm not going to bolt, Buck. I want to get married. Are you going to show up at the rehearsal dinner tonight? You did accept, and there are place cards."

"Who am I sitting with?"

"I have no idea."

"I'll do it if I can sit with Elias and Linda."

"I'll see what I can do. I'm not sure Elias will be able to make it."

"I'll escort Linda, then. I've bought a new tuxedo and all. Valentino. Pretty damn sharp. You ought to invite Redford, too. He's pretty upset."

Oh, for Heaven's sake.

The squeal of the saloon's swinging doors filled the empty bar, followed by the unmistakably solid footfall of good boots.

"Will you look who's here," Buck said.

THIRTY-TWO

Johnny and Shanna Bourbon.

Sunlight filtered through her hair like Helena Bonham-Carter's in some arty Tuscan movie.

Buck, in spite of his bulk, jumped to his feet—he was so happy he was flapping around like an angel—and pulled over a couple of chairs. "Let's get some coffee over here for our guests, Ecstasy."

"Heavy on the cream and sugar, if you please, sister," Johnny called across to the bar, where you could hear the china rattling. When Ecstasy reached the table, her hands were shaking so badly, she tipped over one of the cups.

"It's all right, Ec," Buck said to his sister-in-law. He mopped up the mess while Ecstasy stood stock-still, knotting and unknotting her apron in her bony hands, gawking at the Bourbons. "She watches your show every afternoon," Buck explained to them, "and even though we've had Robert Redford and his crew around here for a week, you're a much bigger deal than he is in Bennett's Fort."

"Well, God bless you, honey," Johnny said to her, and I saw her smile for the first time in my life. "Is there anything I can do for you? Any trouble in your life I can help you with?"

Ecstasy shook her head, too happy to speak.

"This is a surprise," I said. "It must seem like the middle of the night to you."

Shanna nodded and sipped her coffee. She wore large dark glasses and tight, tight jeans. "Johnny thought it was too important to call in about, so here we are."

"What's too important?"

Johnny leaned his elbows on his knees and turned his white cowboy hat around and around in his hands. "After our services yesterday, when I went down to meet with the audience and pray with them, a young woman came to me. She's a regular member of our congregation, but I'd never talked to her before." He glanced at his wife with imploring eyes.

Shanna cleared her throat and turned in her seat, studiously ignoring him.

"It's God's truth, honey." Johnny was full of repentance today. "I don't know this girl. She waited until everyone was gone and then, while Shanna was getting set up, she told me she wanted to talk to me privately."

Johnny shot his attention over Shanna's way again, but her eyes remained hidden behind the glasses. I sensed this was probably an old, familiar tune. She drummed her fingers on the side of her cup. Her nails were filed sharper than arrowheads.

"Stewardess," she said.

"She's a flight attendant, Shanna. Flight attendant. Anyhow, that's the whole point. She flies for Frontier Airlines, and she said she'd seen the picture of Alma and Wade in the paper announcing that Alma had died, and explaining how and all. Anyhow, she said she'd been working the flight from Billings to Roundup that night and the man who said he was Wade Gilhooly . . . wasn't."

I thought my stomach would jump out of my body. "Who did she think it was?"

"Didn't know."

"What's her name?" I said. "I want to talk to her."

"Well, that's sort of the problem." Johnny turned his hat in the other direction. "She wants to remain anonymous. Won't talk to anyone but me." He paused and shot his eyes back at his wife. "As her pastor and all."

"In private, if you can stand it," Shanna jeered. "She's camped out in Johnny's office. Says she wants the sanctuary of the church until all this is over because she's afraid if she identifies the man who did it, he'll come after her. Well, let me tell you something." She took Johnny's cheeks in her fingers, pinched them hard, and talked right into his face. "I'm sick of all this adulterous fornication. We're changing our ways, and if she tries to as much as peek into my man's pants, she'll be *praying* it's the murderer who's coming after her instead of me." She let go of Johnny as if he were a head of lettuce. There were big red blotches on his cheeks. "And, brother, you can take that to the bank."

Shanna's anger had generated a furnacelike energy field. The air around her and Johnny sizzled like an explosion from the sun, and I let it diffuse for a moment or two before I said anything.

"If I give you some pictures," I asked Johnny, "will you show them to her? See if she'll ID him that way?"

"Sure. I think that'd be all right. Don't you, sugar?" he asked Shanna.

"I suppose that'll be fine."

Johnny rubbed his face and looked at his wife and prayed the lightning wouldn't come back and strike him again today.

THIRTY-THREE

I wracked my brain as I drove into town to Mercedes's house. I didn't even notice that there was not a cloud in the sky. My pager went off. It looked like Elias's number at the hospital. I tried it. Busy. I checked the office voice mail as I charged down the interstate.

There was a message from Linda saying to call Elias, that it was urgent. I tried him again. Still busy.

The Frontier Airlines flight attendant who was camped out in Johnny Bourbon's office had saved me a trip to the airport, but she hadn't answered the question: Who had been on the plane?

Was it Duke? While Wade did the shooting and Mercedes made sure the coast was clear? Were they all in it together? There was certainly motive enough, and the fact that Mercedes frequently hightailed it up to Billings to be with Wade and Duke whenever Alma was out of town certainly could imply conspiracy. Why did Mercedes want to see me? We couldn't possibly be getting back to the Russians. Or could we?

Mercedes never moved out of her family's house

next door to my parents', and as I pulled through the gates into her driveway, I could see that, even though her father and stepmother were now gone and she lived there alone, she had changed little about the Federal mansion. The same yellow-silk drapes still hung straight down inside the windows that were as big as doors, the same wrought-iron benches still flanked the front door, and the bell still chimed the same three notes when I pushed it.

I waited what seemed an unusually long time and then heard the sound of strain and wrestling on the other side of the door before it unstuck and flew open, almost flattening a butler so small he looked like a bug. He was practically colorless. His sparse hair, his skin, his eyes behind clear-plastic-rimmed glasses, all blended together in a sort of soulless shade of pale. The only color about him was his suit, and it was gray. He wasn't particularly old and he wasn't particularly young.

"Good morning, Miss Bennett," he said in a vaguely British accent. "Madam is expecting you in the lounge."

Lounge?

"Do you know the way?" He shouldered the complaining door shut. "I must see to this," he muttered and then fought it open again and examined the jamb. "Excuse me." He was talking to me again. "I thought this was repaired. Now, do you know the way?"

"No," I answered. "I don't believe I do."

"Then I'll be happy to direct you."

I followed him up the stairs, past a solid floor-to-ceiling parade of oil portraits of relatives—most of them purchased—in a backwash of constant chatter about the lovely weather and how perfect it would be for my wedding tomorrow. "Madam is so looking forward to it."

"Me, too."

At the landing, he led me to what had been Mr. and Mrs. Rutherford's private domain. When I was growing up, Alma's parents' bedroom had been one of those majestic places we all feel a little uncomfortable entering because it's not our own parents' bedroom and it seems a little improper to be going into someone else's, a little too familiar, maybe even a little disloyal. Consequently, I'd never been in any Rutherford bedroom before except Alma's bitter-apple-green wedding cake.

He knocked on the closed door and then opened it slightly. "Miss Bennett's here, Miss Rutherford," he called and stepped aside to let me pass. "I'll bring the coffee straightaway."

The room was magnificent—what a realtor today would call a stunning Master Suite—large windows and a set of French doors to the balcony all open to let in the cool morning breeze. Outside, beyond the balcony, the formal gardens were exquisitely laid out. Originally designed by the first Mrs. Rutherford, Mercedes's English mother—who must have been astonished to find herself so unbelievably rich from oil profits, but in Wyoming nevertheless—they exploded in a riot of summer's last roses, interspersed with wide swaths of budding yellow chrysanthemums. A fire crackled in the hearth beneath an ornately carved, old French marble mantel.

Mercedes was nowhere to be seen.

The door to the dressing room—which I now assumed to be what he had referred to as "the lounge"—stood ajar.

"Mercedes," I called. It sounded as though water were running in her bathroom. "It's me, Lilly."

No answer. I called again. Nothing but quiet and the sound of water running slowly, uninterrupted, into a sink, not too loud to hear over. I pushed the door slowly.

The doorbell rang in the distant downstairs.

"Mercedes," I called louder, and then I saw her. She lay on the floor as if she were asleep on her side. Her hair fanned across her face, and her legs and arms were in a comfortably half-bent position. "Mercedes?" I knelt beside her and pushed the hair back.

A brightly colored Hermès scarf had been garroted around her neck with a hairbrush. Her face was swollen into a grotesque purple basketball, eyes bulging slightly, lips black. Her tongue had begun to swell and protrude, but her skin was still warm and vital to the touch. Then I heard a noise outside the open dressing-room window. A thud, a *whumph* in the garden. Someone had just jumped from the balcony.

This is the sort of choice police officers face every day: save the life or catch the killer? Always save the life. I loosened the garrote, pulled my phone out of my pocket, punched in 911, gave them the news, then jerked Mercedes over onto her back and began to massage her neck gently, hoping to open her airway. Then I pinched her nose closed with my fingers, sealed my mouth over hers, and began to blow.

It was a minute or two—who knows? a lifetime—before the butler strolled in with a coffee tray, which he placed slowly and deliberately on a small table beside the chaise.

"Do you know how to do CPR?" I said.

"Yes, I do." The man was unflappable.

"Well then, get to work. The police and an ambulance are on their way."

I prepared to hand Mercedes over to him, but at that

moment she began to fight for breath through her damaged windpipe. The sound was as beautiful as it was ghastly. The garish flush on her face faded slowly as blood trapped by the closed jugular vein began to return to her heart. I had gotten there just in time. One more minute and she would have been too dead, the oxygen deprivation to her brain too great. Strangulation/asphyxiation is one of the fastest ways to die, particularly with a garrote. Long-drawn-out strangulation struggles between killers and their victims in movies are Hollywood devices—unless the killer is totally inept—because, in reality, unconsciousness comes within ten to fifteen seconds and severe brain damage occurs within four minutes.

"Mercedes." I took her hand. Her color became more and more normal. Petechial hemorrhages emerged like smears of blood in her eyes. "You're going to be all right. Just stay calm and try to breathe slowly. Can you hear me?"

She drew in more air, each breath slightly easier than the one before.

"Can you squeeze my hand?"

She responded with surprisingly strong pressure.

"Tell me," I said. "Who did this? Was it Wade?"

Her grip tightened.

"Duke?"

Tighter yet.

"Duke?" I asked again, incredulous.

Her eyes opened and her expression was one of terror. And then I got the message.

"Help is on the way, and your man here is going to hold your hand until the paramedics arrive. Don't be afraid, you're fine. Everything's all right."

I got to my feet and hurried to the balcony. Nothing to see, of course. Nobody. But now I knew who I was looking for, and I had to stop him. I didn't even want to imagine what he'd do next if we didn't get to him in a hurry. Panic had hurled him totally out of control, launched him into the stratosphere of stark terror at being found out and captured.

I flew down the stairs two at a time, racing to the front door, which stood open. I could see my Jeep beyond, but two figures standing in the entrance hall blocked the way. I screeched to a stop. Could not believe my eyes.

My mother and Richard's. Both in lovely flowered-chiffon day dresses.

"Oh, Lilly, dear," my mother began briskly. "We saw your car and thought maybe you could come by for a cup of coffee and talk about tonight." Her sentence ended in a whisper because her eyes were on my drawn sidearm. "What in the world?"

"Did you see another car in the drive? See anyone leaving just a minute ago?" I snapped.

They both shook their heads.

"What's going on?" Mother asked.

"Someone's tried to murder Mercedes. Would you wait here for the paramedics? They'll be here any minute. She's up in her dressing room. Show them the way."

"Where are you going?" she called out the door after me.

"Wade Gilhooly's." I put down my car window. "And, Mother, do not discuss this with anyone. And I mean *anyone*. Morning, Alida," I yelled as I drove away.

She gave me a little wave. She loved me.

●   ●   ●

"I'm on my way to the Gilhooly residence on Sunset Drive," I told Jack over the radio as I hurtled down the busy boulevard toward Wind River Estates south of town, honking my horn and flashing my lights. What I needed was a siren. I'd ask for that next.

"I'm on your heels. Wait at the road until I get there."

"Right," I answered. Like I would. For sure. Get a clue, Jack.

The driveway and parking area of the Gilhooly estate looked like a General Motors showroom. It was filled with cars, most of them with Montana license plates, all of them brand-new GM models. I assumed they belonged to friends of Wade's who had driven down from Billings for Alma's funeral, because it was pretty clear Alma hadn't had any friends. And Wade, who had a lot to start with, was now super-rich and, bottom line, everyone had come to celebrate. Duke Fletcher's shiny red GMC Tahoe fit right in.

The white Cadillac convertible sat in the open garage. I slammed up tight behind it, and then walked over and laid my hand on the hood. Hot.

My stomach tightened and adrenaline quickened my heart. What would happen from now on was what made me tick. This is what detective work is all about. Grab the bastard and read him his rights. I could hear myself saying the words in my head.

I drew my weapon and moved slowly along the gray stucco exterior to the front doors, which stood open. But in spite of the full parking area, the entry hall was empty. I stopped and listened. Judging by the salsa band and the festive voices that drifted in, it sounded like the prefuneral warm-up luncheon was out by the pool. I had to hurry. It was almost one o'clock, and they would be leaving soon for the cathedral. I crept quietly inside, past the giant birdcage, and edged down the hall into Wade's study. As I'd told Linda, the flight attendant's statement to Johnny had answered half of my question, and now, looking across the room at the bank of TV monitors, the full picture fell into place.

And then, for a blinding instant, it felt as if a safe had dropped out of the sky and cracked open my skull. Everything went black.

THIRTY-FOUR

I was balled up on a hard, ridged surface that smelled like leather and warm rubber and motor oil. Enticing odors for some, but not for me, especially once I realized my hands and feet were tied and everything was dark and I was locked in the trunk of a car with little room to maneuver.

I squeezed my eyes shut and then opened them. Claustrophobia was an unthinkable indulgence. Certainly not an option. My head was killing me. I shook it to try to bring some clarity but all it brought was more pain. Slowly the fog cleared and I remembered everything. Then I knew I was in the trunk of Wade's Cadillac. And I also knew that if I didn't escape, I was dead, because now I had figured out everything. It was so sad. Pathetic, really. He would kill me, or *try* to kill me, next. Fortunately, he was turning out to be not too successful in the murder department. But he was sure strong on attempteds.

There was absolutely no light. This old boat was built. Sealed up tight as an oil drum and hot as hell.

Like being trapped in an oven with the temperature turned to five hundred. Hot enough to broil steaks. Through my uninsulated metal coffin, I clearly heard the sounds of voices, car doors slamming. How long had I been in here? Where was here?

My fingers began to explore the knots. They were loose and childishly unprofessional—he'd obviously never made it beyond Cub Scouts—and after a couple of minutes of picking at them with my fingernails, one of the hitches began to unloop. In no time at all, I had freed myself. But it didn't matter. I was still imprisoned, horribly cramped in a pitch-black blast furnace.

Cadillac built two hundred of these limited-edition Eldorado convertibles in 1976, all of them white, all with red-leather interiors, and as I ran my fingers over the seams and seals and steel, I understood why most of them are still on the road more than twenty years later. They've got no give. They took all the cushioning and put it in the ride, leaving the trunk hard and functional and heartless as a whore—and as escape-proof as a Vuitton steamer trunk.

The noise outside stopped, and I forced myself to bite back my instinct to yell for rescue. My training told me I needed to explore the few legitimate escape options available before I started to panic and bang on the hood, drawing attention to my predicament, because I had no idea where I was. I could still be in Wade's garage, for all I knew. And I if I were, or if I weren't, I wondered where my own car was and if Jack Lewis were looking for me yet—or not.

I dug around in my pockets. My phone was gone. Well, that was no surprise. My glasses were still there, but I couldn't see anything anyway. And, still there like an old friend, safely strapped on the inside of my forearm, was my knife. My little, featherlight, undetectable, spade-shaped CIA letter opener. So versatile and so strong, I could dig to China with it if I had to.

I slid it from its chamois sheath and went to work.

The Eldorado was big, but its trunk was tiny—Fiat 100–sized—because the top fitted back into it when it was down, and of course Wade had the top down. Can you imagine going to your wife's funeral with the top down? How about a little decorum, Wade? But the fact that it *was* down eliminated an obvious, simple escape route: just slash the canvas pouch and climb into the car. Plus, there was one of those midget, circus-sized, spare tires bolted in, and that took up a lot of space. No room to do anything much. Little leverage.

It was tough going with the knife, lying on my side trying to jimmy the latch. Sweat slid over me, drenching my hands, and every minute or so I had to stop and wipe them, one at a time, on my skirt, all the while being careful to keep the knife jammed into the locking mechanism. It didn't take long for me to realize this was not going to work. No matter how tough the poly-carbon knife was, it was no match for steel. It could maybe saw through thin metal sheeting or certain other types of metal, but there was no way it would hold up breaking steel nuts or bolts or cutting through a 1976 Cadillac body. Forget it.

I blotted my face with my sleeves, then reached my hands behind my head and rummaged around for the crowbar. I was in luck. It was just where I'd hoped it would be, secured onto the top of the spare. I stopped worrying about the noise and went back to work, smashing the wedge as hard as I could up into the lock-ing mechanism and then pushing and pulling and jim-mying it around with all my might. Sooner or later it had to break or turn. Sure enough, the lock gave way and the seal hissed with a quiet pneumatic pop.

Bomphf. I held the truck lid down, letting the bright sunlight filter around the edge and my eyes adjust, and gulping fresh cool air.

The first thing I saw as I peeked straight out the back was blinding light glinting off the chrome grille of Jack's white Ford Crown Victoria. It was practically kissing the Caddy it was so close. But as I raised the trunk more, I saw that Jack's car was empty.

I looked to my right into a vast empty parking lot— empty, that is, except for the GM showroom from Wade's house, a dozen white stretch limousines, Richard's Mercedes convertible, and my parents' sedan.

To my left, at the front doors of the Cowboy Cathedral, two attendants in baby-blue cowboy hats and baby-blue Western suits, spoke quietly to one another.

The looks on their faces were worth the trip when I let the lid go. It flew fully open and I emerged from its scalding depths, holding my finger over my lips for them to keep quiet. They rushed to help me climb out of the trunk. This was no easy feat in a skirt and high heels, which I'm sure looked as if they'd been selected in the dark from some church rummage sale in North Roundup.

"The service just started," one of them whispered to me as we entered the main lobby and stood outside the doors of the cathedral/studio.

The seats were almost as empty as the parking lot, but for a few full rows down in the very front, where Wade's and Alma's friends and relatives fanned themselves with folded programs and listened to Johnny Bourbon give forth on how lucky Alma was, being with the Lord and all.

Her bronze casket, as big and shiny as her widower's car, sat at the bottom of the steps leading up to the stage, and its brass fittings glared like headlights from beneath a yellow-orange rose shroud, on top of which sat a four-foot high pile of red roses, staked with white gladiolus and Boston-fern fronds. It was the gaudiest thing I'd ever seen. I think Shanna must have arranged for it. Dozens and dozens of candles on tall silver sticks ran along the front of the stage, punctuated with more bouquets and wreaths than a state funeral in India. It looked like a carnival.

I stayed in the darkened lobby and watched from the doorway.

"You're sure you don't want me to escort you to a seat?" the attendant asked as I scrawled out a note on a piece of paper he'd kindly provided for me.

"Not yet, thanks. I want you to hand this—as quietly and discreetly as you possibly can—to Chief Lewis. He's the one—"

"I know who he is, ma'am. I'll be right back."

As the young man made his way down the long aisle, I studied the group intensely: Wade sat alone in the front pew staring at Alma's casket and drumming his fingers absentmindedly on the barrier railing.

I'll bet you're preoccupied, I thought. His color had improved somewhat over the last few days. It still wasn't great, but he looked a little healthier and the bruises were now gone. From a distance, he seemed cheerful and relieved to be surrounded by his claque of Billings cronies. Safe in their bosom, so to speak. Just that one last little problem to deal with: me locked in the trunk of his car. He'd have that taken care of by dinner.

Across the aisle from him slumped three middle-aged women, all in dark glasses. They had the rode-hard look of serious-drinking Yellowstone Country Clubbers, with puffed and sagging faces and thick midriffs. I imagined they must be Alma's bridge buddies.

"We brought nothing into this world," Johnny called out, "and it is certain we can carry nothing out." It was early on. He was only getting warmed up.

Just give me a minute, Johnny, I said to myself, and we'll have things really humming around here.

I saw Tiffany and Dwight huddled alone in a remote pew. She was furtively feeling up my deputy, whose head had fallen over to rest on his hands, which grasped the back of the empty pew in front of them. Dwight looked as if he was praying, and I suppose in some way he was. Praying, no doubt, that Tiffany would not stop.

Richard and all our parents filled the row behind the bridge ladies. Richard was sitting on the aisle next to my mother and fidgeting like a child. I knew he was very worried about me and wanted to come out and try to call me. Finally his head turned and our eyes met, and I held up my hands to tell him not to do anything. He understood exactly what I meant and covered his surprised expression with a big phony sneeze into his handkerchief.

"God bless you," Johnny said.

Richard was completely taken aback. Episcopalians never step outside the forms during a service. "Thank you," he answered.

Duke walked up to the podium and unrolled a sheaf of notes. "Oh, Alma," he began. "What an amazing woman you were." And then launched into a eulogy of such complete bullshit, no one in the congregation could believe their ears.

I watched Jack receive the note, scan it, fold it precisely, score it with his fingernails, and tuck it in his pocket. As he did so, his eyes sought me in the distance until they made me out. He just barely nodded in my direction and leaned to whisper to the ubiquitous Lieutenant Evan, who scooted up the opposite aisle like a shadow to alert the contingent of uniformed and plainclothes officers they'd brought along. The net was closing. Our wolf would be brought to bay.

I was ready for everything, I thought, but I guess I wasn't ready for the sound of the voice.

"What are you doing out here?" Aunt Edith Rochester Rutherford screeched. I felt as if I was waiting for a bus in the Bronx. "Why don't you come in with everyone else?"

I grabbed her arm and practically threw her against the wall out of the congregation's line of sight. "Be quiet," I hissed. "This is official police business."

"What?" She was undaunted. "You going to arrest somebody or something? You'd better be careful of my suit. This is a very boring funeral. Good God, what happened to you? You're all covered with grease. Don't get near me. Don't get that stuff on my suit. It's—"

"I know, a Galanos. Look, do me a favor, Aunt Edith," I said, letting go of her arm. "Just be quiet. Don't tell anyone I'm here."

"Who would I tell? They're all a bunch of hicks. Nothing like the classy people I live with at the Del Coronado Hotel in San Diego, California. I'm going outside to have a cigarette." She teetered away in grape-metallic Manolo Blahnik spikes. Just a used-up old mutton decked out as lamb in an orange-and-grape Galanos miniskirt.

I stuck my head back around the corner and kept my eyes on Jack. Finally Evan returned to his side, and Jack gave me the sign. Everyone was moved into place. A uniformed officer appeared behind me to guard the door. The net was closed.

I grabbed a program from a stack at the door—the crowd must have been a huge disappointment to the church staff, if the size of the stack represented their anticipation—and slipped unnoticed into a seat off to the side in the back.

Duke, who'd sifted through Alma's blood-soaked past, somehow kept dredging up nice things to say. "Alma was such a philanthropist. Her generosity to Johnny Bourbon's Christian Cowboys was well known—"

"Amen," Johnny called.

"—as was her generosity to many other causes." Wisely, Duke realized the only other causes she was generous to were right-wing nutballs. He couldn't come out and name the Wyoming Militia because, as any savvy politician knows these days, you don't ever say a word you don't want repeated on the six-o'clock news with all the modifiers deleted.

I sat and watched and listened patiently, taking advantage of the time to pull myself together. I had no intention of making an arrest during the funeral service itself, because that would be regarded as very bad form. Unless there's reason, like the alleged perpetrator tries to escape or grab a hostage or commit another crime, it just isn't done. In this instance, I was fairly secure in the knowledge that our guy wasn't going anywhere and that we could wait until Alma'd been committed fair and square to what I feared was going to turn out to be hell, and then I could step in and take him on his way out.

Things, of course, never go according to plan. Never. And unfortunately, as Duke scratched up more fool's gold from under the various ignominious rocks of Alma's life, Wade became more and more bored and started to squirm and decided he'd turn around and talk to his best bud, Jerry Pierce, the golfer from Billings who had the Rottweiler named Gut. That's when he saw me. All the color drained from his face, and his head turned from side to side as police officers stepped into sight at each one of the exit doors.

Now it was going to get messy. Damn.

THIRTY-FIVE

Wade turned back to me and we stared at each other, then his eyes darted around the room, searching for escape. I rose to my feet and headed slowly down the side aisle. So far, no one else knew what was happening, and then my mother looked up and saw me.

"Lilly Bennett," she scolded. "Where in the world have you been? Do you have any idea what time it is? What in heaven's name has happened to your suit? It's completely wrecked."

"Later, Mother," I cut her off. "This is business."

Wade looked ready to make a move, and I was trying to get to the end of his row before he did.

"Believe me," she apologized to Alida for my behavior, "she's not always like this."

"I think she's absolutely divine."

You ain't seen nothin' yet, Alida, honey, I thought.

When Johnny saw the armed police officers at all his cathedral's exits, his reaction verged on hysteria. His panicky eyes—so big it seemed only the whites were visible, like Daniel's in Raphael's painting of Daniel meeting the lions for the first time—darted around the room and then, like Daniel, he dropped to his knees at the edge of the stage, raised his arms to the sky, and screamed, "Dear Lord, Dear Lord, have mercy. Have mercy."

If seeing armed officers induced this reaction, especially knowing what I knew—that they weren't there for him—I supposed Johnny's prison experience must have been extra bad, worse than he ever let on. Shanna knelt quickly beside him and put her arm around his shoulders, comforting him.

The whole tableau was totally biblical—these two were loaded with forgiveness, and frankly, the way they lived, they needed to be—and if I'd had more time I would have stopped to admire them.

"Don't worry, darlin'," she cooed, stroking his cheek. The eagle-down on her cuff brushed his face like a powder puff. "You haven't done a thing wrong. They can't be here because of anything you've done. Isn't that so, Lilly?" She looked at me, as I drew closer and I could tell she was afraid.

"Shanna's right," I answered, not taking my eyes off Wade. "I'm not here for you."

I reached the far end of Wade's row and he darted out, leaving his cane on the floor, and took refuge behind Alma's casket. Only the top of his head and his frightened eyes were visible over the roses through the fence of gladiolus spears.

"Now, Wade," I said, "let's just do this quietly."

Duke never moved. Not a bristle out of place. He stood righteously, statuelike, at the podium, furious he'd been interrupted. "What in the devil is going on here? This is a *funeral,* for God's sake. Have you no sense of propriety, Miss Bennett? You're the biggest troublemaker I've ever known."

I started toward Wade. Our eyes were locked together.

"And where's Mercedes?" Duke asked. "She told me she was meeting with you."

"That's a good question, Duke," I said. "Why don't you tell him where Mercedes is, Wade?"

Suddenly I saw a tiny flash of light on what looked like a silver gun barrel, and I guess everyone else saw it, too, because there were some shrieks, but nobody left. They all fell to their knees and peeked over the tops of the pew backs. Their heads looked like ducks in a shooting gallery.

"Put the gun down, Wade."

"Don't anybody come near me or I'll shoot. I haven't done anything." He pointed the gun directly at my forehead and his eyes flew wildly around the church.

"Put the weapon down and we'll talk about it." I kept walking slowly toward him. I could feel the whole room holding its breath.

"I'll shoot."

"No you won't. You shoot me right now, you'll get the chair. So far you're just facing one charge of murder one and four attempted murders. You kill me, a federal officer, you're in deep shit."

Wade licked his dry lips and dug one of his hands into the roses. He kept the six-shooter on my face.

"You know we can still use the chair in Wyoming," I said. My heart was beating so fast it felt as if I had a ticker-tape machine in my chest. It was just Wade and me in the room, eye to eye across the top of his wife's casket. "I read about a fellow recently whose face caught on fire and part of his head exploded when they threw the switch—and he still wasn't dead. He was screaming like hell. Imagine it hurt like the dickens. Just think, that could be you, Wade. Put down the gun."

But instead of dropping the weapon, he turned the casket and began to roll it up the aisle with one hand while waving the gun around with the other. I couldn't believe my eyes. "Anybody tries to stop me," he yelled. "I'll shoot Bennett."

I stayed on the other side of the rolling bier, and he was really getting it going pretty good, picking up speed. So much for whatever his illness was, I thought. I guessed he was well, because the thing was starting to cruise like a bat out of hell and I was having to run to keep up. At least the speed made it hard for him to keep the gun aimed, and I thought, Jesus, he could keep on like this all the way to Nebraska if somebody doesn't do something. Why don't they just close the goddamn doors? But everyone was merely watching us open-mouthed, and I was too winded to yell.

Finally I sucked up every bit of energy I had left and heaved myself across the top of the pile of flowers. I grabbed for his tie and yanked as hard as I could. And what happened was, he and I both came to a screeching halt as the casket shot out from under me and I landed flat on my stomach on the blanket of roses with Wade flat on his back next to me, the gun long gone, spinning away out of reach beneath the pews. I jumped with both knees onto his belly, jerked my handcuffs out from the back of my skirt, and slapped those suckers on him so fast he didn't know if he was up or back.

"Where'd you get those?" he squeaked out, incredulous.

"You did a crappy job of frisking me, you stupid bastard," I said as I tugged him to his feet and smacked the other cuff onto the brass railing of Alma's casket.

"Wade Gilhooly." My voice was suddenly strong. If I'd ever felt sorry for him, all that sympathy had evaporated during this little joyride. "I'm placing you under arrest for the murder of Alma Rutherford Gilhooly and for the multiple attempted murders of Jim Dixon, Elias Bennett, Mercedes Rutherford, and me, Marshal Lilly Bennett. You have the right to remain silent. Anything you say can and will be used against you in a court of law. You have the right to an attorney. Any questions?"

I wanted to kick him in the leg, just the way Linda had.

"How'd you get out of the car?" He still could not believe what was happening, still thought his macho Irish bad-boy charm could rescue him.

"You have a way of underestimating women, Mr. Gilhooly," I said. "Why did you hire me in the first place? Why not just let the police department handle it?"

"I thought you'd stop at McGee. You had enough clues and enough evidence to sink a ship."

Lieutenant Evan unhitched the cuff from the casket, turned Wade around, locked his wrists together behind his back, and escorted him to the door.

"You picked the wrong girl," I said to his back.

THIRTY-SIX

Everyone followed us out of the cathedral, evidently leaving Alma for later, because just before I exited, I looked over my shoulder and saw people, my mother and Alida Jerome leading the pack, tromping through the flowers and shouldering past the deceased as though her large casket were simply something in the way. At least it wasn't spinning.

"Why did you do all this?" I asked Wade before Evan guided him into the backseat of Jack's sedan. The bewildered mourners, if that's what you could call them, formed a semicircle around us, with Jerry Pierce and Wade's banged-up executive Jim Dixon slightly closer.

Some of the angry red had drained from Wade's face, leaving it blotchy and fearful. He stared at my shoes. "You probably won't believe me, but I'm sorry I tried to kill you and Elias and Mercedes. I'm not sorry I killed Alma, though. I couldn't take it anymore. She deserved it. I did it out of self-defense."

"Self-defense? Try again."

He ignored my question, saying instead, "Why didn't you just stick with McGee?"

"Because he didn't do it."

"He's done worse. He has a lot to pay for."

"You're right," I said. "But you did all this."

"How did you know?"

"Well," I stopped to organize my thoughts and looked around the crowd, enjoying my moment. I saw Jack look at his watch, which made me enjoy it even more. "I didn't know for sure until this morning, and then two things happened: First of all, the disappearing flight attendant, who"—I turned to the door to see if she'd made an appearance, which she hadn't—"who I believe will tell us you were *not* the man on the Frontier flight from Billings last Sunday night. That it was your vice-president Jim Dixon, who often traveled in your stead. Isn't that so, Mr. Dixon?"

I stared at the Gilhooly GMC executive who'd been at Wade's house the morning I was there and who had crashed and totally demolished his Seville on the way back into town. His face, still bruised and swollen from having the air bag explode into it and practically permanently embed his glasses into his eye sockets, revealed nothing. Even with the bruises, his similarity to Wade was remarkable.

"You knew I was outside your study door, didn't you Wade? That's why the conversation with Mr. Dixon was so stilted. And after you'd watched him pour a highball glass of straight vodka—presumably the first of several, judging by his blood alcohol at the time of the accident—and excused yourself to get your briefcase, you did something to his car. Am I right?"

"He didn't do anything to my car," Jim Dixon said defensively. "He was only gone for a minute or two."

"Wade?"

Wade stared at him and me defiantly. I got the feeling that if his hands hadn't been cuffed behind his back, he would have given us both the finger.

"He loosened your brake lines and disconnected the warning light. He knew you'd get two or three good applications out of it, enough to get you onto the freeway before the brakes went completely."

"Is that true?" Dixon asked.

Wade just ignored him.

"You son of a bitch," Dixon said, his voice was quiet, awestruck. "After all I've done for you." He looked completely dumbfounded. "I've covered up for you a million times. You son of a bitch."

"I've covered for you a few times myself," Wade countered defensively. "Like most mornings when you're too hung over to work."

"Yeah. But I've never tried to kill you. You bastard. You actually tried to murder me." The enormity of this fact seemed to be sinking in. He faced me. "You've got it right, Miss Bennett: I was on the plane pretending to be Wade the night Alma was shot. I stood in for him all the time. Wade Gilhooly never left town at all—said he wanted to spend a quiet Sunday evening with Tiffany."

"I was at the home with my grandmother," Tiffany spoke quickly to Dwight.

"I know. Wade just didn't think we'd ever follow it so far," I said. "You hid in Alma's dressing room and shot her, Wade. And then you tried to kill Elias because you were afraid he'd found out about the sabotage on the car."

Wade leaned against the police cruiser and watched his toe move a pebble.

"Don't you want to get a lawyer or something, man?" I heard Jerry ask him.

"What the hell difference will it make?" Wade said.

"You're entitled," I said. "We can stop anytime you like."

Wade didn't answer.

I continued. "Today it all became completely clear when I walked into your study. Last Sunday, when Alma took me on a tour of the house, all the TV screens in your study were on ESPN. I never made the connection that they were also hooked up to the security system, that each screen was attached to a camera somewhere in your house or on your property."

"So?" Wade might have been down, but he was not out, at least as far as he was concerned.

"I realized you knew I was standing outside the door the whole time, and you tailored your conversation with Jim. You'd probably intended to shoot him right on the spot, right then, but I forced you to change your plan."

Wade nodded. I could tell he was thinking.

"What I don't understand, Wade, is why. Why didn't you just get a divorce? Why did you go to all this trouble with the Russians and, my God, trying to kill my brother and Mercedes and me? Why?"

"Because I didn't think anyone would believe me."

"What do you mean, believe you?"

"I know this sounds crazy, but the truth is, I did kill Alma out of self-defense, and then it seemed like if I did just one other thing, everything else would be covered up and it would all go away."

"What do you mean, self-defense?"

His eyes darted around the crowd. "This is hard for me to talk about. It's embarrassing."

"Try," I said, maybe a little sarcastically.

"Alma used to beat me up." Wade said this so quietly we could scarcely hear him.

"Excuse me," I shouted. "I can't hear you."

Wade looked at me and he hated my guts, but I didn't give a damn because he was a one-man, fumbling, out-of-control crime wave. I didn't care if he was a great guy everybody loved, he'd murdered his wife, shot my brother, and given me the biggest headache I'd ever had in my life. I had a lump on the back of my head the size of a baseball.

"All the black eyes and broken ribs, they weren't from bar fights. They were from Alma."

"Hey, man," Jerry said. "You don't have to tell all this stuff."

"No. I want to. See this scar on my neck? The one I said I got from Vietnam? The truth is, Alma threw boiling water on me one time. Another time she picked me up and threw me across the room like a sack of flour. Okay"—Wade drew in his breath—"I could take all that. I'd learned to live with it. But a month or so ago, I started getting sick, and I realized Alma was poisoning me, and somehow she still is. I'm just getting sicker and sicker, and I don't know what's causing it. But I swear to God, it's something she's done to my food or water or something."

"Well, for goodness' sake," my mother said. "Why didn't you just go to a doctor?"

"Mother," I said. "Stay out of this."

"I did, but they couldn't find anything wrong with me. Said it was just flu. I'll tell you another thing: Whatever weird African juice she's using on me, she used the same thing on her parents."

Whoa. "Alma poisoned her parents?"

"That's what I said."

Jack and I exchanged glances.

"But why'd you have to go and shoot Elias?" I asked. "That was completely uncalled-for."

"Because it was the perfect final setup for McGee. He was there. I had his gun. I didn't try to kill Elias; I just wanted to injure him. And then, when they arrested McGee, it was perfect, but then the idiots let him escape."

Jack's face visibly reddened.

"I don't think Chief Lewis cottons much to being called an idiot," I said.

"Sorry," Wade mumbled.

"What did you do to Mercedes this morning, you little peckerheaded pipsqueak?" Duke broke from the crowd and thundered into Wade's face. He'd balled his big hand into a fist. "What did she ever do to you except be your friend? Always rushing up there to hold your hand."

"Well, she was holding your hand plenty, too," Wade gave a little back. He might have been sick as a dog, but he was not going gently into anybody's good night. Not by a long shot. He was a tough little bastard.

"That's none of your damn business." Duke drew back and would have knocked all Wade's teeth down his throat if Jack hadn't grabbed his arm.

"She called me last night and said if I didn't turn myself in, she'd call the police. I panicked. I didn't mean for all this to happen. Shit, I practically killed myself this morning, jumping off her balcony."

Jack stepped forward. "Party's over."

Lieutenant Evan put his hand on Wade's head and shoved him into the squad.

"Don't worry, buddy, we'll get you a good lawyer," Jerry told him. "We'll get you off. Hey," he said, conveniently forgetting the four attempted homicides, "you said yourself, it was self-defense."

Jack closed the door slowly and started around the

car. He stopped long enough to look at me over the tops of his dark glasses and whisper in my ear. "You'd better clean up if you're going to get married," he said. "You look like hell."

"You're welcome." I smiled.

THIRTY-SEVEN

Mr. and Mrs. Elias Caulfield Bennett III
request the honour of your presence
at the marriage of their daughter
Lilly McLaughlin
to
Mr. Richard Welland Jerome, Jr.
Saturday, the twelfth of September
at five o'clock
Circle B Ranch
Bennett's Fort, Wyoming

THIRTY-EIGHT

SATURDAY MORNING · SEPTEMBER 12— WEDDING DAY

Are you sure you want to do this?"

"I'm sure."

"You really do?"

"Yes." Richard was sounding exasperated. "I really, really do."

"Okay," I said. I was skeptical. "But this can be pretty tough going. I don't want you going all hysterical on me or anything. Or fainting."

"Lilly."

But there was no going back.

"Too late now. Here we are." I pulled over behind the cemetery director's gray jeep.

It was a very quiet, late-summer morning at the Wind River Cemetery. Little breeze and full of birdsong. The lush green lawns unrolled peacefully around us, and the marble and cement monuments appeared to float on the light morning mist.

"Glad you could make it," Jack Lewis said. He held a Styrofoam cup of coffee. "We've been waiting to start till you arrived. Morning, Richard." They shook hands. "Not too late for you to bail out."

"Believe me," Richard said. "I've seen worse things than this."

"I mean getting married."

The Rutherford family did not have a private marble mausoleum with everyone tucked safely behind pad-locked, cast-iron gates, but instead they were buried on a hilltop with spectacular vistas. Their grassy plots lay in the protective shadow of a statue I assumed to por-tray Bradford Rutherford's father, the original oil baron who'd bought the handful of leases from the gov-ernment after Teapot Dome and turned them into what was now the country's most notorious independent. The larger-than-life-size bronze sculpture was of a roughneck leaning against what appeared to be the bot-tom of an oil derrick. His legs were crossed at the an-kles, his arms folded over his chest. His head drooped, and his eyes were closed, his face shaded by a beaten-up cowboy hat. His jeans were baggy, shirt loose, and the bandanna around his neck looked flat with dirt and sweat. Remington's unmistakable scrawl ran along the base like sharp blades of grass.

Below, thin lines of yellow string ran out from plot markers and formed a grid across the grave sites where the sod had already been removed. The thick rolls were stacked like firewood against the statue's four-foot-tall bronze base.

After welcoming each one of us and saying that there was no shame in feeling uncomfortable or queasy and not to be embarrassed to return to our cars because exhumation was a grueling, and often unsettling, pro-cess, Mr. Hastings, the ageless cemetery director, gave an almost imperceptible nod to the head grounds-keeper. At once, the big yellow backhoe revved up and

its custom-made, grave-width shovel tore into the hard
earth as though it were flour.

We remained a fairly solemn group as the backhoe
dug. Mr. Hastings had loaded a large steel canister of
hot coffee and a big box of glazed doughnuts into the
back of his wagon, so we all—Hastings, Lewis, Richard, me, the medical examiner Kim Leavy, and two
morticians—sipped the coffee, scarfed the doughnuts,
and watched.

"You eat many more of those," Jack said, "and
you'll be getting married in a gunnysack."

Everyone laughed but me.

"Why don't you just shut up for a change?" I said.

"She seems a little touchy, today, Richard."

"Tell me about it."

I walked over to the far edge of the plot and looked
out at the city. I was depressed. This was not how I
wanted to begin my wedding day, exhuming the bodies
of my parents' friends and neighbors to see if they'd
been murdered. This case had been so unsatisfying—so
many people with so much money, more than any of
them could ever need in ten lifetimes, and yet it had not
been enough. The thought that Alma had murdered her
parents, poisoned them to share in the control of Rutherford Oil, made me sick to my stomach.

And Wade. Poor Wade. That's how I'd begun to
think of him as Elias improved and my headache less-
ened. An abused husband. Completely trapped, or at
least imagining he was, desperate to protect himself.
Why didn't you just go to the police? I'd asked him.
Because he couldn't afford the publicity. And no doctor
could find anything wrong with him—just kept telling
him he had the flu.

Had there been a conspiracy between Wade and
Mercedes and Duke? They all said no. I wasn't so sure.

Did it matter? Yes, but nothing would come of it. Paul Decker would get Wade off on an insanity plea and installed in a suite at St. Mary's Psychiatric Hospital before the fall roundup was over.

Jack materialized next to me.

"How's Gilhooly?" I asked, interested in discussing something other than the size of my hips in front of a bunch of strangers.

"Okay, I guess. They've got him over at Christ and St. Luke's under observation, waiting for the test results on the toxins. Jim Dixon refuses to press charges, and Decker will probably have Wade at St. Mary's by the end of the day. I wonder if it'll turn out to be true? That that babe murdered her parents."

"I wouldn't exactly call Alma a 'babe.' But I think it'll turn out to be true." I kicked the dirt with the pointed toe of my boot. "I guess Mr. and Mrs. Rutherford should consider themselves lucky she didn't shoot 'em, and stuff 'em, and hang 'em over her fireplace."

The backhoe's forked bucket hit something solid, and the sound made chills run up my spine. We all watched in silence as the grave diggers jumped down into the open grave and went to work, clearing away the dirt and digging around the edges of the vault so the heavy chains could be fitted into the notches. Their shovels grated deafeningly on the cement, and it seemed impossible for me to believe that, just hours before at our rehearsal dinner, Richard, lean and elegant in his black tie, had sung "You're the Top" to me as his toast. I looked over at him leaning against the car, and I could tell he was thinking the same thing. Or would have been if he hadn't been talking on the phone.

The men tossed their shovels up onto the piles of dirt and heaved themselves out of the grave. The backhoe's engine screamed again as it jerked the chains taut and wrenched the heavy vault from the earth where it had lain for two years, not long, but long enough to insinuate itself, take up a strong position. It did not come willingly, but after a couple of minutes the large gray box swung through the air and settled gently on the grass. The men, now sweating, went to work with their sledgehammers.

"The Rutherfords went top of the line," Mr. Hastings said wryly. "Sealed vaults. Most you can pop the top with a crowbar. These things use the kind of glue the Navy uses to glue its ships back together. So we've got to bust them apart."

Watching the process of exhumation, not the first I'd seen, reconfirmed for me that cremation was the only way to go. This was hot, hard, big-muscle work. Nothing spiritual about it.

After a while, the big box took on the abused, pitted appearance of cement bridge supports on interstate highways in New England—the kinds of bridges I'm always sure are about to collapse on top of, or underneath, me—and finally it surrendered to the blows, crumbling and cracking, splitting to reveal the dull bronze casket.

The morticians stepped forward.

"These guys give me the willies," Hastings said behind his hand, as one of the gray-suited gentlemen crouched down and unscrewed the glass identification tube in the casket's lower-right-hand side. "Talk about a whole different breed of human being. I don't know how they do it. You wouldn't believe how much money they make. Practically mint the stuff."

The man stood up and ceremoniously unrolled the tiny paper scroll. "Bradford Rutherford the Third," he announced in a loud, formal voice, as though he were presenting him for dinner and dancing at the Court of

St. James. He then returned the paper to the tube and the tube to its spot, secured a face mask over his nose, tugged on a pair of industrial-weight yellow rubber gloves, fitted a crank handle into a small opening in the lower-left-hand side, and went to work. The top gave way with a sticky hiss. I didn't look as they removed Mr. Rutherford's remains to a body bag and placed him gently in the back of the Cadillac hearse.

The process was repeated for his wife, Mrs. Rutherford, the great big Dane. Again, I didn't look to see if she was still big or not.

"You'd better get home and put your face in a bowl of ice," Jack said. "I don't want to drive all the way the hell out to your damn ranch to watch some bride with a potato for a face stagger down the aisle."

"How'd it go?" Richard said when I climbed into the car. "Sorry I missed it. I got tied up on a call."

"Great, I guess." I slumped down in my seat and rubbed my eyes. I was completely exhausted.

THIRTY-NINE

B etter give this girl a drink," Richard told Buck as we slid into the booth at about eleven-thirty. I laid my head on the table.

"Hey, Ec," Buck yelled. "Bring us three triples of Irish and some of those cold meat-loaf sandwiches you made up this morning." He turned back to me, a smug look on his face. "So, what have we got here? Just what I predicted? Prewedding jitters? Premarital troubles? You all going to back out?"

Ecstasy placed ten shot glasses and a huge pile of sandwiches on the table. "I brought an extra shot," she said. "Even numbers are easier to keep track of."

"Thanks, honey." Buck drank the first one so fast I wasn't sure he'd even touched the glass. Like that old joke: See this? Want to see it again? "That was one hell of a damn party last night. Your mother almost danced me into the ground, Richard. All right, now let me get this straight. You're here because you need some counseling. Okay, so I'll tell you what to do: Read my lips: *Don't do it.*"

I started laughing. Richard and I clinked our glasses.
"No, Buck, we don't need any counseling, and we are
going to do it."

"We've been at the cemetery," Richard explained as
he swallowed. "Watching the Rutherfords be disin-
terred."

"Oh, shit. No wonder you're depressed. Here,
honey." He slid a full glass across to me. "Have another. I'll join you."

"You sure looked handsome last night, Buck," I said.
"I loved your toast."

"Yeah, it was pretty good, wasn't it? Redford wrote
it."

"Who?" Richard asked.

"Robert Redford," Buck said.

"Robert Redford wrote your toast?"

"Yup," Buck said. "He's got a thing for Lilly."

Richard closed his eyes and pinched his forehead.
"This family," he said tiredly. "You're all nuts."

"And you thought fat twin sopranos from Düsseldorf could be a problem," I told him. "Come on, we've
got to get going."

"You going to Christian and Mimi's luncheon at the
country club?" Buck asked through a mouthful of meat
loaf and mayonnaise.

I shook my head.

"I know it's just for the out-of-towners," Buck said.
"But Christian said I could come. Have you met Mimi's
sister from Chicago? Wow. She's as pretty as Mimi.
And that Principessa Pagliacci or whatever her name is
from Rome? Talk about a looker."

"We're going home to get some sleep," Richard said.

"Give everyone our love. We'll see you at five
o'clock. Don't be late."

Buck stood up and put his hands on my shoulders.

His blue eyes twinkled merrily. "I'm really happy for you, Lilly."

"I know, Buck. Thanks." I kissed his cheek above the beard.

He shook Richard's hand, and I could tell he wanted to wish him good luck, but by then Buck was too choked up to speak. So he gave him a bear hug instead and then punched him hard in the shoulder.

The day was so clear and beautiful—the weatherman said it was going to get up to seventy, a heat wave for September—we didn't go directly home. We stopped at the wedding pavilion first.

Manuel, my parents' butler, had gotten his crew up and out early, and now everything was almost ready for our two hundred special guests.

"I can't believe what your mother has done," Richard said as we climbed the steps into the pavilion.

The place was crawling with waiters setting the tables and the florist and his assistants putting the finishing touches on the centerpieces and trimming the brass hurricane lamps that hung from the thick pine-log posts.

"Did you know what she had in mind, or is this what you told her you wanted?"

I shook my head. I couldn't even answer. The fact is, we hadn't communicated much about it at all, except I'd said she should do whatever she wanted because I was her only daughter and she'd been thinking about my wedding since the day I was born. Besides, she had exquisite taste. Much better than mine. Neither one of us likes geegaws and glop, so I hadn't worried that I'd end up with frilly white wicker flower baskets and burgundy lace overcloths on the tables and a bunch of caged turtledoves dangling from the rafters.

Plus, Mother had made it clear that she fully appreciated the constraints of her challenge: I was a grown woman, not the dewy-eyed bride I would have been twenty-five or so years ago, and a ranch wedding could not, and should not, look like a city wedding. But it should also be formal, not casual. She had gone the plain-and-simple route, and the result was breathtaking.

"This is possibly the most elegant setup I've ever seen—even better than our *Traviata* set," Richard marveled. "When the sun goes down, it will be like dancing in a diamond."

The tables had all been lacquered in deep, glowing forest green, so shiny you could put your lipstick on in them, and in the center of each table, sterling-silver spittoons the size of basketballs overflowed with golden aspen leaves. Miniature silver hurricane lanterns surrounded each centerpiece, and every place setting included four gleaming crystal glasses—red wine, white wine, champagne, and water—and a full complement of glittering sterling flatware. The straight, ladder-backed kitchen chairs were lacquered in the same velvet green as the tables, and the floor looked like glass. Coronas of aspen leaves surrounded the brass sconces. Everything had been designed to glow and twinkle.

"Manuel," I caught up with him in the kitchen. "Congratulations. This is magnificent."

He smiled and nodded. "We're getting close."

"How many Valiums so far today?"

"None yet. Your mother is on her best behavior. I think maybe she's taking them today instead of me."

Mother had flown in Daniel Proust from Manhattan to do the cooking, and he was busy tying sprigs of fresh tarragon to long tenderloins of Circle B Angus. Each one looked like a work of art.

"Look at this." Manuel opened the door to the walk-in cooler, where cases and cases of 1995 Puligny-Montrachet Les Courcelles and 1985 Dom Perignon were stacked against the back wall. Six one-kilo tins of Petrossian beluga and fillets of smoked Scottish salmon sat on one shelf. Our wedding cake, a three-tiered concoction topped with a cascade of creamy roses, luscious devil's food invisible behind thick white fondant icing, sat on another.

I squeezed Richard's hand. "Can you believe it?" I said.

"Yes." He squeezed back. "And I like it."

The awful morning was banished. My wedding day had begun anew.

"Check this out," Richard said once we were back in the pantry. He ripped open the top of a case of Domaine Drouhin Oregon Pinot Noir and held a bottle up to admire. "This is fine. This is going to be an excellent affair."

"Go down by the river," Manuel said. "I think you're going to like it. Very simple. Then you'd better go home. There's not much time."

It was true. It was one o'clock. We had to be back at the barn by four.

Richard and I walked quickly down to where the wedding ceremony itself would take place, where my cousin, the Very Reverend Henry "Hank" Caulfield Bennett, Bishop of the Wind River Diocese, would officiate. The altar, actually one of the green tables with a big gold cross, held a bed of pine boughs and two large sterling vases of aspen leaves. There were rows of plain pine chairs with green cushions on the mowed ground.

It was all just as it should be. Beautiful. Solemn. Intimate.

We sat down on the riverbank. The water was at its lowest point, ready to call it a summer and freeze up for a few months. It skimmed along the rocky bed like molten glass.

"I'm glad we came down here," I said. "It's helped things start over."

"You can say that again."

"I'm sorry I fouled up our week so much," I told him. "I had no idea."

"We've all survived. You and I weren't designed to lead boring lives."

FORTY

"**Y**ou're pretty much what I would consider useless as a best man," Richard said to Elias as he followed him slowly up the stairs to our bedroom, where we were dressing. "*You're* supposed to be tying *my* tie, not the other way around."

In spite of the fact that Elias had the constitution of a bull, he had had most of his blood replaced three days earlier and was still a little weak and pale. His arm was in a sling, the wound hidden behind thick packing and bandages.

"I may be useless, but I'm happy." He settled himself onto the chaise in my bedroom and poured himself a glass of whiskey. "I know I should be drinking champagne," he said defensively to my matron of honor Sparky Kendall, who was frowning at him, "but this works better as a painkiller."

"You shouldn't be drinking anything at all," she scolded Elias, then came into the dressing room and started in on me. "You know this manicure cost me thirty dollars. And these little buttons are a bitch. If you'd had Vera Wang make these dresses instead of Armani, she would have hidden a thin little zipper behind them, and they just would have *looked* like actual buttons."

"I don't care. They're worth it." I was standing in my dressing room looking at myself in the triple mirror. "I love these gowns."

"Everybody ready?" Richard called from the bedroom.

"Ready," I answered.

"Oh, my," he said, turning me around. "You are lovely."

All we could do was smile at each other like two idiots.

"Want to get on down there and do it?"

"Let's."

FORTY-ONE

SUNDAY, SEPTEMBER 13, 1998

Lilly McLaughlin Bennett and Richard Welland Jerome, Jr., Wed in Ranch Ceremony

by Pat Collier, Society Editor

If anybody thinks for one second the rich aren't different from you and me . . . think again. Yesterday afternoon, in what will go down in history as one of the West's most memorable and glittering weddings, Bennett heiress **Lilly McLaughlin Bennett** and **Richard Welland Jerome, Jr.,** General Director of the Roundup Opera Company and scion to one of Manhattan's most venerable banking dynasties, said their vows at the two-hundred-thousand acre Bennett family ranch, the Circle B, outside of Bennett's Fort.

Everyone agreed the bride's parents, **Mr. and Mrs. Elias Caulfield Bennett III** . . . our beloved Katharine and Eli . . . pulled out all the stops for their only daughter, and we all know that when it gets down to pulling stops, they have more than most.

Katharine looked stunning enough to have been the bride herself in opalescent mushroom satin . . . Carolina Herrera made three trips to the ranch to make sure it was perfect . . . with every single one of the famous Bennett family diamonds. I don't know which sparkled more, her eyes or the necklace.

The setting for the nuptials was on the banks of the Wind River . . . a fleet of private helicopters and limousines was parked tastefully out of sight over the hill in another valley altogether . . . looking across the vast, historic ranch where a handful of championship Black Angus grazed like props in the distance. The two hundred or so guests . . . I figure they invited one per acre so no one would get that closed-in feeling . . . included the **Duke and Duchess of Westminster**—she had on what one might call a few very important pieces of jewelry, so important, in fact, that a bank guard hovered discreetly in the wings—and **Baron and Baroness Heinrich von Singen und Mengen.** She had on practically nothing at

all, but when you're as young and pretty as
Lulu, you don't need much.

While waiting for the wedding party to
arrive, everyone chatted comfortably from
the rows of cushioned—that Katharine
thinks of everything—ladder-backed pine
chairs, sipped French bubbly, and listened to
rousing selections by Puccini, Rachmani-
noff, and Beethoven performed by the
Roundup Opera Orchestra, known affectionately to those in the know as Richard's
Band.

Right on the money, at five o'clock sharp,
yours truly thought she was in a scene from
Butch Cassidy and the Sundance Kid. As the
sun headed for the hills, the orchestra let fly
with Copeland's *Billy the Kid,* and five rid-
ers in formal charcoal-gray three-piece suits
and black cowboy hats thundered over the
horizon, right out of the setting sun, tail-
coats flying, their horses at a full gallop. It
was that drop-dead gorgeous groom himself,
Richard Jerome, and his men: best man **Elias
Caulfield Bennett IV**, still recovering from a
near-fatal shotgun wound suffered at the
Rutherford Oil annual meeting last Wednesday; Richard's twin sons **Richard III** and
Charles—what lucky girls will nab these two
young studs?—and his team-roping partner,
the bride's other brother, **Christian Bennett**,
President and Chief Operating Officer of the
Bennett empire. They circled the guests
twice at full speed, whooping and hollering
and throwing mud all over the place (but
only in the right direction, not one guest was

splattered) before dismounting and taking their places by the altar, which Katharine had loaded up with pine boughs and aspen leaves. Simple. Simple. Simple. Always is best.

The Bennetts like to keep things all in the family, so on hand to officiate was the **Very Reverend Henry Caulfield Bennett,** Bishop of the Wind River Diocese, resplendent as ever in his red miter and antique pectoral cross with all its rubies. "It's so helpful to have money of one's own when one decides to go into the clergy," Katharine Bennett once confided, and boy oh boy, is she ever right. And we all just knew underneath those red, white, and gold satin vestments, Bishop Hank had that dinner-plate-sized Saddle-Bronc Champion buckle holding up his trousers.

We don't get to welcome many true American aristocrats like **Mr. and Mrs. Richard Welland Jerome, Sr.,** to Roundup. Alida Jerome is such a gracious lady—she was Alida van Rensselaer, one of those original Dutch New Yorkers, the ones who bought the island—and she didn't appear even slightly out of place in the wilds of Wyoming as she went down the aisle on her husband's arm in her Hardy Amies tealength salmon beaded chiffon. Mr. Jerome is the Chairman and CEO of Jerome Guaranty Bank & Trust, that hallowed banking house where it's said one needs an opening deposit of one million. But you get unlimited checking.

And if all this weren't enough, four of the most beautiful gals in town—Matron of Honor **Sparky Kendall** and bridesmaids **Mary Pat McArthur**, former Miss Texas **Pitty-Pat Palmer** and **Mimi Bennett** (Mrs. Christian)—glided up the grassy aisle like swans in full-length, long-sleeved, sage-colored, coupe de velours Armani gowns.

The only thing that could have outdone this group of beauties was the bride herself, and she didn't let us down. Lilly and her dashingly handsome father—the personification of the West in his tailcoat and cowboy hat, reins firmly in hand as usual—arrived in the shiniest buckboard I've ever seen, draped with garlands of roses and drawn by a team of perfectly matched Percherons with roses woven into their manes and tails.

Lilly's gown was the same cut-velvet Armani as her attendants', but fawn-colored, setting off those Bennett blue eyes like laser guns. She carried a tumble of fully blown, teacup-sized Oceana roses and wore her great-grandmother's pearls. The simplicity of the bride's dress and jewelry defined the elegance of the occasion perfectly.

No one could ever say that Lilly Bennett, one of the country's most successful security consultants, rushed into marriage, and this was a match and an occasion worth waiting for. Not a dry eye in the house as her elegant, dignified father handed her off to her handsome groom, considered to be the Last of the Twentieth Century's Most Eligible Bachelors.

•   •   •

"Did you hear that?" I said to Richard, as we shot our
way into the morning sun in the G-5 at six hundred
miles an hour, headed for France. " 'The Last of the
Twentieth Century's Most Eligible Bachelors'?"

"You didn't know that?" He poured me a glass of
champagne. "What else does it say?"

> For the guests, the wedding was just the be-
> ginning of an evening of sheer fantasy: what
> we all would do, if we could.
> Katharine's florist, that divine genius
> **Kenny Wallace,** must have stripped an entire
> forest to provide the gigantic bouquets of as-
> pen leaves, which were at their absolute
> peak of color. Thousands of candles. Unlim-
> ited caviar and champagne. A stupendous
> dinner prepared by New York's unparalleled
> **Daniel Proust** and nonstop music from **Bob
> Hartwick** and his full sixty-piece orchestra.
> And the guests themselves were as glit-
> tering as the occasion. All of Old Roundup
> was there, including **Mercedes Rutherford,**
> who reports her company's Siberian venture
> is off once and for all, and her escort, presi-
> dential candidate **Duke Fletcher** . . . looks
> like there could be something serious going
> on there. Mercedes looked remarkably well
> considering her brother-in-law had strangled
> her almost to death only two days before.
> Ah, the wonders of makeup for concealing
> all manner of things. And **William Hewitt**
> was there with his fiancée, our favorite ro-

deo superstar, **Miami McCloud,** who, just in case you've forgotten, used to be a Texas high school football star before that doctor in Montrose, Colorado, turned her into one of Wyoming's prettiest gals. It appears William's mother, the formidable **Victoria Hewitt,** has given her blessing for his and Miami's nuptials, which are scheduled for Christmastime. I hope Miami's doing some serious planning, if she ever hopes to top this affair. Watching her and Alida Jerome chat was worth the price of admission.

A contingent of Roundup's finest, including **Chief Jack Lewis,** was on hand, as was the Commandant of Fort Hickock, **Brigadier General John Taylor,** whose arm bridesmaid Pitty-Pat Palmer (Texas)—now divorced from number three—never let go of once the ceremony was over. The general has replaced Richard Jerome as Wyoming's most eligible bachelor. Another also-ran in the Lilly Bennett Stakes (if you choose to believe the gossip) was Chief Justice of California's Supreme Court, **Wink Harrison,** whose wife, **Jayne,** never took her razor-sharp eyes off hizzoner the whole time.

Joan Chamberlain—not there with estranged husband number five, **Dickie,** who attended with a dishy young thing—left the dance floor long enough to tell me she had done her best to grab Richard herself.

Televangelist **Johnny Bourbon** and his wife, **Shanna,** were locked deep in conversation with our own Perry Mason, **Paul Decker,** probably discussing Decker's latest client, truck tycoon, ex-golfer, and all-round bad boy **Wade Gilhooly**, whose recently late wife, **Alma Rutherford Gilhooly**, was expected to bequeath a bundle to Johnny Bourbon's Christian Cowboys. Don't look now, Johnny, but a little birdie told me she's left the whole caboodle to the National Rifle Association. Why is no one surprised?

Nobody wanted the party to end, but at eleven o'clock, after a final toast by Elias Bennett, and after Lilly had tossed her bouquet to a tall redhead who'd been tending to him all evening, the newlywed Jeromes kissed their families and friends good-bye, climbed into the family's navy-blue helicopter, and headed off to spend their wedding night at the Grand. By the time you read this Sunday morning, they will be on their way to a friend's chateau in Burgundy—nonstop on the family's navy-blue Gulfstream-Five—and a well-deserved rest from this exhausting ranch-style life.

One last note . . . As I stood there watching the chopper sail away into the stars, a familiar voice behind me said, "Story of my life. I never even got to meet her. One of these days I'm going to get the girl."

It was **Robert Redford**.

If you enjoyed Marne Davis Kellogg's **NOTHING BUT GOSSIP,** you won't want to miss any of the tantalizing mysteries in the Marshal Lilly Bennett series.

Look for the latest, **BIRTHDAY PARTY,** at your favorite bookseller's, coming from Doubleday in hardcover in December 1999.

ABOUT THE AUTHOR

A fifth-generation Westerner, MARNE DAVIS
KELLOGG lives with her husband in Denver,
Colorado, and Norfolk, Virginia. *Nothing But
Gossip* is her fourth Lilly Bennett mystery, and
she is now at work on her fifth, *Birthday Party*.

Visit the author at her website:
www.marnedaviskellogg.com

SUE GRAFTON

"Once again, the finest practitioner of the 'female sleuth' genre is in great form...."
—Cosmopolitan

"Ms. Grafton writes a smart story and wraps it up with a wry twist."
—The New York Times Book Review

___27991-2	**"A"** IS FOR ALIBI	$6.99/$8.99 in Canada	
___28034-1	**"B"** IS FOR BURGLAR	$6.99/$8.99	
___28036-8	**"C"** IS FOR CORPSE	$6.99/$8.99	
___27163-6	**"D"** IS FOR DEADBEAT	$6.99/$8.99	
___27955-6	**"E"** IS FOR EVIDENCE	$6.99/$8.99	
___28478-9	**"F"** IS FOR FUGITIVE	$6.99/$8.99	

"The best first-person-singular storytelling in detective novels."
—Entertainment Weekly

Ask for these books at your local bookstore or use this page to order.

Please send me the books I have checked above. I am enclosing $____ (add $2.50 to cover postage and handling). Send check or money order, no cash or C.O.D.'s please.

Name _____

Address _____

City/State/Zip _____

Send order to: Bantam Books, Dept. BD 26, 2451 S. Wolf Rd., Des Plaines, IL 60018
Allow four to six weeks for delivery.
Prices and availability subject to change without notice.   BD 26 9/96